Spring Into SciFi 2021 Edition

A Cloaked Press Anthology

Published by:
Cloaked Press, LLC
PO Box 341
Suring, WI 54174
https://www.cloakedpress.com

Cover Design by:
Steger Productions Design
https://fantasyandcoffee.com/SPDesign/

.

Cloaked Press is proud to present:

Jason Lairamore
Mike Adamson
Tom Howard
Linda M. Crate
Andrew P. McGregor
James Pyles
Eamonn Murphy
Alex Minns
Gregory Allen Mendell
David Cleden
Louis B. Rosenberg
Matthew Chabin
Tony Conaway

Contents

The Girl from the Pier

by Jason Lairamore

Gus Treadway, a senior at Newtown Medical College, sat on a bench at the Newtown Sports Quad on the Bay watching the girls gallivant about showcasing their summer-wear finery. He was deciding on which one to go talk to and hopefully ask out on a date, when he saw her.

She wore a black wetsuit. Her hair was black and reflected the sunlight in a greenish hue. She had on a pair of enormous sunglasses and lugged a bulky, black backpack. Whatever was in the pack was heavy. She leaned forward to keep her balance.

Something about her intrigued him, so he stood and followed her as she walked from the arena and toward the ocean. She stepped on the pier and walked to its very end.

There was nowhere else to go. Here was his chance to go talk to her.

She climbed the railing and jumped into the ocean, backpack, sunglasses, and all.

Rushing forward, he looked down into the rolling waves. Nobody else seemed to have noticed anything. He waited for her to resurface, but he never saw her come up. He looked to his fellows on the pier again while he thought about calling the authorities.

"Don't worry yourself, lad," an old fisherman said. The man chewed on the end of a cigar and had more sun wrinkles than Gus had ever seen. "We figure she has some kind of scuba gear in that pack. It's not the first time we've seen her."

He nodded his thanks, turned and walked back down the pier. He thought about going back to the sports quad. There was more than one fish in the sea, after all. But, he decided against it.

He was halfway back to school when his mind clicked on what had originally intrigued him about her.

He had been studying nonverbal communication since he had been a kid. Eighty percent of human communication was expressed that way. He had been fully confident up until that moment that he knew every nuance and deviation of the human walking pattern.

The girl had thrown off signals and cues he had never seen.

#

The buildings of Newtown's Medical School stood both tall and proud in the middle of downtown. The campus itself looked like a bright, red bud of healing growing in the middle of the dying detritus that was the city.

The Allied Health building was dark and empty. Quiet halls and gloomily lit walls ruled. There was one exception to the quiet, and that was the Therapeutic Applications Lab. Gus knew the Advanced Gait Training course was in session because he'd taken the class himself as a junior. He also knew the professor. Dr. Cowlter was one of the most intelligent and prudent people he had ever met.

He barged into the lab, not thinking of the interruption he would cause. Nine students sat around two rows of tan, plinth tables while a tenth student gave an accounting of a public posture analysis. A picture of a man was projected up on one of the tan walls. All eyes turned toward Gus as he rushed forward.

"Dr. Cowlter, I am so sorry for disturbing you," he said.

The class looked at him like he was a crazy person fresh from the insane asylum. Nobody barged into Dr. Cowlter's class. To say that the doctor had a reputation was an understatement. Not that Gus had ever had an issue with her. Dr. Cowlter just had a drive to improve and could not tolerate a lack of 'intensity' in her students.

"Class," Dr. Cowlter said, "for those of you unaware of the identity of this young man, I present Mr. Gus Treadway, one of our most promising students."

Gus slowed his racing mental pace enough to nod a greeting to the class

"Please," he said. "I need a moment." He glanced around at the awe-stricken class.

Dr. Cowlter raised an eyebrow. "Please use this time wisely," she told the class as she ushered Gus into the hall.

His legs felt weak now that the moment was upon him and she was standing before him. His knees ached. His jaw ached too, like it didn't want to move right.

"Mr. Treadway?" Dr. Cowlter prompted. It was now or never.

"I saw a girl this morning," he said, then told of what had happened at the pier.

"The girl was something different," he said. "I've never seen anything like her before." He paused before continuing.

"I don' think she was human."

Dr. Cowlter exhaled. "Mr. Treadway, did you hear of the farmer's market riot this morning?"

What did that have to do with anything? Sure, times were hard and people were starving. Yeah, the finances of every country worldwide were collapsing. He'd heard similar stories every day his whole life. It was always the same. The girl, however, had been something different.

"Why are we here?" Dr. Cowlter followed.

"To learn medicine," he replied.

"And how does what you've just told me help us do that?"

"But-,"

"You are extremely smart and will go far in whatever field you decide to follow," she said. "We haven't the time to explore the depth of difference between each and every individual of our overpopulated race."

"What are the three directives?" she asked. Her intensity was a palpable thing.

"The three D's," he answered. He knew what she was about to say.

She held up three fingers like he was in kindergarten and needed a visual reinforcement. "You diagnose the patient's problem. You define the minimal necessary treatment. You deliver care."

"This isn't about efficiency," he shot back.

"That's all everything is. We seek equality of care to all, for all, with as little variance as possible. We can't afford variance."

"Wait-,"

"Our job is to treat everybody the same as fast as possible," she said as she pulled out her portable.

"Dr. Medlief has advisor hours now. Go see him to clear up your misconceptions."

She turned back down the hall toward the Therapeutic Apps Lab.

"She was real," he said to her back.

Dr. Cowlter put a hand on the door and glanced back at him. "Doesn't matter," she said. "We have enough problems to deal with. Go see Dr. Medlief."

She left him standing alone in the deserted hallway.

As he walked away from the building, he realized that she, in the course of only a few minutes, had come to mean more than the flesh and blood he knew her to be. She reminded him of the wonder the world had to offer.

#

Administration was one of those places that made people nervous for no good reason. It was imbued with an uncanny intimidation, as if a spell had been cast over its sharp angles and polished surfaces.

It didn't help that it was summer and staffing was down to a minimum. Increased human presence diminished the overpowering sense of transmitted superiority.

"May I help you?" The secretary asked. She behaved much like the avatar of the building itself.

"Gus Treadway," he said. "I'd like to see Dr. Medlief."

"One moment." She picked up the phone and had a short conversation.

"Follow me," she said.

They didn't go far. The hall was filled with 'any-use' offices that the professors used for counseling duties.

The secretary knocked on one.

"Come in," Dr. Medlief said through the door.

He nodded his thanks to the secretary as she turned to go.

"Mr. Treadway," Dr. Medlief said in greeting when he opened the door.

"Dr. Medlief, I -," and he told the doctor of what he had seen right there in the doorway.

Dr. Medlief didn't seem the least bit surprised. The doctor just nodded and tee-peed his fingers in front of his face. Gus shut the door and sat in one of the chairs facing the desk.

"Nikki," the doctor said and shook his head. "She loves those new legs of hers. I knew she'd get caught. Not that it matters now."

"What?" Gus said, shaking his head.

"Dr. Cowlter sent a message saying that you would be stopping by."

"Who is Nikki?" Gus asked.

Had he heard Dr. Medlief right? New legs?

Dr. Medlief clapped his hands. His eyes widened. A smile played across his features. Gus gripped the armrest of his chair.

"I bet Dr. Cowlter sounded just like this," the doctor said.

His face melted away. His whole head turned to putty.

It reconfigured into a perfect replica of Dr. Cowlter. The whole process took less than a breath.

Gus got to his feet and around to the back of his chair fast.

What once was Dr. Medlief raised a hand. "Hold on," it said. "I bet Dr. Cowlter sounded like this."

The voice was a mockery of a British accent and sounded nothing like Dr. Cowlter. "We must march forward into oblivion. Ya, ya ya. Efficiency and uniformity will save us from blah, blah, blah."

Gus grabbed the doorknob.

"STOP" The voice was Dr Medlief's again. Gus glanced back before ripping the door open. Dr. Medlief had a gun pointed at him.

Gus eyed the gun and froze. It was like some subconscious force had taken command over his ability to move. He knew he needed to get far away fast, but something about the gun and the look on Dr. Medlief's returned face kept him firmly in his spot.

Dr. Medlief shook his head. "I need more practice."

Gus couldn't speak, not while the gun was on him.

Dr. Medlief squinted at him. Gus's heart raced. His hand was sweaty on the doorknob. Dr. Medlief extended the gun forward, towards Gus.

"No," Gus managed to say.

"People die every day," Dr. Medlief said, his smile growing. "Don't worry."

There was a pop, then starbursts…

#

Sight came in flashes. Sounds, when he heard at all, were muffled. Waves of vibration rang like silent gongs, some in his very bones. Everything pulsed and moved.

He jolted and found himself in a gigantic space that he could feel more than see. People lay everywhere, strewn about like dead leaves.

The floor was metal, and it vibrated. The light was soft and diffuse. He couldn't see more that twenty or thirty feet in any direction. Sounds echoed.

He stood much easier than expected. He would have bet good money that gravity was less than normal. That left but one explanation, but he didn't want to think about that.

None of the people lying about were anybody he knew. After some soft stepping to avoid any of the bodies, he found a winding path.

He started walking.

It felt like an hour passed. He couldn't believe the number of people he saw. The longer he walked, the larger the space seemed.

A more substantial light pinpricked up ahead. He hurried, but kept quiet. He was the only one awake out of the seeming millions of people lying about. It was pretty obvious that he wasn't supposed to be up and moving. The element of surprise was all he had.

The light grew and revealed an opening the size of a garage door. What he saw on the other side what unfathomable.

A metal decking extended about ten feet from the door. Beyond, there was space, and floating there, was Earth.

The view shifted. Earth got closer. He could see coastlines and cities. He could see home.

"Ready for the show?" Dr. Medlief asked. Gus startled, but kept quiet. Dr. Medlief hadn't seen him. It was a good thing he'd spoken or Gus would've just walked out and got caught immediately.

Dr. Medlief had asked the question to his two companions. One was a man Gus didn't recognize. The other was the girl. She still had on her sunglasses and backpack.

"Have you ever done this before?" she asked. Her voice was light, but hard around the edges.

"No Ma'am," Dr. Medlief said. "This is a special case." He extended something towards her.

"You want to push the button?" he asked. "One little finger and all those bombs fly. Boom! The video will be a hit to every sentient!"

Gus tensed. They planned to blow up Earth. What was it Dr. Medlief had said? 'People die every day.'

The girl shook her head. "You should do it."

Gus edged forward. He couldn't let this happen.

"It's not that big a deal," Dr. Medlief said. He glanced at his other companion and shrugged. The man shrugged back.

The girl, Nikki, Dr. Medlief had called her, sighed.

Gus couldn't wait any longer. He couldn't sit there and watch an alien destroy his world. He jumped from hiding and landed on Dr. Medlief's back. The doctor crumpled under Gus's weight and squished into the decking like play-dough. The controller flew from the doctor's hand. Two quick strides and Gus had it. There was only one button and it had a protective cover plate. Gus shoved the controller into his back pocket and turned to face the other two. Dr. Medlief remained a contorted pile on the floor.

The man held up his hands and took a step back. Gus rushed him and punched him in the face. It felt like punching one of those squishy stress balls from the health food store.

The girl laughed.

"A little help here?" he heard Dr. Medlief say. "It takes a lot of energy to keep myself looking good, you know."

Gus turned around to do further damage.

The girl, still chuckling, stepped in his path. He grabbed her by the shoulders, intent on moving her aside. She took hold of his wrists. When he tried to push her, she didn't budge.

"That's enough," she said, though she still wore a closed-lipped smile.

Gus tried to jerk her to the side then tried to pull his hands clear, but succeeded in neither. She remained unmoved without any sign of strain. Behind her, Dr. Medlief was back to looking exactly as he always had.

"The tranquilizer in that gun must have been out of date," the doctor said. He gave Gus a nod. "I never had a chance to use it you see, so, when you came along pitching a fit about Nikki and we were about to round up everybody anyway, I thought I'd try out some of my acting skills. I scared you didn't I?"

"You saw me?" Nikki asked.

Gus looked down into her sunglass-covered face. She smiled big, showing him a row of teeth that would have made a shark proud. He pulled away from her and she let go of his wrist. Her hands went to her mouth.

"Sorry," she muttered.

He stumbled back a few steps to gain some distance. The other alien he'd been beating on had regained its original figure and was once again standing silently next to Dr. Medlief.

Gus checked his back pocket to make sure the controller was there. It was.

"Well, now I'm starving," Dr. Medlief said to his alien companion, who nodded.

"What's going on?" Gus asked.

Dr. Medlief pointed a finger toward the view of Earth.

"Your planet is overpopulated, has been for years. We're helping out."

All Gus could think about were the bombs.

"By nuking us?"

"Fake nukes. They have a big blow, lots of debris, but no radioactive garbage to wait out. Sure, you'll have some cleaning up to do, but no biggie. It'll keep the rest of you in the dark about our little mass abduction."

Gus glanced to the Earth and back to Dr. Medlief.

"The people back there?"

"We're dropping all of you off at another planet. You know, give you guys some room to stretch your legs," Dr. Medlief said.

"Why?"

"To help out."

That was the rub. People, alien or no, didn't go through that kind of trouble for nothing. There was always a price.

"Why?" he asked again.

Dr. Medlief snorted and glanced to his companion, who gave him a conspiratorial wink that did nothing to improve Gus's opinion.

"Listen," Dr. Medlief said. "You guys aren't ready to join the more advanced races yet and the way things are going you are all going to breed yourselves to death before you learn how to get to another planet and colonize. There is endless real estate out there, so we figured we'd give you a little leg up."

"And while there is no shortage of habitable places, intelligence is a rare thing," he continued. "That is why we are helping."

Gus shook his head. He wasn't ready to buy that line.

Dr. Medlief threw up his hands.

"Believe me or don't," the doctor said. "I don't care. Nikki, you talk to him. I *have* to eat."

He turned to his companion. "You want to join me?"

The other alien nodded and the two smacked together like two pieces of clay. In a matter of seconds, they formed into an eight foot tall monster of a man that Gus would not have believed could exist had he not been looking right at it.

"Push the button whenever you figure out that it's the right thing to do," the thing said in a deep voice. "That's your planet down there, after all."

It walked around the gentle curve of the platform and was soon gone.

The girl, Nikki, glanced at him sidelong. Gus's mind had had about all it could take. He could feel what he assumed to be the crashing effects of a body depleted of its endorphins. His mind didn't want to think about anything anymore. It was all just too much.

"I used to be a mermaid," Nikki said.

He laughed. Of course she had. Why not?

"My father raises unicorns," he replied, "but only the normal kind."

She chuckled. "I get it. It's a lot to take in. Here goes the rest of it."

"This backpack is my aerator, which is connected to the gills located against my ribs. My eyes -," She pulled her glasses down.

Her eyes had no color around the pupil. They were solid black, and where the whites should be, it was bright gold.

"I didn't say I didn't believe you," he said.

"I know," she said. "I just wanted you to know."

"Okay," he said and turned to gaze out at the Earth.

"The aliens are going to fix me up the rest of the way soon," she said, "make me fully human."

So this is what shock felt like. It was an odd sensation.

"You saw me walking?" she asked. He glanced her way. She had taken a few steps closer.

"Yeah," he said. "I was at the sports quad when you came strolling by."

"Why were you there?"

He shook his head.

"Push the button," she said. "Earth will heal up fine and the humans will gain another planet."

"I don't' trust Dr. Medlief," he said. The alien wasn't telling him the whole story. He was trying to keep the humans on Earth in the dark about the existence of other intelligent races in their midst for some unspoken reason. And what of those who would wake up on a new planet. They would know right off that some higher power had taken steps without their permission.

Nikki shrugged.

"Does it matter?" she asked.

He pulled the controller from his pocket and eyed the single button.

"All the people back there sleeping are going to wake up to quite a surprise," he said.

"Yeah," she said. "It's already a done deal. If you don't push the button then the aliens will just do it themselves before we leave. It's not like you could stop it anyway. At least this way you can say you were the one to start things in a different direction."

He popped the cover from the button and sighed.

"I was at the sports arena to meet pretty girls," he said.

He glanced at her and saw her smiling.

"I tell you what. I will push this button on one condition," he said.

"What?"

"You and I go on a date when we get to wherever we are going."

"Before or after I'm fully human?" she asked.

He shrugged. "Both."

"Okay."

He pushed the button. The bombs streaked whitely across the sky and blew up in great dusty clouds that filled most of the entire globe.

Nikki grabbed his hand as the world changed, hopefully for the better.

Jason Lairamore is a writer of science fiction, fantasy, and horror who lives in Oklahoma with his beautiful wife and their three monstrously marvelous children. He is a published finalist of the 2012 SQ Mag annual contest, the winner of the 2013 Planetary Stories flash fiction contest, a third place winner of the 2015 SQ Mag annual contest, and a Writers of the Future contest Semi-Finalist. His work is both featured and forthcoming in over 80 publications to include "Perihelion Science Fiction," "Stupefying Stories" and Third Flatiron publications, to name a few.

Elusive Target

by Mike Adamson

"Think of my ship as the deerhound, and yours as the hunter," the big man said, very softly.

Captain Jenna Craig squinted over the rim of her glass in the officer's club of the Transport Guild tower in Jocasta, the spaceport city of Alcubierre's World. A half-hearted dust storm blew against panoramic windows, ghosting out the blocks of the city against the dun overcast. The woman was petite, in the black jumpsuit of the guild, her dark hair worn on the collar, face the smoothness of a recent round of rejuvenation biotech.

Her eyes narrowed as she breathed softly. She had been fully briefed before leaving Susa by corporate courier, to take over command of the heavy transporter *Kerala* here at the Jocasta docks, but now the final details could emerge. Only she and the man she faced would be aware of them—such was security a year into the human race's first alien war.

AD 2496 had come in raw and violent, with simmering battle all across the outer frontier, after a deep survey ship had been intercepted by an insular alien people known only by their name, the *Sendaaki*, a race otherwise shrouded in mystery. None knew how diplomacy had failed or how to repair relations, but massive mobilization was in effect throughout the colonies of the Middle Stars. Every measure was being pursued to learn something about the enigmatic foe who barred the way to potentially rich worlds in planetary clusters deeper into the galactic arm.

Craig downed a shot of smooth Irish malt and set the glass down, its click on the hard table top the only sound for long moments. "They told me no one aboard has the first clue what the *Kerala* is carrying. They'd probably turn in their guild cards if they did. But the command crew are all ex-military and primed to be ready for anything, so when I give the order…"

11

"They jump to, no questions asked." Harlan Meroe was square-cut, a career spacer whose bearing spoke of the military. One could take the man out of the service, but not vice versa. He was descended from the first colonists out this way, his genes a pleasing admixture of African and Polynesian, and his hair was civilian length—clearly a cover. He was Fleet Intelligence to the soles of his feet.

They were perfectly matched for this assignment; they had known each other forty years ago on the routes of the Middle Stars, had their quality time and gone their separate ways. But each was a consummate professional, and, after his time in uniform, Meroe had known precisely who to recruit for this daring, desperate ploy.

They were alone in the corner of the bar, and their wristies had swept the place for surveillance tech. They were clean, neither monitored nor overheard. Craig shifted in her seat and beckoned the serving robot for another round. When they chinked shot glasses, she enjoyed the burn of the spirit and nodded faintly. "It's these goddamned *foo-fighters*, isn't it."

"Of course," Meroe returned with the ghost of a smile. "We know they're enemy probes, scouting for their fleet, but that's all. Are they machines? Are they directed energy?" He shrugged. "Maybe they really are the same tech that showed up on Earth five hundred years ago, following bomber streams on night raids, in which case the Sendaaki have been watching us *at least* that long. Whatever, finding answers is our job. We've studied the pattern of their appearances—they may be enigmatic objects but the intelligence behind them operates in accordance with conventional logic, and that means we can second-guess them."

"Bate," Craig whispered

"Bate," was the soft affirmation. Meroe toyed with his empty glass. "Intelligence has spent months setting the trap. A locality out toward Paradise Wells where you'll be making a delivery. They always show up when ships are busy, we think it's their way of obfuscating—they dodge around like flies, and ships give them spatial references to play with. So far our defensive fire hasn't been able to touch them, our predictive tracking is inadequate."

"The *Kerala* changes all that." Craig breathed a soft sigh, glancing at a wall chrono. "We're due out of here in ninety."

"One for the sky?"

"No thanks," she returned easily. "Maybe after." She reached across the table and lay a hand over his, a silent communication that reminded them both of who they had been generations ago, and who this war compelled them to become. It was also optimism, the promise they would come through whatever lay ahead. Meroe smiled, did not move his hand, and they enjoyed their moment as long as they could.

They rose and the big agent pulled on a jacket with a rasp from the zip. "I'll see you in the air, then," he said softly, with a tight grin. "Remember—like grouse to the hunters."

#

The Jocasta docks served most of the southern hemisphere, a sprawling industrial wasteland of concrete and plasteel where ships loaded and offloaded, service was performed and the military rubbed shoulders with the merchant navy of space. Twenty ships could be in port at any one time, a tempting target surely high on the Sendaaki agenda. Their probes had appeared on this world with increasing regularity as if a major push was to be expected—though double-think suggested the deployment of probes may divert attention from some real objective.

Yet, as Craig walked the dock beneath her command, she felt in her bones that all this—half a century's worth of human industry—was too ripe to ignore for long. The docks stretched a hundred square kilometers, criss-crossed with transport arteries, gantry cranes taller than the pyramids, warehouses and container stacks, rail links and canals, transhipment points for airship pickup...

The *Kerala* was one of the uglier vessels she had ever seen, little more than an 800-metre long flying drydock for thousands of cargo modules, the vast sled driven by three interlinked fusion piles powering titanic antigrav drives and conventional spacefolding synchrotrons. The whole was cased in filthy metal hull plating, her faded stencils and codes sand-blasted by touchdown on angry worlds across the Union. A command bridge rode high above the container stacks, most of the way back to the stern, and Craig looked up 150 meters to the upper antenna masts, field grids and waveguides. Heat beat back off acres of concrete and she felt the air sizzle with the AG field under the monster.

To inspect the vessel was a Captain's privilege, and she had presented her credentials to the First Officer on arrival that afternoon. The crew was returning from shore leave and the craft would rise from the docks through the dust when the last man was aboard. She took an elevator shaft at the vessel's flank, rode up in air conditioned comfort. She breathed deeply and tried to steady her heart as she caught a glimpse of Meroe's ship at a hardstand far off, the *Swallow*, aptly-named, a small and elegant hull designed for rapid transit of high-value goods. She was nimble, and would serve admirably to drive the prey *to the guns.*

#

Meroe's crew could smell an op. They were ex-fleet, many merchantmen staffed ex-military personnel in these days of strife, when any civilian vessel within five lightyears of the warzone was deemed at risk and ran armed. They were bringing the ship to flight-standby, going through the checklists for departure, and logged a parallel vector to the giant container ship which would leave ahead of them. Meroe sat back in the command seat behind and between the pilots in the streamlined nose; the more casual he was, the more they sensed a fight coming.

Jocasta Traffic Control called the airspace restricted and they watched the *Kerala* launch from her moors, half a million long-tons rising with the grace of a wind-blown leaf, her industrial-yellow hull stained and scorched to a patterning of filth and wear. Her own length clear of the yards, her drives fired up and she moved off, stately and magnificent, gaining speed for her run into the western continent, to offload goods before turning her gaunt bows for space and a five-week passage to Aquarius. The monolithic craft shone as she cleared the dust palls, a great haze of light about her triple engines under the stern decking.

She glided into the sky with a distant peal of thunder, and soon Traffic Control called the air clear. *Swallow's* departure was half an hour on in the schedule, and the skipper rubbed a hard chin as he thought. *They'd come*, they would not be able to resist the bate—a lumbering container ship closing on a center of human activity in which high-power military com-nets had been active for months? The double-think was meant to suggest a hidden installation, well worth a close look, and the ship gave the enemy their opportunity by playing to their tactical pattern. The flightplan took the ship directly through the zone of densest signal emanation, and charged grids in the desert had been prepared to reinforce the illusion, dummy installations, many underground... All they needed was one solid chance.

When clearance was called, Meroe closed his shoulder harness with a clash. "Let's go," he grunted, and the pilots hauled the ship into the air on streaming thrusters, turned her west and sent her into low-supersonic flight to gradually overhaul the giant. They were timed to pass through the zone more or less simultaneously, they must appear casual—together but not obviously so.

"All right, people," Meroe grunted as the distance paid out under the *Swallow's* elegant wings, "we have a job to do, and I don't mean deliver three tons of machine parts to Paradise Wells."

Around him, the two pilots, the flight engineer and systems tech glanced over their shoulders with wry looks, and one rubbed fingers at another. "Twenty, I believe."

A chuckle went through the group but Meroe raised a hand. "You want a crack at the bad guys? Of course you do. Well, unless we're way off-base, they'll be putting in an appearance in about fifteen minutes."

Lund, the copilot, turned her lint-blonde head. "That's about when we intersect with that big mutha out ahead."

"Correct. I want the weapons on standby, everybody sharp. If they show, we go for them like a hungry raptor."

The senior pilot, Li Pei, cracked his knuckles and adjusted his flying gloves. "Always happy to oblige, boss, but a little warning would be nice."

"I know. Not possible, my friend. You know how it goes."

"Need to know, huh? And the grunts who get tossed at the bad guys are the last ones to find out?"

"If you like." Meroe's tone brooked no dispute, they knew how it worked.

"Not really, but it'll do," he replied evenly, and eyed Lund with a crazy grin. They were not working an armed trash-hauler on the closest colony to the zone for nothing. They had often wondered why the military had let experienced veterans go as the war was brewing, they should have been stop-lossed straight back in. Now they understood— they were not really out, just coming at the enemy from a whole other direction.

The ship lanced through the blue, crossed a wide sound between land masses and bored on into the dry western wastes. They had the *Kerala* on track out ahead, she was hard to miss even at this distance, and Li Pei brought them onto a parallel vector to pass the giant at 5000 meters on her port beam, the same in altitude above the sands. The scanners were on passive track. The systems tech, Bikila, was watching for the first hint in the EM bands of the kind of incursion with which they had become familiar. Short of an actual Sendaaki landing, and the fleet reported no alien contacts this side of the zone of exclusion, it could only be the wandering globes of light scathingly dubbed since the twentieth century as *foo fighters*.

Closer, closer, the radio sky was quiet… Now they were over the western desert, heard the signal traffic from townships on the coast, saw ribbons of trackways and canals, the glimmer of air lanes; but the sudden burst of x-rays that heralded an alien probe emerging from hyperspace like a round from a canon was absent. At five minutes' lag time they could see the heavy hauler in the blue, a speck against the horizon haze off the starboard bow, and every heart thudded like a mallet. Were the aliens too canny to be taken in?

Meroe sat forward against his straps, itching to be into the fight, willing it to happen, and the very air was charged as the *Swallow* gradually drew up with the mighty *Kerala*, over the target region of the parched, dun waste.

Bikila's rich voice broke the tension like a bolt from the blue. "X-ray signature! Loud and close!"

"Guns up!" Meroe snapped, and before the weapons deployed a ball of golden fire streaked across their canopy, arced savagely for the freighter and entered the death-dance, flitting with the agility of a housefly around the giant as it scanned the desert beneath. Ranging shafts of active particles licked from its brilliant corona to paint the wastes in broad strokes invisible to the eye but plain as day on the scanners.

Meroe balled a fist as Li Pei and Lund sent the ship at the alien in full thrust and the engineer, Mawson, brought up the predictive tracking grid. "If the thing makes a break, we get in its way," the skipper grunted. "Just keep its back to the freighter—and it'll never know what hit it!"

#

"Captain! We have company!"

The duty officer's call broke the spell for Craig and she was out of her seat in an instant. The bridge of the *Kerala* was a wide-windowed frontage in the streamlined module which rode above the containers on twin pylons, and the ball of golden light danced about the ship before them.

"Alert stations!" Craig snapped and the duty officer, a burly ex-Marine named Stinson, hit the klaxon contact with the heel of his hand.

"Mr. Stinson, your system key please," Craig barked, taking her own from the neck of her uniform and striding to the master bank, behind the pilotage consoles before the armored viewports. The bridge watch swapped glances filled with meaning, and the captain raised her voice. "Just keep your heads, this is what we're here for. It's all automated, let the system do its job." She nodded to Stinson as they inserted the keys. "Turn." The system recognized command authority and the captain entered a simple code. On a projection screen over the console, indicators flashed and stabilized—*combat mode active, predictive tracking online.*

All across the hull, panels withdrew and hidden guns ran out, and the upper layer of containers blossomed like opening orchids to deploy gun after gun, tracking arrays and other sensors, and in five seconds reactors hidden among the cargo were coming online.

Stinson's eyebrows rose into his cap but he had to grin as the diminutive captain reached into the display and tapped the glowing letters commit? A second more and every gun on the ship opened up with one voice, pouring a torrential stream of laser and particle fire after the foo fighter.

"They can evade one predictive system, Mr. Stinson," Craig said tightly, "but the *Kerala* has been rigged with five, interpolating every decision, coordinating over a hundred fluid-mount turrets. Let's see what they make of this!"

If it was a machine, it was a smart one, for it doubled back close to the hull to reduce the number of turrets which could bare at any one time. The ball of goldy light streaked back and forth under the drive sled, scanning the desert every moment, and the *Swallow* looped low to send its fire laterally, skimming the big ship's underside and forcing the alien thing to the starboard beam where turrets waited to acquire it in an ever more lethal crossfire.

In the end, all it had was maneuverability and speed, the ability to change vector from one second to the next so defensive fire was never on target—it was in a race, its maneuvering ability against the system's firing solution. Even a thousandth of a second slow and the guns would have it, and unless the alien systems were of inconceivable capacity, it could only be a matter of time.

The strange engagement continued for long seconds, the guns vomiting fury that streaked the sky and desert all about, the agile freighter maneuvering hard to add to the fire quotient, but the alien stayed ahead of the solutions, seemingly with ease. "Come on, come on," Craig gritted through her teeth, knowing the margins were tight and growing tighter for the alien as the passage of time eroded the odds by which random chance played in its favor. If alien math was anything like that of humans, the controlling intelligence behind the probe knew the envelope was becoming untenable—

The guns shut down. In the sudden, shocking quiet, Craig and Stinson stared at their instruments, before their eyes went involuntarily to the wide viewports, and abruptly they understood why the system was still in full combat mode but not firing.

The pilots were silhouetted in a broad corona of golden-orange light around a sharp, bright core that hung just outside the plasteel barrier. They almost felt alien laughter, as the thing computed and found the weak spot in the attack. "It must have observed that as it crossed the hull, the guns automatically stopped firing to avoid hitting the ship's own structure," Stinson whispered. "Therefore it need only take up a position where no guns can fire."

Craig stepped forward hesitantly, past the pilot stations to the very inner arch of the plasteel wall and stared out at the softly pulsating spheroid of energy, raised a hand and placed it to the cool transparency. "What are you?" she whispered, feeling as if its instruments must be scanning her to the bone marrow. She was face to face with a Sendaaki thing, the enemy, whatever words described it, and she was cold to the core with strange dread.

The tableau held for seconds that seemed years in length, then the globe staggered in the air as fire cannoned into it from the ship's port side and Craig caught a glimpse of *Swallow* against the sky, weapons streaming flame to shove the probe with terrible force away from the safe space. The freighter's guns hammered as one and the probe raced away in a descending arc, bracketed and straddled with fire, until it smacked into the desert in a shallowing arc that buried it in the drab dust and grit of a dune.

All guns went silent and the tracking grids were clear, a cam feed showing only the settling dust pall over the impact site.

"We got it," Craig said in a small voice, trembling somewhat. "I don't believe it, we got the bastard!"

#

"Hold position," Meroe hissed, eyeing the data feeds about him. Their guns covered the impact site, at the first hint of motion they would open up again, but long moments stretched out and the energy signature of the alien probe flickered at a low ebb. He threw a glance at the main situational board and found the *Kerala* now several kilometers downrange from the impact point and speeding on. No one spoke, every breath was held, but as the ship passed ten kilometers and the airspace remained clear, Meroe gestured to the desert. "Set us down, and fire EMP."

The ship dropped on vectored engines to a swift contact, then her energy grids reconfigured and Mawson toured the systems on a final check. "Internals shielded, all secondaries locked out, firing now."

The electromagnetic blastwave washed outward in a savage blow, trained for maximum effective discharge into the dune, and as the systems stabilized the sensors cleared and Bikila raised an eyebrow. "No signature. I think it's dead…"

"If this was a battlefield we'd be checking for a pulse with all the fire at our disposal," Meroe mused wryly. "But we want it reasonably intact, so…" He opened a secure channel. "This is Deerhound 1 to Briarpatch. Your package has been delivered. Feel free to unwrap."

They appeared across the wasteland from one of the underground bunkers, a convoy of squat, camouflaged vehicles, army engineers lugging gear to secure the area. They established a perimeter, air traffic was diverted, Fleet fighters appeared overhead in a standing patrol, and *Swallow* was backed off five hundred meters before Meroe deplaned and met the detachment commander. The techs went in with heavy equipment, a mini-dozer digging away the soft matter of the dune, and Meroe and the officer watched on their coms as sensor readings confirmed they were almost on top of the inert alien craft.

A message flashed in and Meroe tapped the com at his right ear, traded nods with the officer and acknowledged, and moments later the whistle of jets announced the *Kerala's* captain's gig coming down from the blue to a formation landing alongside the larger *Swallow*. Craig joined them, tight-faced but optimistic.

"You really don't need to be on-site, ma'am," the detachment commander, Klaus, said britlly. "Unnecessary risk."

"I stood face to face with that thing, lieutenant," she replied, nonplussed. *"Before* it was damaged. And now I'd see it for myself."

He was not happy but bowed to rank. On their com screens the engineering drones had excavated down to it, revealing a metal orb, evidently the core of the visual effect. "Getting good data," Klaus mused as he saw streaming feeds from the instruments his drones were applying. "Definite latent subspace field, no ionizing radiation… The way it ploughed in it must have a lot of mass despite not being very large. That makes sense, the energy requirements for the way it flies would be enormous. If we can get it back to a bunker we'll take it apart, I'm expecting antigravitational systems, some sort of repeller drive, a subspace generator and AI core—all of that packed into something two meters across!"

"It's alien," Meroe murmured.

"No kidding?"

The tech robots swarmed the site, deploying instrumentation, beaming data back to shielded computers in the bunkers, and the digger quickly cleared away the soft dirt until the probe droids stood about the object with overlapping sensory fields, soaking up data. The surface was imaged to fine resolution, lidar mapped the proportions, and instruments observed in every part of the spectrum.

Across the desert, the officers stood back with the supervising technicians, and Meroe knew they were itching to get at the thing themselves. But caution was the rule, none could forget for an instant that this was not only enemy technology, it was also the product of entirely alien thought processes. The situation could not be trusted no matter how safe it may seem.

The apparently inert craft lay silently for long minutes as the robots worked, but every com feed was alerted as the sensors detected energy in the strange sphere. "It's not dead," Klaus whispered. "Low level energy signature—it may be coming back online. It doesn't appear physically damaged by your direct hits, the energetic envelope must have deflected them, though at serious penalty to the vehicle."

"You might need to lock it under something too solid for it to break through," Craig mused. "A bunker, perhaps?"

"That's the plan, ma'am," Klaus murmured. "Levels rising, the latent subspace field seems to be reenergizing."

"Is it making a break for space?" Meroe asked sharply. "Better to blow it to hell and study the junk than let it go."

"I'm not sure…" Klaus squinted at the data feed. "It may be damaged, the field should be symmetrical but reads as anything-but. No subspace field I've ever seen is sustainable without also being symmetrical—for every 120° of field eccentricity you square the energy demand."

"Field radius?" Craig asked sharply.

"3.6 meters and increasing, but oscillating wildly." Klaus looked at the others. "I don't think we should be standing here."

"Rate of increase?" Meroe asked, a hand at his com.

"Exponential."

"Everybody aboard!" Meroe roared with a sweeping wave of his arm. "Leave your gear, get aboard, now!" They turned for the *Swallow's* wide, dark shadow and pounded up the ramp, Craig calling her own pilot a hundred meters away to launch immediately. The technical crew poured aboard and Meroe took his command position, Craig and Klaus slamming into spare seats toward the back of the bridge as the techs secured in rear compartments anywhere they could.

Mawson was pale-faced as he read the emanations from the alien. "It's going wild, my guess is a self-destruct to avoid inspection if it's incapable of escape." He eyed the systems enunciators. "Ramp sealed, aft compartment reports secure!"

"Go!" Meroe snapped, and Li Pei and Lund brought the ship off hot-standby. Engines belched thrust and she heaved into the air, turned on the spot and the throttles came up as gear retracted. She left the zone like a bullet from a barrel, but static arcs were burning over the alien probe as energy mounted to insane intensity—and the subspace field collapsed with a thunderclap, transducing from dimensional energy to heat. The fireball was a hundred meters wide, raw energy fused silicates in the sand to globules of glass, radiant heat was in the thousands of degrees and a blastwave slapped the streaking vessel out of the air with impunity.

Systems went down as breakers blew, and emergency power kicked in, Mawson fighting the internals for control as Li Pei struggled for dynamic stability. All was roaring wind against the airframe as, engines flamed out, the craft went through a full stall spin, turned over and dropped like a stone. Desert and sky flicked across the canopy in sickening flurries, then auxiliary power reached the helm and the vessel was snatched from its death-drop into a savage glide that ended with a rending impact as she skated across a dry lakebed in a geyser of grey-brown dirt, thrown up in a great rooster-tail from beneath the hull.

She gouged a four-hundred meter rut in the flats before coming to a rocking halt, dirt rained high over the canopy, and in the sudden quiet Lund reached to overhead panels, threw the main breakers and released fire foam in a dozen locations.

Meroe panted, dragged his spinning thoughts back to focus, and released his harness. "Radiation?" he barked, and at the rear starboard station Bikila shook his head groggily.

"Soft x-rays only, when the subspace field collapsed. The detonation was not nuclear. Though it was nuclear sized."

"Anybody hurt?" Meroe called through dust and smoke wisps.

Craig raised a hand with a grim smile, and the pilots high-fived—any landing they could walk away from. Meroe staggered aft, looked into the rear compartment and found technicians tumbled and sprawled. "Lund, we need a med kit, aft, on the double! Mawson, call it in, wideband, any help, we have injured."

A moment later the ship rocked again as a secondary blast wave went over, a roaring windstream that slugged the vessel mercilessly. When the racing wall of dust had gone by, Meroe reached to an overhead escape hatch, primed and blew the panel, dropped the ladder and squeezed up into the space. He whistled softly, and found Craig at his side a moment later, eyes shaded, to take in the still-rising mushroom cloud of smoke and dust, some twenty kilometers behind them.

They climbed onto the hull and stood staring in more than a little shock, and Craig felt the man's arm go around her, bringing a futile yet far from unwelcome sense of protection. Klaus profaned softly as he appeared at the hatch to look up at the spectacle.

"This trick won't work twice," the woman said softly. "Did we get anything to justify the effort?"

"Good data," Klaus whispered. "Not as good as taking apart an intact probe, but better than nothing."

"That's as much as we can hope for at this stage in the game," Meroe muttered.

"I could hope for a lot more," Craig said with a disgusted edge to her words. "We cost them a probe, they learned we are capable of deception. Not much of an exchange."

"Six months work, two ships and crews, a dummy installation…" Meroe sighed. "Something tells me we came off a long way second in this."

Klaus joined them and they watched the now-fraying cloud as high altitude winds began to pluck it apart and the fallout rained. There would be a vitrified crater at ground zero. It seemed a somber testimonial to human ambitions—flame and ash.

But the war had a long way to go, and there would be many more disappointments before the day came the colonial fleet made real headway; and none could guess what stroke of luck, what inspiration of diplomacy, might ever bring this conflict to an end.

For Craig and Meroe, the memory of a warmth long ago was abruptly the most precious commodity in a galaxy whose daily existence had grown precarious, and in that simple human feeling they know what they were fighting for.

Survival.

Mike Adamson holds a Doctoral degree from Flinders University of South Australia. After early aspirations in art and writing, Mike returned to study and secured qualifications in marine biology and archaeology. Mike has been a university educator since 2006, is a passionate photographer, master-level hobbyist and journalist for international magazines.

A Unique Opportunity

by Tom Howard

The aliens' arrival flooded the news. They landed at several world capitals, representing strange and exotic star systems. No two aliens leaving their ships looked the same. They appeared tall and thin, glistening blobs, or furry and spiked. They belonged to a homogeneous group of civilized worlds called the Unity. Being stuck way out at the end of the Milky Way spiral, they'd stumbled upon us by chance. If it hadn't been for one of our probes blasting random speeches as it passed through one of their wormhole conduits, they'd never have known we existed.

In my office, I pulled myself away from the most amazing event in history and pulled up the Taylor-Snead contract. After six decades, an old lady had a rep to live up to.

"Miss Combs," my secretary, I mean my executive assistant, said from the door. I think her name was Millie. After so many years of admin folks coming and going, they tended to run together.

I didn't mind her interrupting. I could use another cup of coffee. My doctor would never know. "What is it?"

"There are some men here from the government."

"Send them to Otis. He handles Fed contracts."

Millie turned to look behind her, her eyes wide. "I'm sorry, Miss Combs, but they insist on speaking to you."

Another client suing us for something they'd done wrong. I nodded, and she stepped aside. Two men in nice suits entered.

"We're sorry to bother you, Miss Combs," the Vice President of the United States said. "Could we have a few minutes of your time?"

I must have looked like a toad struck by lightning with my mouth open and my eyes bugging out.

23

I stood. "Vice President Munoz, what can I do for you?"

He smiled and took a seat, and the other man escorted Millie out of my office and closed the door.

"Your government needs you," Mr. Munoz said. "You've heard about the aliens from the Galactic Unity, I assume?"

I paused, distracted by his mane of white hair. He was even better looking in person.

"Yes, of course. What does that have to do with me?" And your being here.

He leaned back in his seat, expressing casual body language. I'd seen that "I'm a regular guy" posture before. I was being played, but I didn't care. He was the freaking Vice President of the United States of America.

I sat down before my legs gave way.

He looked around as if people stood in the hall with their ears pressed against my door, striving to learn what state secrets he had to share with me. If the Secret Service wasn't here, I suspected there would have been a crowd huddled outside my door.

"We have an opportunity here, Miss Combs. The Unity folks want to make a deal, and we hear you're the best in the business."

"A deal?" I envisioned bad science fiction movies of aliens invading Earth to carry off young women in bikinis. "What kind of deal?"

He leaned forward in a conspiratorial move. "We think it's a trade agreement, but we're not sure what they want from us. Their technology is so advanced anything we have to offer seems ludicrous. Right now, they're looking for something they might want."

After half a century, my dedication and long hours hadn't won me many friends or endeared me to my children, but I had gotten the job done. But this was way out of my field. "I'm sorry, sir. I don't think—"

He jumped to his feet. "Damn it, Combs, they're looking for contracts with almost every country on Earth. We must find a commodity they want before the others do. It's your duty as an American."

This guy needed acting lessons. Yelling people made terrible negotiators. He had FBI reports on me to ensure my participation. Little did he know, the subject of aliens was reason enough. I could double my rates afterward. "What about my firm?"

"They'll be compensated. They and you."

"A percentage of the deal if I broker one?" I asked.

"Don't push it," he said with a grin, the first real emotion I'd seen since he'd walked in.

I smiled back. "When do I start?"

"Tomorrow morning at 9 a.m. in front of this building. Will that work for you?"

I nodded. "What will I show them?"

"We're thinking of promoting ourselves as a tourist location. Show them the wonders of the world, focusing on United States features if you can, but nothing is off limits. The United Nations has given them worldwide travel authority. If you find they're interested in a specific resource, please let us know, but we're thinking tourism is our best asset."

It would be an interesting story to tell my grandchildren, but I had doubts. If these aliens could travel to planets made of diamond and watch rainbow-colored suns set on the horizon, what would a backwater world like Earth have to offer? "Tomorrow morning. Just me?"

"Well, we wanted to give you a military escort, but the aliens said no. You can have one admin assistant and one government representative."

"You?"

He shook his head. "No. The President requested one of his Freethinkers accompany you."

Great. If one of the government's ideology watchdogs was traveling around the world with me, they wanted to make sure I didn't say anything bad about the government. Freethinkers were only free with their thinking when it occurred within their strict guidelines of loyalty.

"What authority will I have? Can I close a deal? And will it be binding for an entire planet?"

"If we approve," the Vice President said. "Do you agree to work for us?"

"I can give you two days, and there better be lots of zeroes in that offer."

"I'll make sure of it. If you need anything, your government escort will contact us. Would you like a federal executive assistant?"

"No," I said. "Millie will be fine." If not, an avid science fiction fan in the office would give a testicle or ovary to go with me.

He paused. "One last question, Miss Combs. How is your health?"

The bastard. He knew I'd been treated for cancer three times. If it came back, the next time would be my last. "I can't run a marathon, Mr. Vice President, but I can still make them sign on the dotted line. Don't worry about me."

#

The next morning, I almost changed my mind. I was too old to be traipsing around the world with little green men, but the contract had arrived the night before during my second glass of wine and the zeroes had been staggering. They knew how to motivate me. I dressed in black slacks and a suit jacket and wore my most comfortable shoes. I'd checked online the night before for places to show our tourists. I'd see what piqued their interest. Might be young men in speedos.

When I arrived at the office, Millie waited for me at the front door, a bag over her shoulder. She wore a beige jacket, cargo pants, and a hat.

"You look like you're going on safari," I said. "Are those combat boots?"

"Hiking boots," she said. "I wasn't sure where we'd go today."

"As long as you have your cell phone and a notebook, I don't care what you wear. Are you ready?"

She nodded. "I can't believe this is happening, Miss Combs. Thank you for taking me."

"No problem. If we end up sharing a yurt in Mongolia overnight, I wanted someone who didn't snore. You don't snore, do you?"

Before Millie could answer, a tall man in a suit walked up. "Miss Combs? Miss Binderswith? I'm Mr. Dodge. I'll be accompanying you on this trip." He smiled, but it appeared to hurt his face.

He addressed Millie. "Binderswith, is that an American name?"

"I guess so," she said. "My parents are from Wyoming."

Before I told him not to interrogate my employees, a silver orb descended from the sky like Glinda the Good Witch arriving in her shimmering globe. It sank to the parking lot without a sound. During the night, the front of the building had been cordoned off, and the press corps and bystanders watched as the ship landed. Like a soap bubble, the globe popped, leaving two figures standing by a silver column.

"One small step," I said and strode forward. What if they drooled battery acid or spoke by emitting disgusting odors? A hairless pale green alien wore a red kilt. His friend was naked. Or I assumed he was naked, being covered from head to toe in thick brown fur. He reminded me of Cousin It from the Addams Family.

"Miss Combs," the green one said in perfect English, "so pleased you are taking us on a tour. We hope it will be beneficial for everyone."

"Thank you for inviting me," I said. "This is Miss Binderswith and Mr. Dodge. They will be accompanying me."

"I am Grex," the green man said. "These are my noble companions, Mr. Bzzz, and 62018." Surprisingly, the silver column between them was another alien. I hadn't seen any cybernetic life forms on the news. Perhaps a colony of small creatures lived inside the hovering silver tube.

"Please call me Six," the silver column said in a deep voice. "I am pleased to meet you." Lights traveled up and down the tube as the creature spoke. "Excuse me if I break taboo, but I thought your planet only had two genders."

"That's correct. Mr. Dodge is a man, and Miss Binderswith and I are women."

"But you do not look like Miss Binderswith," he said.

"I'm older," I said. "We change in appearance as we age. Someday young Miss Binderswith will look more like me." I hoped she wasn't insulted.

Mr. Dodge, who had been staring at the aliens, asked, "Which of you is in charge?"

"In charge?" Mr. Bzzz asked with a voice that sounded like hundreds of bees buzzing. "Do you mean who owns us? No one can own another."

"The Unity is a symbiotic organism," Grex explained. "We're equals here. No one is in charge."

"Then how do you make decisions?" Mr. Dodge asked. "How do you accomplish anything?"

I wanted to hear this.

"We go where there is need," Grex said. "We follow compassion in all things."

"Sounds like a good plan," I said but wondered if we were negotiating with children. "If you'd like to begin, I thought I'd show you the Grand Canyon."

As fast as the bubble disappeared, it reappeared around us. I took Millie's arm as the ship zoomed into the sky but felt no acceleration. The smooth walls flowed into chairs and everyone sat except for Six and Mr. Dodge. He seemed disturbed the alien government was a symbiocracy.

"Do you need directions?" I asked. "It will be—"

"We've arrived," Grex said. "It is quite lovely."

I looked down at the deepest canyon in North America. Sitting in an alien bubble hundreds of feet in the air with beings from light years away, the eroded striations below weren't as impressive as I'd hoped.

"My parents brought my brother and me here when we were children," Millie said. "They had burros who took you down these narrow little trails to the bottom, but I was too frightened to go."

"Do you still travel together?" I asked.

27

She started, unaware she'd spoken aloud. "He died in Afghanistan."

"That is so sad," Six said. "An accident?"

"A war." She looked down into the canyon.

The aliens looked away as if the concept of war embarrassed them.

Mr. Dodge cleared his throat and scowled at me as if I weren't doing my job. "The government spends millions of dollars every year on national parks like this for our legitimate citizens to enjoy."

What did he mean by that? Illegitimate citizens had to visit the ditch in the next state?

"Is that a lot of money?" Mr. Bzzz asked.

They learned every language on the planet, knew how to deal with people with contract negotiating experience, and they didn't know how much a dollar was worth? He was pulling Mr. Dodge's leg. I liked Mr. Bzzz.

"Have you seen the canyons on Mars?" Six asked. "They go down for miles. What's next, Miss Combs?"

The aliens were not impressed with our little depression in Arizona. Aliens would not be coming here to spend their hard-earned credits to see rust-colored rock.

I showed them the Great Wall of China next, although Mr. Dodge gave me the hairy eyeball for taking them outside America.

When the bubble dissolved, we joined thousands of human tourists atop the wall.

"Extraordinary," Six said. He floated forward. "So many people."

Not what I wanted to show him. "This wall is 4,000 miles long. It can be seen from space." I'd done my homework.

"Does it change colors or produce harmonic sounds throughout the day?" Mr. Bzzz asked.

"No," I said.

"Too bad," Grex said. "That would have been lovely."

Next, we tried Mt. Everest, then the Pyramids at Giza. The visitors were pleasant but unimpressed.

Maybe I wasn't the right person for the job. Millie took pictures of the aliens at every place we visited, more excited at seeing the aliens than the greatest wonders of the modern world. I didn't blame her. Mr. Dodge tried to stay aloof and professional but had stopped providing worthless bits of information about how our government had contributed to everything. If he hoped to catch me saying something "un-American," he was going to be disappointed. I'd been telling people what they wanted to hear since he wore diapers.

Shifting from man-made wonders back to natural ones, we visited

Victoria Falls, Hawaii, and the North Pole. Although our visitors made kind comments, I felt Earth had nothing to offer interstellar sightseers. I had no idea how to read the client. Grex seemed cheery and interested, but his expression never changed. Mr. Bzzz's fur rippled, and I guessed it was relaying an emotion, but I didn't know if he was repulsed or attracted. Six's lights blinked. I needed a key to unlock these guys.

We stumbled across the key by accident. Millie needed to use a bathroom on our way to see the Christ the Redeemer statue in Peru. A religious icon might get their attention.

We landed in Santo Joya in Brazil for people to stretch their legs and use the facilities at a roadside service station. The owners and customers stared at us but didn't comment when we entered. We humans did our business while the aliens shopped. We'd have to think about food soon, and I had no idea what they might like. Maybe gastronomic delights would land these particular fish.

"What is this?" Grex asked me when I left the ladies room. He held up a key ring with one of those rubber balls where the eyes bugged out when you squeezed it.

"It's a colorful trinket used to keep our keys together. We use keys to unlock our homes, cars, and businesses." I dug mine out of my pocket and showed him.

Grex squeezed. "This one looks like a Lipharian."

"It does!" Mr. Bzzz agreed. "I want one. Do we barter for them?"

"We'll pay for it." I took two of the colorful key rings and handed them to Mr. Dodge. He might as well make his government credit card useful.

"Mr. Six, would you like an Earth memento?" I asked.

"No, thank you," he said. "I've been collecting data since we arrived. I've plenty to remember Earth by."

Millie joined us as Mr. Dodge bought the key rings, and we returned to our bubble in the parking lot.

We passed over acres and acres of jungle, Grex slowing the bubble to let Millie take pictures.

"What happened here?" Grex asked. The bubble hovered over a series of denuded hills. Stumps from thousands of trees dotted the landscape, interrupted by spirals of crude dirt roads dug into the countryside. Rain had washed deep red gashes into the clay.

"They're cutting down trees," I said. "This rainforest used to be untouched. Now, it's being hacked down to provide farmland and timber. They're losing thousands of acres a year."

"Thirty thousand," Millie said from the transparent wall.

"But doesn't this forest provide your planet's atmosphere?" Six asked. "Why is it being destroyed?"

"It's a renewable resource," Mr. Dodge said. "It will grow back."

Millie shook her head. "Not in time. They're cutting it down faster than it can grow."

Mr. Bzzz's fur rippled, and the three of them stood speechless. What had gotten them so excited?

"This isn't rational," Grex said. "You're cutting off your *xccryx* to spite your *inbratia!*"

I didn't need that translated. "We humans don't always do the smartest thing where our planetary resources are concerned."

"Climate change is a hoax," Mr. Dodge said.

"I rest my case," I said. Perhaps they weren't accustomed to seeing a race intent on instant gratification, but it gave me an idea.

Lunch was forgotten as we visited the dying Great Barrier Reef, the smog bank over Beijing, and the great island of plastic floating off the Pacific Coast. With each stop, the aliens grew more and more excited.

"This is incredible," Grex said when we paused over the toxic electronic dump site in Ghana. "So much self-inflicted destruction." The smoldering ruins went on for miles, and people sickened by the toxins picked through the wreckage.

Mr. Bzzz agreed. "I've read about such planets but never expected to encounter one."

I felt a surge of hope. Maybe our planet's mistreatment was reason enough to attract alien tourists. We could show them how we were working to scrub our air, repair the ozone layer, and clean our oceans. We'd be an inspiration to the galaxy, a backwater planet struggling to regain harmony with nature.

"It is terrible," I said. We'd look at the shrinking ice caps and the strip mines in the afternoon. "Perhaps you can help us heal our planet faster." That would be the compassionate thing to do.

Six blinked. "When we encounter a planet, which has suicided like this one, they are lifeless husks. Our scientists will welcome a chance to observe it as it happens."

Grex turned to me. "We're willing to discuss terms for the use of your resources. We'll need to establish research centers, spaceports, and full satellite coverage."

"With the United States?" Mr. Dodge asked.

"With all countries," Mr. Bzzz said. "This is a unique opportunity for the Unity."

I should have insisted on a percentage. "We can arrange that."

Grex turned the bubble around, and the Washington D.C. skyline appeared. "We've found lifeless worlds after the inhabitants stripped the planet of its resources, but we've never found one at the tipping point. If we can determine what caused it, we might prevent it from happening to other worlds."

I didn't like the sound of that. "Tipping point? You mean the point where we can still save ourselves?"

"Oh no," Six said. "It's much too late for Earth. I've been running atmospheric scans and checking environmental data bases. Your scientists are wrong about how much time you have left. You've gone over the tipping point. I don't know why we didn't see it sooner."

"We never thought to look for the signs," Mr. Bzzz said. "They seemed so rational."

"That's preposterous," Mr. Dodge said. "Are you saying we're doomed? I told you global warming is wrong. We can prove it."

"Shut up, Mr. Dodge." Let him report me. "How long do we have, Grex?"

"Our scientists will do what they can, but I'd say you've less than a hundred Earth years before the planet becomes unlivable." He lowered the bubble where we'd departed this morning. It seemed like years had passed, and they pressed down on me.

Six blinked as the bubble popped. "We'll discuss this with the rest of the Unity. Your planet is a remarkable find. You are very unique."

"Yeah," I said, "we're going to be uniquely dead in a century. Good for us."

Mr. Bzzz rippled. "I understand we will need contracts for the temporary facilities we intend to build here. Should we contact you tomorrow, Miss Combs?"

"Yes, that would be fine." I was numb. There were places I wanted to go and people I needed to see. I had grandchildren who might live to see the end.

Mr. Dodge looked pale. He left the platform without a word and walked away, whether to report to his masters or to take his family to church, I didn't know. I didn't care.

"What will we do, Miss Combs?" Millie's voice trembled as if she wanted to cry. She joined me on the steps, and we watched the bubble disappear into the sky.

"I don't know about you, but I'm going to open a bottle of 700 Pipers Scotch I've been saving." Although I'd technically won this contract negotiation and my reputation remained intact, I didn't feel like celebrating. I wanted to drown my sorrows and not think about the future, something we humans were good at.

Maybe the Unity needed a good contract negotiator.

Tom Howard is a science fiction and fantasy short story writer living in Little Rock, Arkansas. He thanks his family and friends for their inspiration and the Central Arkansas Speculative Fiction Writers' Group for their perspiration

Be Brave

by Linda M. Crate

"Be brave," she said. "They will never harm you. Not as long as I am here to protect you, and I will always protect you. Even when I'm gone, I will be here," she remarked, placing a hand on his chest.

"Bionica, come, we must find you protection," his father insisted.

His mother shifted from his father's arms and remained on her knees, hugging her son tightly. "Be strong, I will never leave you."

"But mother, everyone dies."

"No, they always live," she corrected. "They can never die. As long as you hold them in your hearts, they will always be alive. They can never take me from you. As long as you're breathing, so am I. You may not understand me now, but you will one day."

"Mother!"

"Be brave."

"MOTHER!"

"Be brave, I love you. Be brave," she insisted, tears dancing down her cheeks. She sniffed horribly, grabbing a tissue from her pocket, dabbing at her eyes. "I love you," she whispered.

"We have to go before they find you."

"It's too late," she gasped. "Look!"

"MOTHER!" Grant cried out, waking up drenched in sweat. He looked over to his wife Ida who looked at him with great concern. "Don't worry."

"What's wrong?"

"I had another dream about my mother."

"What do you think it means, Grant?"

"I think it means Earth is nearing its end. Every time I've had this dream, the planet I was living on has died. I don't want Earth to die, I don't want you to die. I don't want the children to die," he protested. "I have to leave before they find me."

"Grant! Don't be absurd. Where will you go?"

"It's me they want. They tried to send me away to protect their planet, but they killed them, anyway." He clenched his fist, running a hand through his long black hair. "It's me that they want," he whispered, his bright hazel eyes flashing darkly.

Ida sat up on the bed, her long blonde hair an unkempt mess. He had always admired how she looked perfect even with her hair a complete and utter wreck. He loved the way she smiled, the light that shined in her eyes, the way her body and his seemed to fit perfectly against one another. "You can't go. We love you."

"I love you, too," he answered. "But I'm going to tell you something. My mother loved me enough that she died for me. It is my turn to be brave. To protect you all," he whispered.

"You can't leave me."

"I love you, be brave," he whispered. He would not make his mother's mistake and linger too long. She screamed his name, but Grant ignored it. As much as it killed him inside, he knew it was him that they wanted. He turned. "I love you, be brave," he remarked, throwing down his necklace his mother had given him. "Keep it, to remember me." It was a golden chain with a golden pendant with stars and crystals etched in and a large diamond in the center. "Goodbye, my love, good bye forever."

"You think we're just going to let you go. I love you, you idiot. Come back here."

"There is no time, Ida. I cannot explain it fully as I wish I could. There is no time. They'll be here, they have destroyed planets in pursuit of me before. Do you really think I want them to destroy Earth over me?"

"Don't be so arrogant. How can you be so sure that it was you they were after? It seems a bit preposterous to me that they should destroy entire planets to get to you."

"My father killed five thousand nine hundred alien planets and my mother helped him to protect the human race. I don't think it's so ridiculous that they would chase me down until I was dead," he answered with a hollow laugh. "And now I've waited too long. It's too late, they are here."

"How can you tell?"

"That blue light, that's how it always starts." He grimaced. "There will be asteroids, there will be death. They will kill people openly during all the chaos without showing them any mercy, they'll probably kill you right before my eyes."

"Don't talk like that. It's so morbid."

"It's the end of the world, did you really think there would be magical skipping pink butterflies and silver unicorns dancing on streams of rainbows?"

"Stop it," Ida hissed, eyes suddenly alive with an intensity and a fire. "Am I really supposed to just lay down here and die because some alien scum decides to set my planet on fire? We'll fight, of course."

"It will be futile."

"I don't care, I am not going to lay here and be some damsel in distress simply because you tell me to be. Don't be stupid. If you're going to fight then so am I."

"They might not take you too seriously in a night gown."

"They will if they've ever seen me fire a gun," Ida smirked. "It's the end of the world, who said I had to be fashionably correct?" She walked over, kissing Grant hard on the mouth. "Just give me a kiss, first."

"You just took one."

"Maybe I'd like another."

"Ida."

"Shh."

"There's something I've never told you. Or even showed you." He stepped away from her, revealing his true appearance. His long golden locks he had inherited from his mother and the vividly intense blue purple eyes he had gotten from his father. But the most horrifying thing he knew would be his skin. His skin was blue and purple as his eyes. His teeth were jagged and gold in appearance, as well.

"You monster!"

He laughed darkly. "I thought you loved me."

"That was before I knew the truth!" she growled.

"Is there any such thing?" he demanded. "Everyone lies."

"Well, if I were an alien, I wouldn't lie about it."

"Wouldn't you?" he asked, eyes sharp as daggers. "How long do you think people would have let me live if I walked out like this. Hmm?"

"I—hadn't considered that," she remarked, looking away.

"Does it really change anything? I'm still your husband. I'm still the father of your children."

Ida considered his words. They were true. She still loved him. No matter how terrifying she found his true appearance, she had fallen in love with his beautiful heart and his beautiful spirit. She pulled his mother's necklace from the ground and put it on with delicate grace and kissed him full on the mouth. "You were right, but you should have told me the truth long before this."

"You accept me for what I am?"

"How could I not? What you said was true. You're still the father of my children and the love of my life. I love you. I always have."

He smiled. "Thank you. My father was an alien, my mother a human. I'm not really like either of the races." He looked away. "I suspect that's why the children never get ill on this planet, their bodies are stronger than a humans." He looked apologetically at her.

"Well, that's a perk," she smiled.

"What was your mother's name? You've never told me much about your parents."

"Bionica."

"What wasn't she a cyborg?"

"I suppose that doesn't make her completely human, either, does it?" he snorted. "But yes, she was. I always have visions that come true, it's something I inherited from her race. I only wanted to spare you. I only wanted you to live and the children, too."

"Everyone dies."

"No, everyone lives," he smiled. "As long as you have them here," he remarked, placing a hand on her heart. "I must go."

"I've already told you no."

"Last time I checked, my will was my own. I love you, my stubborn flower." He kissed her fully on the mouth one last time before he walked out of the house. He closed his eyes and appeared at his home planet or what was left of it. He knew that Ida would never forgive his decision to leave her, but he had to. To his immense relief, he saw that the blue light had left Earth. It was coming nearer and nearer to his home planet, however.

There wasn't much left to be destroyed.

Only him.

"I'm being brave, mother," he whispered. "Like you always told me." He snorted. "I was almost selfish. I almost stayed. She would have made it so easy. Makes me wonder why father was so willing to do the right thing and send you away. But maybe his love for you was more pure than the love I've shared with Ida. He had always been truthful to you about who and what he really was." He ran a hand through his long golden hair, glancing at his blue and pink skin with a grimace. "But I suppose it's not easy to be brave, is it, mother?"

"Why do you love me? I'm nothing special."

"Ida, don't be silly. You're special to me and to everyone who knows you. You are so beautiful, so smart, so talented. How could you not see that in yourself?"

"I don't know. I've never been self-confident."

"Well, I'll give you lessons."

"You will, will you?"

"But they won't come for free."
"They won't?"
"No, you'll owe me a kiss for each one."
She laughed. *"Very well then, I suppose I could do with sharing my lips more with you. They really seem to like you."*
"They do, do they?"
"Indeed," she admitted with a roguish grin as she pulled him into a forceful kiss. *"And for the record, I love you, too."*

"I suppose you think you're being brave, don't *you?"* came a cruel voice.

Grant turned to find himself facing an alien woman with thick long purple hair and golden eyes. Her body was much like that of a human woman except she had leathery black skin accented with gold and purple and a tail that looked as if it belonged to a scorpion.

"What do you think bravery is?" he demanded.

"Dying for your men. Defending the honor of your tribe. Dying with dignity in battle like a true warrior. Not dying for a woman. That is weakness. Women are weaker than men. In dying for one, it shows that you're just as weak. It is truly pathetic what the humans did to you. Your mother was brave, your father was brave, but you are pathetic."

"Forgive me, but I wished for a more peaceful life. I wanted love, I wanted life. I wanted a chance to feel the sun on my face without it burning straight through my skin," he snorted. "Not everyone can be a martyr in war. Who would I have to fight for? You killed my entire race when you killed my parents. Who would my men be? Just because I am dying in the name of love doesn't make me weak. I am not only dying for my wife, but my children, the people of Earth, my country, and all the countries that are represented on that crazy planet. So, you see, I am braver than either you or your men could possibly be. You kill peaceable people simply because they don't agree with you or your ideals of what is right and what is wrong. You are a violent race driven by war and the need to dominate. It will give me great pleasure when I see your race eradicated from every galaxy that has ever been created."

She scoffed, slapping at the ground angrily, forcing blue rooted plants from their slumber. "These hearty plants have more backbone than you. Pity they will die just as easily. Get off that rock," she snarled. "You will face me like a man. I will not kill a child. There is no honor in that. You will fight for your life or your death whichever will claim you. Do not speak to me of bravery, you are starting to sound like a human. Not surprising when you consider how many years you've lived with them."

"They are more tenacious than you think," he whispered. "This may not be their apocalypse but your own."

"Don't be stupid when we're finished with you, we will destroy your precious Earth including your stupid wife and children."

"There are some lines you should not cross, woman, and that is one of them. Never insult my family, ever again," he growled.

"So you do have a temper? Good. I was beginning to think I was going to fight a little girl and that would be terribly boring. Show me that you're a man! Let me see you bleed," she snarled.

"I will show you that you're only a woman." He glanced as he followed her direction, his eyes widening in horror. "No, what have they done?!"

"Earth is in our way, I thought I told you before that they would die. My men are ready to take them out when I am finished with you. I am not going to miss that for the world," she laughed wickedly. "Or lack thereof, perhaps?"

He punched the woman hard in the face without thinking.

She smirked. "Ah, so it begins does it? I suppose you should have a weapon, no? I will make this a fair fight."

"With that tail of yours, is it really going to be fair?"

"I suppose you have a fair point but that's not my problem, it's yours," she smirked. She raised her tail to strike him but he dodged fairly quickly. "Agile, I see. Good, this will make this an interesting fight."

"I'm not interested in fighting," he snarled, shoving his fist straight through her chest. He used the bionics he had inherited from his mother to use her own organs against her.

The alien woman shuddered against his attack and gasped as she glanced over her shoulder as all her ships and her men were destroyed one by one. She glanced at the fire in his eyes. "You combined the powers of your parents to destroy my race?!" she shrieked.

"Yes," he smirked. "Not so weak now, am I? Dying for the ones I love," he whispered.

"What?" It was then that she realized her tail had slammed into his heart when she had turned. "I suppose we both get to die with honor," she whispered as her eyes closed and she fell hard to the soils of his home planet.

Grant smiled as he reached for the stars. "Thank you for everything, mother," he whispered before his eyes stared forever toward the heavens.

Linda M. Crate's works have been published in numerous magazines and anthologies. She is the author of seven poetry chapbooks, the latest of which is: *the samurai* (Yellow Arrow Publishing, October 2020). She has also authored two micro-collections, and three full length poetry collections.

Fantasy Film Investigations Inc.

by Andrew P. McGregor

Senior investigator Louis Leckie shook his head in disbelief. Judge Andrews was a biased bastard, but for once he'd exercised some discretion and gotten it right. The director of 'Hot Pursuit,' a mediocre film to begin with, slumped in his seat as many in the audience in the packed courtroom cheered and clapped. Judge Andrews finished reading his verdict and a couple of officers clamped cold metal cuffs around the director's wrists. They prodded him towards the white-walled room's side-door.

With a wide grin, prosecutor Cassandra clop-clopped in her shoes right up to Louis and flung her arms around him. "Told you I could put the prick away."

"Well done," Louis told her through gritted teeth as a small crowd of human reporters and accompanying micro-drones surrounded them. Louis stepped out of her embrace. "I really thought Andrews was going to go against you this time."

"It was your evidence that put the director away. He's been making dodgy films for *years*. It's about time we got him."

Louis nodded and smiled, but didn't quite feel the same way. He'd been working on this particular film for almost a year, gathering evidence and trying to prove, beyond a doubt, that director Collins had falsified his actor's physical limits. Along with the money he'd just lost in a bet with her, he couldn't help feeling guilty of putting potentially innocent people behind bars.

Louis looked over at the wide-eyed actor, the leading man whose physicality had been the subject of such intense scrutiny, and whose lucrative career had just been crushed by the verdict. As rounded as his belly and limbs were, Louis still had the aching suspicion that maybe, if pushed, a person of the actor's physical dimensions could have performed the stunts in the film. Some simulations even stated it was possible, albeit unlikely. The entire case had hinged on Louis' evidence that the plump hero could not have climbed a thousand stairs with one broken leg and been able to jump around, kick people, and shoot a gun with accuracy when he reached the top. Judge Andrews' verdict implied that such feats were physically impossible when put together in a consecutive fashion.

"He should have purchased a fantasy license," Cassandra said to the assembled reporters while Louis stood by and watched. "Now he has to pay the price."

"Don't you think jail-time is harsh?" A woman with a mop of curly hair asked.

"Do you know how many people have made horrible life-choices based on their heroes?" Cassandra asked the reporter. "It's all common knowledge, look it up if you need to. Potential doctors ditched their careers to become bad crime scene investigators, a brilliant astronomer joined the army. Young kids are trying all the drugs they can get their hands on, because that's how super heroes are made and *it happened in the movies.*" Cassandra took a breath before the reporter could back down and make an escape from the prosecutor's wrath. "Children have fallen to their deaths pretending to be superman or ironman. If irresponsible films by people like Collins continue to be made, then mark my words, poverty on a massive scale will return, wars will start, chaos will ensue."

"That's a powerful statement," a taller man over the back called out.

"Well, she's a strong prosecutor," Louis said. His comment was met with scattered laughter and he tapped Cassandra on the shoulder to distill her rage. "Come on, I can't stay much longer."

She glared at him, but the lines around her eyes softened, and the smile slowly returned. "Sorry Louis."

Louis agreed wholeheartedly with what Cassandra had said. In fact, he'd been there since the beginning. The Screen Entertainment & Media Integrity Commission, SEMIC for short, had been founded on one guiding principle: misrepresentation is dangerous. He just wished Cassandra was a little less aggressive.

On their way through the small throng of reporters, Louis deflected a couple of questions about the investigation and ignored the floating cloud of micro drones that followed them out of the courtroom. A handful of the larger, more expensive finger-nail sized drones followed them all the way to their waiting airship. The drones would record in detail, he knew, every minute sound and every movement so that the news sites they belonged to could report on their tiniest facial expressions.

Louis took comfort in the fact that the drone's handlers had to send a copy of their recordings to the state's police department so they could spot any falsified data. Should the news reporters try to manipulate their images, they would be caught.

The drones eventually stopped and returned to their handlers. Louis and Cassandra boarded the airship along with dozens of other officials and police officers, identically clothed in dark navy jackets and black pants. The uniforms looked rather casual but were equipped with all the latest protective material and communication gear. Backup attack drones were never far away. You could never be too safe when dealing with non-complying film studios.

"So, you'll be launched from the bridge," Cassandra said as they sat in a small four-person booth lined with red leather. A slim white table floated down from the ceiling.

"Yes, the bridge. Water, please," he said to the table. A tall white cup sucked itself out of the centimetre-thick table and water swirled upwards from tiny pores inside the cup. The table decreased minimally in size as the material from which it was made converted to water.

"How long will you be gone?"

"A month, two months tops," he blurted.

"Confident, are we?" She smiled and ordered a beer.

"Allowance now reached," the table's quiet voice spoke from speakers embedded throughout its surface.

"Already?" Cassandra snatched her white cup of pale beer.

"Easy there, I'll shout you my allowance. I think you've earned it," he told her.

"That's a breach of regs, Louis," she said before slurping the liquid in her cup.

"So they'll fine me another beer for the week, I won't be around anyway." He drank the cool water in his cup and felt it soothe his dry throat.

"What's the case, anyway? And why do you have to go all the way to Ceres?"

Louis sighed, "It's the film studio that made 'Second Stand.'"

"Oh, that one." Cassandra rolled her eyes.

"Yeah, I guess that's why they didn't bother assigning you to prosecute this one, too easy. We've got them cornered now, so they're trying to negotiate. The director, Wesley Mavrin, has invited me to come see the set where they made the film. He thinks he can prove to me that the stunts were real, somehow."

"That'll be a tough one," she said between sips. "I assume you've already run the actuaries?"

Louis nodded, "I ran the actuaries and got permission to run full-scale tests in near-Earth orbit. I even had a whole simulator to myself for a couple of hours. There is no way Mavrin can worm his way out of this arrest."

"Mmm, sounds… dangerous," she winked at him. They'd always imagined doing exciting things like this when they were children, dreaming of becoming space-ship captains or rocket-racers.

"Hardly, I'll have to wear a slop-suit the whole time and I'll be riding in a converted Orion-craft."

"Ah, now that's comfort!" She laughed at him.

"That's mean." He mock-frowned at her, then gave her his best impression of an impish grin. "Guinness, please."

The table morphed upwards near his hands and a white cup started filling with Guinness formed out of materials from the table itself.

"Now *that's* mean, you know I hate that stuff."

"Well, don't be mean to *me* next time. Enjoy the drink." He got up from the table and frowned as he transferred a large sum of money to her account using the computer embedded at the base of his brain.

"About time you paid up. Hey, want to make another bet about your new case?"

Louis shook his head at her suggestion and walked to the far side of the airship's viewing platform. He could barely make out the large inflatable dome of the airship's gas-filled top above them, but could easily see the ship's propellers rotating near the rear.

Below the floating ship was a vast expanse of interconnecting buildings fed by the various roads, tubes and rails stretching in all directions across the city. It was five-thirty in the evening and the darkening city came to life with glow-foil strips and the occasional power-guzzling street lamp.

As his gaze shifted to a new point in the distance, the airship's smart-glass illuminated each of the tiny buildings for him with a label appearing next to each.

Approaching rather quickly was the city's SEMIC Towers. Almost two kilometres high, the giant skybridge that connected the towers had several transfer vehicles on its top waiting for launch. From this distance, the vehicles looked like teeth for the bridge's mouth. Even to Louis, who worked at SEMIC's towers, the place appeared ominous.

The tune *Gonna Eat the Sky* started playing in his mind.

"Still, why is it you have to go all the way out there? Bring the bastard back to Earth or drop the case. It was a shit film, and the flight out would cost more than the movie's entire budget and takings put together."

Louis glanced to the side where Cassandra had joined him at the viewing window. "It did okay at the box office. More importantly, this case could bankrupt the company and all its backers."

"So?"

"It's *big*, Sandra. The producer was Myla Sincrow if you recall."

"Yes, I remember the name. So Sincrow's what? Some mining executive out in the rocks who financed a movie because she got bored?"

"She's *the* Sincrow." Louis sighed when Cassandra returned a blank stare.

"She isn't just some mid-level executive. She has a majority stake in Space-Tech as well as Prime Mining. She *owns* Ceres, Sandra. If I pull this off, I shut down two of the biggest interplanetary companies in the Solar System."

Cassandra stared at him a moment longer, her mouth opening, and then grinned devilishly. "Need a prosecutor?"

"Greedy," he said and wagged a finger at her. It was the case of the decade and even if he didn't win, he'd be famous.

He bid Cassandra goodbye and entered his home tower's quarantine. He stripped naked and sat in a scrubber bath. High-detail scanners ran up and down his body while he looked up his grandkids on his neural net and exchanged messages back and forth with them.

They were excited about his trip but, he admitted to them, he didn't share that excitement. Maybe a hundred years ago when he'd dreamed of this kind of thing, but now? He felt... not tired, just well-worn. Maybe if he were exploring deep space or going on a cruise, it would be a more interesting endeavor. But this was a job, one job in a long line of many jobs. Perhaps he would retire after this one. It was, after all, the largest case he'd ever been involved with.

After two hours a bell chimed inside the small blue decontamination room, rousing him from a quick sleep.

Time to go.

#

His fears were confirmed the moment the shuttle reached orbit and he glimpsed the vessel that would take him all the way to Ceres.

He'd gotten a taste for what was to come when he'd smacked his head on the shuttle's door and then endured the junk-heap's rattling when it launched from the SEMIC Towers' giant skybridge. The gee-force of the ascent he could handle, but the rattling, no.

He knew there'd been budget cuts. That could be the reason for the shuttle's shaky ascent - some engine parts or a glitch in the shuttle's computer probably hadn't been checked. Or, more likely, it had been checked but deemed unnecessary to repair. "Damned accountants," he muttered.

The engine cut out and weightlessness arrived. His stomach felt as if it was trying to escape through his ears. "Couldn't you make this thing spin a little?"

"Approaching destination," the shuttle's computer informed him.

"Oh… pus," he said as the 'destination' came into view. It was little more than a white star at this distance, but the optics in his eyes optics enhanced and sharpened the vision. It was the *Surge Advocate*. Louis groaned. The *Surge Advocate* was one of the oldest ships in the fleet, something that was new when he was a child. Short and dull-grey, it had a large pusher plate for propulsion. Modern vessels used nuclear valves for thrust, which were both far more fuel efficient and provided a smoother ride for their passengers.

The arrow-headed shuttle swam up and snuggled next to the white monster's head. A docking tube extended from the head and clamped onto the shuttle's underside.

Louis unclipped and lurched forward out of the couch, then waited for his stomach to catch up when he reached the airlock. He heard a hiss, some mechanical sounds, and then the lock spiraled open.

The docking tube was scored with tiny pockmarks, created by stellar radiation suffered over the decades of unshielded space travel. His neural data assured him the defect had been rectified and a new, albeit thin shield had been installed on the outside of the tubing. Only marginally reassured, his knuckles turned white while he floated down the monster's maw.

The feeling of dread intensified as he reached the monster's interior. The crew cabin was tiny at four metres wide on each side. The walls appeared to be solid metal where he'd been expecting the usual spongiform smart walls.

For a moment his humour returned and he smiled — he felt like he'd entered a wooden sailing ship in the age of aircraft carriers. "Let's set sail then, shall we?" He tried to get comfortable in a couch that probably had feathers for cushioning while reviewing flight plans and mission goals. Two small tug boats arrived from Century Station. They latched on to the *Surge Advocate*'s anchor points and slowly dragged it out of Earth's orbit.

The technology was so old and dangerous, he'd practically been dragged beyond the moon's orbit by the tugs instead of the usual fifty thousand kilometres. While he waited, he slept, ate, exercised and gave periodic updates to his children and grandchildren on his flight status. Telling them he'll be *fine*. He used to do this *all the time*. Even the older great grandchildren could see the sweat on his face.

It took three days for the *Surge Advocate* to reach a safe distance before it could start up the main 'engine.'

"You may now engage flight mode," one of the automated tugs told him.

"Acknowledged," the *Surge Advocate*'s computer sent back. "Engine is ready, Louis, engage?"

Louis gulped. "Go for it."

#

Thump... Thump... Thump...

The monotonous sound echoed throughout the ship.

Thump... Thump... Thump...

Day after day.

Thump... Thump... Thump...

Like a heartbeat.

The nuclear explosions flashed bright-white every three seconds, sending energetic pulses into the ship's pusher plate. The Orion Drive, despite being designed almost two hundred years ago and dangerous to any nearby habitable areas, was still one of the most effective methods of space travel. A pity the design didn't allow for more noise dampening. At first Louis couldn't sleep and couldn't think straight. A relentless headache set in. Noise-cancelling ear plugs helped, but he could still feel the thumping through every surface.

An entire month of this crap? He thought to himself.

He distracted himself by playing virtual games and listening to classical music. 'Classical' was an insult, many of the songs were No. 1 hits in his youth. It made him feel the weight of his years. His fingers cramped at the thought, long overdue for de-ageing treatment. He may be old, damn it, but he had another good twenty years of service in him yet.

At that thought, he popped some pills for the pain and his kidneys.

At last the ship reached the half-way point. The Orion Drive ceased its endless thumping and the small gravitational push disappeared. Louis' stomach shifted upwards towards his throat and he clamped his mouth shut. The ship flipped one hundred and eighty degrees so that the engine was facing the opposite direction, and he almost lost his brown-paste breakfast. The pusher plate extended again, and he felt a small shudder as the nuclear packages started firing again.

Thump... Thump... Thump...

The gravitational push reappeared and Louis sighed. He would have to endure two more weeks of skull-pounding thumping. Having exhausted much of his scheduled entertainments, Louis had one last option. He was going to have to go over the details of the case yet again to make damn sure he knew what he was doing when he arrested the movie's director. And, all things going to plan, the magnate Myla Sincrow herself.

#

"Beacon engaged," the asteroid's robotic flight controller broadcast to the ship. "A berth has been cleared in bay five, please allow Ceres Station direct control."

"Alright, alright, you damned robot." Louis punched a few of the ship's archaic controls. While he hadn't been overjoyed to begin with, his mood had taken a turn for the worse since the ship had flipped on its axis. Once the constant thumping had ceased, a permanent headache had remained for the past few days.

"We have you, *Surge Advocate*," Ceres Station called. The ship moved without the onboard computer's input as the station's computer took control. If the ship sensed it was in danger, the link could easily be broken and control returned. Ceres Station's computer fed correctional course data into the *Surge Advocate's*, guiding it towards the station's docking tubes.

"Robot... Ceres Station, please ensure two police officers are assigned to the *Surge Advocate's* docking tube as per the request I forwarded yesterday."

"Officers are ready and waiting, Mr. Leckie."

Louis nodded. "Good."

He felt the small vibrations of the ship as its thrusters made minor course corrections. Space suit components hissed and clicked as he connected them around his body. He patted the hard, inner shell of his suit, making sure it was secure, and started zipping up the off-white outer suit. The suit clung to him as if static electricity had added a charge to the fabric.

The *Surge Advocate* played a soft symphony for him from its tinny speakers, rising in tone the closer the ship came to Ceres Station. "A bit dramatic, don't you think?"

"A bit of fun, Louis," the *Surge Protector* replied as the 'Jaws' theme song increased in volume.

"Cut it out."

"Yes boss."

The *Surge Advocate* slowed to match velocities with the rotating habitat and a soft docking tube extruded itself from Ceres Station, snaking its way towards the ship's habitation section and latching on like a hungry snake, forming an air-tight seal. The hissing and clunking sounds of air pressures equalising on either side of the *Surge Advocate's* hatch were audible through Louis' sound-dampening helmet.

"Piece of junk," he muttered. If the *Surge Advocate* had been a modern cruise liner, he would have needed auditory enhancers to hear the air on the other side of the docking hatch.

"Pressure equalised," the ship announced.

Louis nodded. "Open."

The docking hatch *clunked* as the locks disengaged and the hatch ground open, screeching on its hinges.

The docking tube was black, as if covered in soot. Rings of dull light, like dusty ribs, lit up the circular tube all the way to Ceres Station.

"Well, here I go," Louis said as he pushed off and floated down the black alien gullet.

"Tell me, Louis," the *Surge Advocate* said, "does it feel like you're being eaten, or being reborn?"

Louis sighed. "Eaten, if I had to choose." The 'Jaws' theme song started playing again. "Shut up and power down. I don't need distractions right now."

"Yes, sir." The song stopped.

The suit automatically puffed small amounts of air to push him down the centre of the tube. A light at the end shone through the dusty ribs, beckoning him onwards. When he neared the end of the dusty tunnel small puffs of air slowed him until it was safe to grab the railings at the tunnel's base. Louis grabbed the dust-covered metal bars and eased himself inside Ceres Station, taking care not to bump his head.

"Mr. Leckie, welcome to Ceres Station," a woman in police-rated power armour said.

Louis grunted as his feet hit the black, dust-covered floor. The suit's boots magnetised so he didn't bounce back into the air. "Thanks," he replied without feeling particularly thankful.

"Do you need refreshments?" A young man, also in a faceless blue set of power armour asked him.

Louis shook his head and looked around the large, dark airlock while the hatch closed behind him. Hissing and grinding sounds accompanied the shutting of the hatch and opening of the Station's main hatch. The grinding noises were worse here, as if the station's hatches hadn't been serviced for a couple of decades.

"Do you know why I'm here?" he asked the two officers.

"Yes sir. We are to accompany you to see Wesley Mavrin and Myla Sincrow in relation to a movie they directed and produced," the young man said. "I'm afraid Mr. Mavrin could not be located."

"That so?" Louis said and frowned. A warning chill started forming in his chest. "Is Miss Sincrow available?"

"She is nearby. Do you wish us to take you to her before we continue the search for Mr. Mavrin?"

"Yes, escort me so I can arrest her."

"That's what I said."

"Is it now?" The chill ran down Louis' spine. The young man's tone sounded odd, too formal perhaps. It was hard to tell with their accents.

"He did," the older female officer confirmed. "We will escort you to Myla Sincrow."

"And *arrest* her," Louis reiterated for her. Silence followed.

The inner hatch for the airlock opened and the three of them clomped their way out into the cavernous reception area. The area was filled with bright monitors and thick cords tied together, running the length of the walls. Paths of fine black soot on grey tiling showed where traffic traversed in and around the monitors with higher frequency. The facility appeared to be abandoned. "So, where is she? Will it be far?"

"Right here," an older sounding woman hidden behind one of the monitors said. Louis almost jumped when he heard her speak. He squinted into the darkness, against the glow of the monitors. She floated above the monitor so he could see her face. The monitor she'd been working at lit up the age lines and strands of grey hairs on her otherwise brunette head. She wore dark grey work clothes, and a blackened respirator over her nose and mouth to protect her lungs from the fine dust of Ceres Station.

"Miss Sincrow?" Louis asked.

"You know damn well who I am," Myla spat as she floated to her full height and put gloved hands on her hips.

"You are aware of the charges filed against you?"

Myla smiled. "Of course."

"Will you come willingly to Earth or must we use force to detain you?"

"Oh, I'll get to Earth, but it'll be on *my* terms."

"Is that so?" This time it was Louis' turn to put hands on hips. "I'm not going with you."

Louis' shoulders slumped a little. "I thought as much. Myla Sincrow, you are hereby charged with producing a movie with fantastical elements and profiting from it without a fantasy licence. Officers, please detain Miss Sincrow."

Neither officer moved to do as ordered. Myla's smile remained.

"Officers, do your duty!" Louis raised his voice.

"Yes, officers, do your duty," Myla said. This time Louis was sure her tone implied sarcasm, but the fact barely registered. The two officers took a step to each of Louis' sides and looped their armoured arms through his, holding him in a firm but gentle embrace.

"Let go," he barked at them and struggled against their mechanical grip.

"They won't. That's the thing about a small mining community, Mr. Leckie. Everybody knows everybody. These officers are my friends and neighbours and as far as we're all aware, you're the one trying to illegally kidnap me."

"*Kidnap?*" Louis spluttered and his eyes bulged.

"Yes. Look, I'll make this short. No harm will come to you. But if I let you go, the full force of Earth's justice will come screaming all the way up here to grab me, won't they? So how can we resolve this?"

"By coming with me," Louis said through gritted teeth.

"Do you really believe the movie needed a fantasy licence?"

"Don't be stupid, I wouldn't be here otherwise. I've studied your so-called 'movie' from opening scene to final credits. There are far too many physical impossibilities for it to be realistic."

Myla's smile widened. "But that's where you're wrong. Two years ago my movie would have been impossible but with recent advances we have made on Ceres, I've made it possible. You see, Mr. Leckie, in the old days before litigations and fantasy licenses, art used to inspire reality. Then art *became* reality. Think about the ancient dreamers, Daedalus and his son Icarus who flew too close to the sun."

"What about them?" Louis snarled.

"Humanity's dreams came true. We can fly now."

"That does not excuse the fantastical elements in your movie."

"They are not fantastic elements," Myla snapped, her smile vanishing. She turned to her cronies. "Bring him to the emergency life boats. I'll prove him wrong."

"Oh no," Louis said as the officers pulled him away

"No, don't worry, we're not going to harm you."

"Then what are you going to do?" Louis asked her.

"Let you watch. You see, I'm going to prove that my movie doesn't require a fantasy licence.

#

"Here we go, Mr. Leckie," the young officer said as they floated around a bend in the soot-covered corridors. The words 'Emergency Life Boat 3' were plastered in neon around a large, circular hatch. On the other side of the hatch was a compact spherical room containing several acceleration couches.

"Wait, you're serious about this?"

Myla, floating next to the circular hatch, gave him a thin-lipped smile. "I told you, I'm going to prove the film's scenes are possible."

"You're going to take a lifeboat all the way to Earth and then crash it there? The movie's lifeboat only had enough supplies for a week. You'll die of oxygen deprivation before being burned up in Earth's atmosphere."

"Well, you'll just have to watch and see, won't you?" She climbed through the hatch, twisted in midair to turn back and look at Louis, then pressed a button and closed the circular hatch.

Louis shook his head. "You're going to die."

Broadcast through the station's speakers, Myla–said, "That's what the director thought. I proved him wrong too."

Louis frowned. "You sound like you've done it before. There are no records of a lifeboat crashing to Earth from Ceres."

"Just watch," the older officer said.

A moment later they heard a *thwump* from the other side of the hatch. The lifeboat had launched.

"Got something I can watch?"

"Thought you'd never ask," the older officer said. She pressed a few buttons on her wrist display and a translucent screen opened on the wall next to the lifeboat hatch. The screen turned on and an external camera somewhere on the surface of Ceres zoomed in on the lifeboat as it shot away from the station.

"Whoa," Louis said without meaning to. The lifeboat was rocketing away from the station at an incredible pace. "How is she doing that? The boat must be pulling ten gees."

"Micro fusion reactor," Myla responded over the speaker, sounding strained. "Only about five gees, not ten."

"That's still a lot."

"Enough to get me to Earth in a bit over a week."

"But the gees—"

The image changed from the external shot to a shot of Myla's flattened face. She seemed to be struggling to breathe, let alone talk. "The micro drive will slow to one gee soon."

Louis tugged his arms away from the officers at his sides. He had to follow her, track her progress and try to catch up to her. "I need to get to my ship."

"Yes, Mr. Leckie," the older officer said.

In a hurry, Louis almost managed to out-pace the station officers. He swung around corridor bars and kicked off walls like a man one third his current age. Used to the Ceres environment, the officers trailed behind, panting as they tried to keep up.

They reached the hatch to the *Surge Advocate*'s airlock and Louis reactivated his boots' magnets, halting his mad dash through the lifeless station. "Open it," he demanded, his arms crossed.

"You're the boss," the female officer said, still panting.

"Fitter than he looks," the younger man said when he caught up.

"Open the damn door," Louis yelled.

"Yes sir," the female officer replied. The hatch popped open and Louis marched forwards, into the dark airlock.

"Good. Oh, and by the way, you're both fired."

From their body language the officers looked worried for a second but relaxed as the hatch closed.

The air inside the airlock matched pressure to the waiting black tube and the *Surge Advocate* in record time, but it felt longer than the trip to Ceres had. The outer hatch opened, and he flew through the tube into the ship. "Ship, power up and track that lifeboat."

Lights flickered on and something deep within the monstrous vessel groaned, reverberating throughout its white shell.

"Hello Louis," the ship said.

"Catch that boat," he yelled at the ship.

"What ship?"

Louis groaned in exasperation as he sat in the ship's acceleration couch. "Haven't you heard a thing that's been going on?"

"You ordered me powered down. I powered down."

"Idiot," he said, not entirely sure who the remark was aimed at, himself or the ship's AI. A modern computer would have at least recorded everything and analysed it as soon as it powered back up. The *Surge Advocate* had recorded nothing while it was powered down in standby mode.

"Sir?" the computer asked, sounding upset.

"Nevermind. A lifeboat launched from Ceres Station. Find it and track it. We need to capture its occupant."

"Found it. Warming up the thrusters. We have clearance from Ceres Station."

"That was easy," Louis said. The station probably wanted him gone. The *Surge Advocate* performed an emergency spin to align it for a transfer orbit to Earth. The thrusters pushed the ship as hard as they could while a lone tug boat from the station arrived to pull it into empty space.

"You have a transmission coming from the lifeboat."

"Put it on."

Myla Sincrow's face appeared. Her short hair and face were no longer flattened against her acceleration couch. She looked as if she were lying down on a bed on Earth. "You won't catch up to this boat in that old thing, Louis, but you're welcome to tail me all the way to Earth. I wouldn't bother asking for backup, either. The flight plan was registered with Century Station two months ago."

"That's when my flight plan was approved…"

Myla smiled. "Yes, it is. You could say I've been waiting for you."

"But… why?" If she'd known he was coming to get her this whole time, surely she could have proven her point some other way?

"There's no better proof than seeing it with your own eyes, wouldn't you say?"

"That depends. Are you really on that lifeboat or are you still on Ceres Station?"

"Being on Ceres Station would defeat the purpose of trying to save my movie and my property. No, I'm definitely in here. I'm going to keep broadcasting on this channel all the way to Earth. If you still feel the need to arrest me, you can do it when I land. If you've seen the movie, you know where that'll be."

Louis' eyes sharpened but instead of coming up with a useless retort, he nodded and turned off the communications link. "Ship, record all of the lifeboat's broadcasts. I need to send a message to Skybridge Command."

"What is your message?"

Louis sighed and opened his sloppy space suit. He was feeling the bruises he'd accumulated during the mad dash back to the ship. *Damn, being old sucks.*

"Tell them Ceres Station's officers illegally detained me, and Myla Sincrow will enter Earth's atmosphere in approximately eight days." Louis wracked his memory for details of that detestable film, trying to remember exactly where it was supposed to end. He did not want to watch it again, not even a few seconds, just to find out that little piece of information. "Tell them she's going to attempt splashdown in the Atlantic Ocean, somewhere in the Sargasso Sea." *And obliterate herself in the process,* he thought to himself.

#

True to her word, the *Surge Advocate* could not catch up to the much smaller boat. Having lived in space all her life in micro-gravity environments, at one gee of acceleration Myla Sincrow was suffering. Blood-flow to her extremities had slowed, her joints ached from the added pressure, and she seemed light-headed and delirious. After a day, the lifeboat's micro-fusion drive powered down to a tenth of a gee so she could recover.

"Tell me, Mr. Leckie, why did you think this lifeboat only had enough supplies for a week? It *is* a lifeboat."

She had him there. Then he buried his head in his hands. The lifeboat in the movie had been damaged, with low power and no air recyclers. The lone survivor of the movie couldn't have lasted more than a few hours or days even with spare air tanks.

Myla's lifeboat wasn't damaged.

In a way, it relieved Louis. Cassandra would laugh at him for forgetting a basic detail like that, but at least he could still prove the movie incorrect. He smiled and turned on the ship's communicators to reply to her. "That damn dumb movie of yours may have been the reason. This whole thing is a farce, isn't it? Just a way to give yourself a few more days of freedom before you burn up over the Atlantic."

"You'd think but no. Have a look at this," she moved out of the way of the lifeboat's camera to show him what had happened to the rest of the boat. Access panels had slid aside, exposing air filtration equipment. It was wrecked, as if someone had taken a hammer and smashed it repeatedly.

Louis scrunched his eyes up. "Idiot."

"No, this is proof."

"If you survive."

55

Myla shrugged. "You didn't believe this little boat could get to Earth in time until you saw it launch, why is this any different? You'll recall, the movie's hero calmed his heartbeat, didn't move, and slept most of the way?"

"Did you have to remind me? It was terribly boring."

"It's *real*. It may have seemed impossible, Louis, but since when did movies have to describe every little detail? Why should the movie writers have to be math geniuses and explain everything to the audience just so they understand how a police officer from the early 21st century can kick in a door? Movies shouldn't have to talk down to the audience about everything. Just let them enjoy the damn thing without a blasted fantasy licence."

Louis chuckled. "I don't think either of us are enjoying this little spectacle of yours."

"No but that's because I'm trying to prove a point. I'm going to go to sleep now."

"You're still going to die."

"Oh, Louis, do you really believe that? Have you any idea of the genetic engineering progress our scientists have been making? Think about it."

Myla did exactly what she said she would do. She went to sleep.

The lifeboat sent Myla's medical data to the *Surge Advocate*. Her heart rate slowed to a handful of beats per minute, and she took only one or two breaths in the same time.

Louis, having had enough of her petulant–and downright foolish behaviour, also caught some sleep with the aid of a handful of headache pills.

The frenetic action of the past few days had taken its toll on him, he ended up sleeping far longer than he had intended. When he awoke, he was surprised to see that the lifeboat had already reached the halfway point and decelerated.

Still feeling groggy from his overlong sleep, Louis sipped on a coffee tube while he caught up on the recordings, news and messages from the past few days. There were several worried messages from family members, the usual murders and political nonsense engulfing the SEMIC's skybridge and its towers. He scrolled through messages from the SEMIC until he saw one that caught his attention.

He tapped on the screen and Cassandra's face popped up. The video was paused but Louis could see that she was standing behind a crowd of people in front of the Justice Centre. Several small drones hung poised above the crowd, no doubt attempting to disperse them.

The video started playing.

"Well, you've stirred up a hornet's nest down here, haven't you?"

"What have I done?" Louis said to himself as the video recording continued.

"It's not being reported widely yet, but Myla Sincrow's escape and demonstration has really caught the attention of the filmmaker's guild and a good number of their fans. They want to peddle unrealistic movies without fantasy licences. Can you believe it?"

"I'm starting to," he answered and glanced at the sensor readings for the lifeboat. It was still intact and Myla was still alive. Healthy, even.

"There's going to be hell to pay. The licensors office is going to crucify us."

"That's if she lives." He said with as much confidence as he could muster.

#

Several days later, Myla Sincrow woke and, true to the movie she was trying to replicate, steered the lifeboat manually into a safe angle for re-entry to Earth's atmosphere.

"She's mad," Louis said. No space-based lifeboat would have a strong enough exterior to survive re-entry.

The lifeboat did not burn up as it screamed down through several layers of air.

"How's she going to stop…?"

The lifeboat's parachutes deployed.

Louis raised his eyebrows while he watched the recordings of the lifeboat as they were beamed to the *Surge Advocate* from Earth. "Now why would a deep space lifeboat have parachutes?" But Myla Sincrow had them installed to prove her point.

The lifeboat deployed air bags to keep afloat. And then, with an impossible calmness, it splashed down.

A medical drone found the lifeboat several hours later. Louis stared at the medical readings in disbelief. The mad woman was alive and still healthy, if a bit afraid of the rocking waves. Her heart was working double time in Earth's gravity, but nowhere near dangerous levels.

She was going to survive.

It conflicted Louis. In part he was relieved, even elated at her survival. On the other hand, he wondered that it wouldn't be better for her to have burned up in the atmosphere. He'd built his entire career on prosecuting filmmakers for making outlandish and unrealistic movies.

Now his entire trip had been one expensive and heavily publicized embarrassment.

"Shit."

#

One month later, after following Louis' return to Earth and recovery from his trip, Cassandra came to see him in his office at his home tower overlooking the skybridge and its set of shuttles.

"It's official, Myla Sincrow's movie is now an intra-system blockbuster."

"A Guinness for my guest," Louis said as Cassandra sat down on the other side of the stark white office room. The digital overlays on his eyes disappeared.

"No way, not this time, Mr. Leckie," Cassandra said. "Table, I'll have your second best single malt whisky. Use my allowance."

Cranky and tired after the events of the past few weeks, Louis took notice of his old friend's chirpy mood. "Now, now Cassandra, that's against regulations, drinking on the job."

"You were the one about to force Guinness down my throat. Besides, I clocked out for the rest of the day. I'm celebrating."

"Really?" Louis' frown, one he didn't know he'd had, softened.

"The Licensors Office is happy with what's going on. They want to thank you for letting Myla do the demonstration."

Louis almost choked on his saliva. "*Thank me?* And I *let her?*" He was dumbfounded.

"That *is* what's in your official report, isn't it?" Cassandra crossed her legs and sat back to watch his reaction.

"I, uh…" he couldn't recall exactly what he'd put in the report, but he was absolutely certain that allowing her to demonstrate is not what he would have said.

"I just read it; don't you remember? You had a bit of an argument with Ceres Station officers, but they let you watch."

Louis smiled at how ridiculous she made it sound. "That so?"

Cassandra shrugged. "That's what your report states. In any case, there's no official reprimand coming your way. Looks like you've dodged a bullet there. The courts are loosening up and they predict fantasy licenses to come down in price by ninety percent. Imagine that! We're going to be flooded with supermen and dragons again. They might even go back to old school computer-generated graphics."

Louis shuddered at the thought of entirely computer-generated movies being the norm again. "The Licensors Office can sell more licences. This is a nightmare."

"Not really. There'll be a lot more people pushing the boundaries now, and there'll be several levels of licences. It's going to get confusing for a lot of filmmakers out there. That's a lot more work for people like us to. The future looks bright, my friend."

"Hmm…" Louis mumbled. It didn't sound so bright to him. Perhaps, he thought, he'd become a relic, a hangover from a simpler time, when the line between reality and fantasy had been black and white. "Not for me," Louis said, making his mind up then and there. He reached across the table, grabbed the glass that had extruded itself from the table, and gulped the liquid down his mouth. The whiskey stung his throat, and he coughed. "I've had enough of these clowns. I'm retiring while I'm still under a thousand years old. Maybe I'll cruise the stars."

Cassandra looked stunned when she realised he meant it. "But you hate space. What about your family? When would you ever come back?"

Louis shrugged. "My family has known me long enough to grow weary of me. I think I'll cash in my assets to buy a ticket to Alpha Centauri. Maybe I'll come back when Myla Sincrow's ridiculous fantasies have *all* turned into reality."

"You know that'll never happen."

"I thought I knew, but then I watched her survive that trip. Hell, I may even learn to enjoy these fantasy movies on the journey to Alpha Centauri."

Cassandra frowned at him. "You've lost the plot."

"I guess so."

"Table, a pint of cider, please."

The two friends stared at each other while the cider formed on the table, then burst out laughing. "What's wrong with beer?" Louis said as Cassandra offered the glass to him.

Cassandra shrugged. "Hope I see you again, someday."

"Maybe you will, in a film from Alpha Centauri." A thought formed in Louis' mind. "I'll be a superhero of some sort. You'll see."

Cassandra covered her mouth but laughed, anyway. "You're going to give me a heart attack."

Louis sipped his drink, swore at the taste and threw the rest away. "Let's go for one last walk on the bridge and then watch the next shuttle launch."

Cassandra smiled with a hint of melancholy. "It'd be my pleasure, Mr. Leckie."

Andrew P. McGregor lives in the rural town of Inverell near the East coast of Australia. He writes science fiction and dark fantasy short stories, most of which are collected in "Tales of Starships & Apocalypse."

Wayback

by James Pyles

London, 1884

Herbert George Wells stood in the cellar of a brownstone in Kensington, knowing that he would never see Amanda again. Holding his beautiful lover, sixteen years his senior, tightly in his arms, through teary eyes, he gazed at the object of her own invention. Illuminated by gas lamps, it was resting in the center of a brick-lined room, cluttered with tables containing chemicals and laboratory equipment. The floor was littered with tools, stray bolts, and metallic sheeting, all used in the construction of her time machine.

"Take me with you," he murmured into her auburn hair.

Amanda Westcott turned her head, resting it against his chest. "Your life is here. Mine is in another world."

"But if it works, you will re-create the world in your image. Can you at least come back to me when you are finished?"

"You won't remember me, my love, but without you, I would never have acquired the means to correct a terrible wrong."

"I would not deny you justice, but was I merely a tool to an end?"

"Because I needed your help liberating my father's prototype from where it has been languishing?"

"We're not three blocks from the Normal School of Science."

Amanda looked up at Herbert, and he was again startled by her vivid green eyes.

"I love you my young scientist, so I won't lie." She placed her hand softly on his cheek. "Restoring my father's legacy is everything to me."

Herbert drew her lips to his, pressing Amanda's robust figure against his slender frame.

Then she broke away. "No lingering farewells."

He took several steps backward, memorizing her appearance. Amanda's hair was suspended high around her head. Her alabaster-colored blouse was in contrast to medium complexion. During their months-long affair, he had seen far more of her skin, and enjoyed her pleasures lasciviously.

The engineer turned toward her time machine. To Herbert, it resembled a sled sporting a plush velvet couch, sitting behind a series of brass controls he found totally baffling. After the pilot's seat, the power source, a glowing metal cylinder the size of a large flagon of ale, was at the rear of a large upright copper disk the height of a man.

She looked once more at him and mouthed. "I love you," and then took the control seat. "You had best leave now." Amanda manipulated the levers and knobs. Steam hissed out of the piping, as the disk hastily spun up to a screaming wail.

Fighting back sobs, he scampered up the stairs to the ground floor. Swiftly donning his jacket and hat, he dashed outside, trotted down the steps, and stopped when he was across the deserted street.

It was a dawn in early Spring. He shivered as he looked back at Amanda's inherited home. There was no sign, but he knew she had departed to whatever fate awaited her. Wells shoved his hands into his pockets and made the forlorn walk to school through choking clouds of fog and smoke.

Balancing Point Institute, the Far Future

"Temporal Event Indicator's lighting up, Wyatt. Seems we have another trip in our near future." Josue Hunter put his hand on his partner's shoulder to get his attention, while pointing to their left at the brightly flashing yellow globe suspended in midair.

"Or our past." Six-foot-two, pale, slim Wyatt Ellison towered eight inches above his fellow Historian, enough to be able to look down on his rapidly expanding bald spot. Josue seemed to compensate by cultivating a thick mustache.

"Always with the jokes, and can't you come to work dressed like a normal person?" As Hunter and Ellison strode the few meters toward the luminescent sphere, virtual displays and controls twisted and elongated, their entire holographic workspace wrapping around them.

"I thought sure you'd figure it out. Today, I'm Captain Kirk from the 1960s television show…"

"Never mind. Look. This time it's the Sky Disc of Nebra." He waved his hand under the global indicator causing it to rise a few inches.

Wyatt stood just behind him, straightening his golden tunic. Josue wore the same navy blue suit pants and jacket with a gray sweater every day. Leaning over his shoulder, he reached to Hunter's right. "That means it's…" Inserting his index finger and thumb a few inches inside the indicator, he opened a readout "…1999, near former Nebra, Germany."

"The discovery by the two amateur metal detectors." Josue ran a finger inside the globe calling up the names of the unwitting perpetrators, while reaching left and pulling over a virtual list of the Factory's inventory.

"We can't let them get their hands on the real Disc. If it's authenticated, it would indicate an advanced knowledge of astronomy for the period of origin, disrupting the timeline as we know it." Wyatt gestured to his right, summoning a large, three-dimensional image of the actual Disc decorated with blue patina and gold inlaid symbols, while pushing away a replica of an ancient white board listing the Institute cafeteria's lunch menu. "That's our job. Suppress discoveries of temporal oddities that would change the trajectory of history."

"Sending the Disc's specifications to the Factory for manufacture. Come along. Just take a few seconds." Josue peered up at Wyatt's bare face, his rakish looks adorned with a mop of uncombed blond locks.

"No, I'll get the Wayback ready." Wyatt waved his right arm causing the far end of the holographic space to shimmer. It reformed as a dimly glowing rectangular doorway with a multicolored neon sign blinking "Wayback" suspended above.

"Why you have to call it that?" Josue's smile reversed to a frown.

"It's the name of a fictional time machine from…"

"Don't tell me." Hunter rolled his eyes at Ellison's peculiarities. "Be right back." Retreating from the Wayback, he made an arm motion, opened another portal, and walked through.

Wyatt returned to the Wayback's arcane controls as Josue re-emerged carrying a copy of the Disc. Snapping his fingers, he closed the gateway. Only the Institute had trans-dimensional technology, the ability to create virtual links to any place on Earth. He had no idea the physical location of the Factory, their workspace, or even the cafeteria.

Josue saw Wyatt at a set of levers and knobs, some as large as his palm, pushing buttons until the numerals "1999" appeared on a replica 12-inch television screen.

"You really don't need that. The indicator automatically uploads the exact timespace coordinates into the portal." Josue strolled over and stopped at Wyatt's left.

Ellison chuckled. "Where's the fun in that? We'll go back a month before the actual event. Then replace the artifact with our duplicate so it will eventually be revealed as a fake."

"Program's set to deliver us in the middle of the night. It's a remote area, so no need for special costuming or language enhancements. Got your unitool?"

Josue patted the left side of his jacket at the lapel. "Right here, but since your costume doesn't have pockets, where's yours?"

"Velcroed to my waistband." Wyatt lifted his shirt so Josue could see the six-inch long blue, cylindrical all-purpose instrument attached to his trousers.

"Vel...oh, I remember. You really are on a 20th century kick today. What's the period for tomorrow?"

"It's a surprise. Ready to avert another time anomaly?"

"Preserving the one true timeline is why I'm here. Let's get this over with. Mom's watching the kids tonight so I can take Camille out to the theater, a 22nd century play."

"Sounds boring, just like this incursion. If it doesn't have action and explosions, I'm not interested. Adventure is why I became a Historian. Preserving the timeline is just a fringe benefit."

Josue sighed. "You're such a child."

"Thirty-nine and forever single, Josue, old fellow." He slapped Hunter on the back.

"Forty-seven isn't old."

"You're married and three kids old."

"Let's go," he groaned. Side-by-side, the duo walked through the greenish glow of the Wayback portal and then vanished.

Seconds later they returned, Josue carrying what looked like the same object he left with.

"I'll check the indicator for verification, you power down the portal."

"Roger that, Josue." Ellison snapped off an exaggerated salute, and then attended to the completely ridiculous control panel.

The older time traveler walked across to the indicator, now showing a faint white. "Incursion successful. Time anomaly averted. I'll take the Disc to the Vault."

"Wait a second, I'm coming." Wyatt quickly finished the Wayback's shutdown sequence and strode over to Josue. The latter waved his hand, a doorway appeared, and they stepped through.

"I'll get a catalog assignment." Hunter absentmindedly moved to his right toward a virtual terminal. Showing the Disc to the hologram, he called the on-duty Custodian. while Ellison found himself endlessly enthralled with visions of yesteryear.

"There used to be a museum called Smithsonian that contained a staggering number of historical artifacts, early aviation technology, natural science exhibits, even a zoo before they were banned." Wyatt's eyes went wide. Every fifteen seconds, the holoimages in the large, circular, lobby displayed a different exhibit of the Vault complex. He watched a dragonfly called Meganeura boasting a two-foot wingspan as it and the rest of its swarm buzzed about its habitat. His grin grew wider as he turned his head to face a river dwelling, 40-foot-long Sarcosuchus Imperator or "super croc."

"Want to stay for a while and visit some of the showrooms?"

"Hang on a second." A virtual doorway replaced the holographic console, and a familiar figure appeared.

"Hi, Randa. Didn't know you were working today." The newcomer seemed younger than Wyatt, but Josue knew the Custodian had been at the Institute longer than either Historian. Her short-cropped hair was medium-brown with a reddish tinge. She was what Ellison called "full-figured," with curves concealed by a loose smock.

"No rest for the wicked." She smiled flirtatiously, teasing him just because he was married. "Pitt and Giorgio have been keeping me busy."

"The ones who brought back the Titanic?"

"Yes. This week alone, they've performed three major incursions. My team has been working overtime just to construct the new environments."

"Anything interesting? Asking for a friend," he nodded toward Wyatt.

Her tone became conspiratorial. "The Ossuary of James was easy, but it's taken days to create the correct display for the abandoned starship. My biggest headache is the Leviathan they found dining on a Sperm Whale back in the Bronze Age."

"Are they cataloged?"

"I haven't made them searchable yet. No chance Wyatt will discover anything for another week.

"Good," Josue whispered. "I'd never get him out of here otherwise." He handed the Disc to her. "Why don't they automate this process?"

"The Secretary set that up from day one. All artifacts shall be personally accounted for by a Vault Custodian." She paused, swaying slightly. "Guess I'd better find a home for this. See you next time."

"Josue, I thought you said we didn't have all day. How about a peek in the World War Two museum? They've got a new Manhattan Project exhibit."

"Can't leave the indicator unattended."

"Come on. The automation will notify us if it's triggered."

"You'll keep me here for hours, and I've got to get home." Hunter gripped Ellison by the arm. Wyatt marveled at the five TBM Avenger bombers taken off the Florida coast in 1945. They'd never been told the fate of the pilots, but Ellison thought he knew.

Wyatt stumbled toward the aperture, still trying to look back at Amelia Earhart's Lockheed 10-E Electra.

"You could write the book on Artifact Fever." A small smile twisted Josue's lips.

"Those were the days. The first time travelers didn't just preserve reality, they preserved history. This represents everything I became a Historian for."

"They made plenty of mistakes, too."

"Wyatt winced. "Like the time a Megalodon got into 1877 Chesapeake Bay."

"Or Little Boy was dropped on Berlin right before D-Day."

Wyatt turned to Josue, scowling indignantly. "It ended World War Two in Europe a year early."

"DeGaulle accused Roosevelt of war crimes."

"They changed it back, one of the first incursions to restore the timeline. Have to admit those early events were really crazy, especially the big timeline jumps."

"You mean cascading Time Storms like the Westcott-Liechtenstein Engine?"

"Those Historians found all that out by accident. The first indicators were terribly inaccurate. Even the modern ones would have trouble if we still had Time Storms."

"It was because of the Storms that the Temporal Location index derived coordinates for the Westcott-Liechtenstein machine from other high significance events. That could have led to the Tesla-Curie collaboration decades later, which would have been disastrous for our timeline."

"If Westcott and Liechtenstein had perfected their production unit, it would have changed everything. Glad we have the big engine here in the Vault. The Institute won't even let us turn it on."

Josue tugged playfully at Wyatt's arm. "One more temporal catastrophe averted. Besides, they corrected the agriculture industry so that farming practices didn't lead to global heating…"

Both men froze as their unitools simultaneously vibrated.

"Crap." Wyatt had his pulled off his belt, as Josue reached into his jacket. "Another incursion."

"So soon? It better not be complicated. Camille will kill me if I have to work overtime."

#

"A time machine?" Josue stared as the indicator coordinates bounced around like popcorn. "Impossible, Time travel wasn't invented until the founding of the Institute fifty years ago."

"People invented time travel lots of times, and the Institute has always uninvented it." Wyatt regarded the indicator's fickle display.

"So how did we miss this?"

"The readings won't settle down enough to tell."

"Are you saying the Secretary can't clean this up?"

"Does that pattern look familiar?"

Josue's face paled as he glanced up. "A Time Storm. But that hasn't happened since...why now?"

Wyatt gently moved his friend back to get a closer look. "The destination points are all over timespace, but look at the distribution around the origin."

Josue peered upward, the tip of his nose entering the hologram. "From somewhere in Western Europe."

"And the dates?"

"Between 1860 and early 1940s." Josue's puzzlement transformed into dismay. "You don't think...?"

"According to..." Ellison scrawled equations using the unitool on a virtual white board, erasing part of the lunch schedule, "...these calculations, the most likely source is Kensington... London...1884."

"H.G. Wells attended school in Kensington. He would have only been eighteen. His novel 'The Time Machine' won't be published for another eleven years."

"His short story 'The Chronic Argonauts,' an earlier version, came out in 1888 when Wells was twenty-two."

"But his location is stable across the timeline."

Suit up, Josue. We're visiting 1884 London." Wyatt skipped backward, twisting several sections of his unitool. Moments later, his Kirk costume morphed into the outfit of a 19th century gentleman, complete with bowler, while the unitool elongated into a cane.

Hunter grimaced as he adjusted his own device. In contrast to Ellison's men's brown tailcoat, he chose a longer jacket, dark blue with matching tie.

Wyatt bowed. "Inspectors Ellison and Hunter of the Metropolitan Police Service, what eventually became…"

"…Scotland Yard. But what will we say to Wells? We're looking for a time traveler? He'll think we're nuts. Besides, you're guessing at the date."

"I did the math." Ellison marched to the Wayback controls. "We'll arrive in late summer which…"

Josue ambled toward his partner. "Normally the indicator feeds the portal exact geo-temporal coordinates."

"Which it can't determine this time."

Hunter's frown caused his mustache to droop. "So I have to trust your math."

"Which one of us got higher marks in trans-temporal calculations?"

"Only by five percent."

"We'll encounter Wells as he exits the physics building after class and offer him a deal he can't refuse."

"I just hope the air won't be too bad. They burned a lot of coal in London back then…"

"London Fog they called it," interrupted Wyatt. "We won't be there that long."

"Fine." An eerie glow shone from the Wayback's portal, and he had to rush to follow Wyatt through.

"Are you out of your mind?" A freezing wind was driving snow and ice almost sideways into them under a shale sky. They were on a sidewalk facing a residence half obscured by the storm. A quaking Wyatt was already gazing at holographic data from his cane, while Josue wrapped his arms tightly around his shivering torso.

"A snowstorm in August?"

"It's…" Wyatt checked again. "…early morning, Sunday, January 8, 1933, Chiltern Court, Baker Street, Westminster."

"Wells' home?"

"Come on before we freeze to death." Wyatt grabbed Josue's icy sleeve and pulled, while pointing the cane toward the nearest doorway.

"But we're nearly fifty years late. Should go back and…"

Ellison was manically banging on the door as snow piled up around them.

After a frozen eternity, it opened. "You gentlemen seem quite impatient."

He was older, heavier, but it was Wells.

"Whatever are you doing out in such weather?" Then he got a closer look at their clothing which hadn't been adjusted for the period.

Ellison produced his identification, which had been updated moments before, presenting it to the sixty-six-year-old author. "Wyatt Ellison, Scotland Yard. My associate, Joseph Hunter. May we please come in?"

"Of course, gentlemen." Wells pulled the door open wider, stepping aside, and then closed it after they'd staggered in. "I have a fire in the study. Perhaps you would enjoy warming up there."

"That would be wonderful, Mr. Wells," Hunter's teeth were chattering. A trembling Wyatt and Josue removed their hats and used them to brush snow off of their clothes, before hanging them up.

Their host bid them both to sit in well cushioned chairs facing a blazing brick hearth. A small table between the chairs. Wyatt leaned forward on his cane, and then looked back at Wells.

"May I offer either of you some tea?"

"No, we're quite fine," Wyatt lied. "However we do have some business with you."

While Wyatt engaged Wells, Josue left his seat and squatted closer to the fire, seemingly to warm himself. With his back to the novelist, he took out his unitool and began working.

Sitting next to Ellison, Wells inquired, "To what do I owe this visit from Scotland Yard, if that's who you really are?"

"Our identification is authentic and our business official."

"Forgive me, Mr..."

"Inspector Ellison."

"But neither you nor your companion are dressed for the weather or modern times."

"This wasn't how we wanted to meet you." Wyatt face was hot with embarrassment. "We just have a few questions."

Josue stood and turned, not bothering to conceal his device. "Mr. Wells, we'll come to the point. We want to know where and when the time traveler has gone."

Wyatt half-stood and then sat again. "What are you doing?"

"He knows who she is and what she's planning."

"How do you know?"

"The Westcott-Liechtenstein Engine. Rolf Liechtenstein died a year before his partner Carson Westcott finished the Engine in 1850. The same year, his wife gave birth to their only child, Amanda Westcott. It's all right here." He lifted his unitool.

Ellison rose, facing Wells, and then turned toward Hunter. "The Engine's inaccessible. Westcott couldn't have known about it, and what's that got to do with…?"

"The first time I saw Miss Westcott, Amanda, was February 1884. I suppose that explains your outlandish clothing." Wells exhaled slowly. "She hinted that, like her, others might traipse throughout history."

"Mr. Wells, we believe she's going to do something extraordinarily dangerous. We need you to tell us what you know."

"I have little to say, Mr. Hunter. We had a brief love affair in the early part of that year. I was a young student, and she was an exciting older woman."

"How did Amanda Westcott build a time machine with late 19th century technology?"

Wyatt knew history was resistant, but not immutable. Normally what a rogue time traveler changed, the Institute could repair. But what had Josue discovered about Wells, Westcott, and the Time Storm?

"There was a device, about the size of a small barrel. It came into the possession of my school's physics department decades earlier. I was friendly with the instructor responsible for its safekeeping. No one knew its purpose, but its craftsmanship was extraordinary."

"You told Westcott about it?"

"She already knew, Mr. Ellison. I'm not sure how. Amanda convinced me to purloin it. She said she needed the mechanism to correct an injustice."

"Or cause one," Josue's tone was caustic.

"We spent weeks constructing her time machine. To this day, I have never met anyone with such a brilliant, insightful mind. Her knowledge of physics and engineering were without peer."

"Did she say where and when she was going?"

"Not then, Mr. Ellison. However it's done now, so I suppose I can reveal to you that I last saw Amanda several weeks ago."

"What?" Josue visibly shuddered.

"That's why we were thrown forward to 1933, a residual path from 1884." Wyatt loomed over the seated Wells. "What did she say?"

"Nothing specific. I believe she knew, even hoped you would be visiting me."

"Why?"

"My former lover was as young and radiant as when we first met. She said she had gathered everything she needed to restore her father's legacy, and this time, you could not stop her."

Josue finally put away his unitool. "If she succeeds, we won't be able to follow her."

"Why not?" Wells slowly stood.

"When a temporal agent visits a time period, it can never be revisited."

"Thank you for your time, Mr. Wells." Wyatt thought about shaking the writer's hand, but merely nodded.

"I can't wish you gentlemen luck. Amanda believes in the rightness of her cause. She promised a new world where men didn't depend on social struggle or war."

"Good-bye, Sir." Ellison turned and followed Hunter out of the study. Wells didn't go after them.

"We'll return from here," Hunter insisted. "Even if Wells sees us, it won't matter."

"Josue, how did you know about Amanda Westcott?"

"I linked up to the Institute library hoping to get some sort of idea why meeting Wells here and now was important."

"And?"

"A few seconds after we left, the Westcott-Liechtenstein Engine disappeared from the Vault without a trace, creating a temporal anomaly. There's no such thing as a coincidence in time travel, so I played a hunch. We've confirmed that Wells knows about Amanda, but not where she is, and we can never re-visit those few minutes in the Vault to prevent the Engine's theft."

"It's not over yet, Josue."

#

"The Secretary still isn't answering messages, Wyatt."

Josue was perusing a virtual obituary in their lab. "Liechtenstein died of a heart attack in Surrey, the evening of Thursday, March 1, 1849."

"Rheumatic fever as a child weakened his heart. Carson Westcott's a different story. After Liechtenstein died, Westcott continued his work."

"Liechtenstein was the real genius. In the alternate timeline, he was a student of biologist and chemist Antoine Lavoisier, who escaped to England in 1794 to avoid being executed during the French Revolution. Later, he became ill, a recluse, finally dying in 1820..."

Wyatt moved to Josue's right. "His eleven-year-old neighbor Rolf did chores for the Lavoisiers. Antoine became impressed with the child's quick intellect, agreeing to tutor him. After Lavoisier's death, Liechtenstein inherited of all his papers, but didn't have the funds to develop his theories, great advances in everything from rocketry to life prolongation."

"That's where Westcott came in. Ten years younger than Liechtenstein, brilliant but unmotivated, he lived off of a modest inheritance. They both met at university."

"Liechtenstein needed funds and Westcott craved notoriety. He was smart enough to see the potential in Liechtenstein's inventions."

"This was one of the Institute's earliest incursions. We acquired the Engine as Westcott was preparing it for a demonstration at the 1851 Great Exhibition, but I can't find any record of what happened to Westcott."

Wyatt stepped back from the displays, both he and Josue were still dressed in 1884 attire. "Someone, probably Amanda Westcott, invaded the Vault and took the most dangerous technological artifact in history. How did she do it?"

"There is no set of calculations that will let me form a stable point-to-point link between us and anywhere around London during 1850. We can't go back and see what happened."

"If Westcott turns that Engine on in the past, all of history will be changed."

Josue's eyes were wet with tears. "Our lives, all that we know, my wife and children, all wiped out if we fail."

"Where and when would Amanda Westcott take the Engine?" Wyatt slapped his forehead. "Of course. The Great Exhibition. Her father planned to demonstrate it there so naturally..." Ellison rushed over to the indicator and spun it out of standby. Then a moment later, "Bad news."

"The blackout extends across to 1851."

"Wait. If she's activated the unit in 1851, why are we still here?"

"Maybe there's a way to salvage all this." Josue stepped to the left, near the unopened aperture to the Vault, used his fingers to manipulate a small virtual panel, and then scanned a list. "The Custodian responsible for managing the Westcott-Liechtenstein Engine was Miranda Higgins. Randa."

"So what? She inherited the assignment. Pitt and Giorgio brought it back nearly 50 years ago, and they're close to retirement.

"Cross referenced and verified. Randa Higgins is registered as an employee since the founding of the Institute."

"That's one heck of a facelift."

Josue kept looking at Randa's profile in the personnel directory. "You seriously think Randa had something to do with the Engine's disappearance?"

"She's got access, and Vault Custodians have a higher security clearance than Historians. Do we have any life prolongation displays?"

"Not that I know of, and believe me, I'd know."

"Not if it wasn't searchable," Josue muttered, remembering his last conversation with Randa.

Wyatt joined Josue at the various displays, settling on Randa's image. "You know, I've never really looked at her before."

"Too busy with the artifacts. We've got to let the Secretary know." Josue's hand reached toward a communications node.

In the workspace center, a doorway appeared, and a figure stepped through holding a unitool. She manipulated it briefly, and the reddish glow of the security system activated.

"Randa." Josue felt his breathing quicken. "How did you find out we were contacting the Secretary?"

"Because, she is the Secretary."

A startled Hunter swung toward Ellison. Returning his gaze to Randa, he saw her nod.

"Actually, I founded the Institute, but that information is behind dozens of layers of encryption." As she spoke, her unitool transformed into a plasma weapon.

"Care to clue us in?" Wyatt remembered he'd left his own unitool as a cane sitting on the floor beside the indicator. He doubted Josue could reach his in time to keep them from both being vaporized.

"No, except to say that your involvement has been anticipated."

The controls of the Wayback abruptly shifted. "The answers you want are on the other side. So is my mother, Amanda Westcott." She waved her weapon toward the portal, and the pair reluctantly walked through.

They stood on the south bank of the Thames, facing Westminster Bridge. An overcast sky rendered the cityscape charcoal. On the street to their left, self-propelling carriages zoomed by, issuing hissing steam and a bluish glow from small rear-mounted cylinders.

A combination of zeppelins and bat-winged bi-planes were soaring overhead, the hum of fast moving motors creating a pleasant vibration.

Josue's voice rattled. "Notice that?"

"There's a lot to notice."

"They don't burn coal, and this is clearly the 19th century. I wonder when we are?" He pulled aside his lapel and started reaching inside.

"1886." Her voice came from behind them. Josue jumped, snatching his hand out of his jacket. Wyatt gritted his teeth and spun around.

"At least you're not armed," Ellison quipped.

"I was hoping she wouldn't resort to that, but Miranda was always strong-headed."

"Westcott," Josue growled. "Do you know what you're doing?"

Amanda's lavender skirt matched her jacket and wide brimmed hat, and her frilled blouse was ivory white. She carried a closed umbrella propped over her left shoulder.

"This way, please." Seeing no approaching cars, she crossed the street toward a large manicured park.

"Let's find out what she wants," Wyatt whispered as they followed. "We can always use your unitool to get home."

"Randa will be waiting."

A stone path led them into a copse of large oaks.

"You can stop whispering like would-be assassins."

Wyatt took a position on Amanda's right with Josue on her left. "Miranda said you would explain."

"True, but I imagine by now you've guessed most of it."

"We know about your father's invention, and that you want to recreate the timeline it would have caused, but how did you know about the Engine once our timeline had been established?"

"Because, Mr. Ellison, I was already a time traveler and operating father's latest invention when Pitt and Giorgio purloined the Engine after murdering Daddy." Her voice was laced with subtle anger.

"Historians aren't authorized to harm anyone." Josue spoke with genuine puzzlement.

"They killed to preserve your precious quantum reality," Westcott confirmed Wyatt's long-held suspicions.

"Our quantum reality is the only valid timeline." Josue kept his voice low and threatening.

"The victors invariably write the history books." Amanda lowered her umbrella, and then opened it. "My daughter provided me with some of your technology to serve my explanation."

Holographic images familiar to Hunter and Ellison expanded around them in a half globe. "This is the shape of past and future history. Going back far enough, you can see we shared a past up until a certain point."

The two men watched with rapt fascination as the centuries unfolded before them.

"This point represents a divergence for you, but normal history for me. Lavoisier arriving in England, his relationship with Liechtenstein, my father, their collaboration. I grew up in the world that it created, a combination of steam and cold fusion that made the fantastic happen. No coal, no dirty skies, enough energy to power a dozen Londons."

"It's still wrong." Hunter's fingers gradually crept up the outside of his jacket.

"Let her talk." Wyatt glared, and Josue lowered his arm again.

"We have hunger, strife, political intrigue, and war. Not a perfect world, but a better one." She gauged Josue's reaction and then went on. "Notice a multitude of similar timelines in parallel to this one, each taking its own course. One of them is yours. Centuries later, your reality invents time travel. Your Institute starts encountering what you think of as anomalies, and 'corrects' them."

"The anomalies were convergence points between our two timelines."

"Yes, Mr. Ellison. Time travel technology is rare. It only exists in our two realities. When your world achieved this capacity, it began to interfere with ours, and those convergence points became an entangling. The actions of your Institute overwrote my history."

"We kept chasing down time anomalies causing the two histories to converge. But how…?" Josue' breath caught in his throat.

"I was isolated from the changes because I was using father's temporal device, returning to 1884 from the future. The incursion caused my machine's power source to fail, and I was stranded. I carried two sets of memories, one from each reality. When your agents invaded 1850, they were unaware of the small scale prototype. It still existed in the altered history over thirty years later, and I used Herbert Wells to get it."

"Randa?"

"I had a daughter with Herbert, Mr. Hunter, not that he ever knew."

"You visited him in the 1932. Why didn't…?"

"In spite of Herbert's numerous dalliances, he is a good man. It would have disturbed him greatly to discover he had a child out of wedlock."

The holographic imagery ceased, and they regarded each other under large, wide oak branches.

"How did you get Miranda into the Institute?" Wyatt walked around Amanda so he could stand beside Josue.

"I knew I would need a trusted confederate inside your organization. Time travel has multiple benefits, including amassing wealth by using future knowledge in the past. I left my daughter with members of my mother's family, paid them well, and gave them detailed instructions as to raising her. That included what she would need to become a founding member of the Institute."

"Why not have Miranda stop Pitt and Giorgio?"

"That was never my goal, Mr. Hunter. For my plan to work, I had to make time travel impossible in your reality at a very specific point."

Josue took quick steps backward, drew his unitool, and pointed it at Amanda. Noticing Ellison tense, he cautioned, "Don't."

Westcott casually rested her now closed umbrella over her shoulder again. "Killing me will change nothing. Once you went through your time portal, Miranda used it to send a highly specific energy pulse through all of the temporal interconnections from your present backward half a century. The physics are complex, but the result is a slight but effective change in the underlying fold of timespace your portals access. Your technology no longer works. It will never work."

"I'm sorry, but I can't let that happen." Josue aimed the unitool and pressed. His brow furrowed, yet the tool remained inert. Then he lowered his arm. Wyatt watched his best friend's body crumple like tin foil.

"You bitch!" Hunter launched himself at Amanda, but Ellison was ready, body slamming him to the grass. They struggled briefly, but Wyatt jumped up first.

"Calm down, Josue."

"Calm down?" He scrambled to his knees, ready to commit murder.

"I can send you home, Mr. Hunter," Amanda blurted out. "Your family, your life is still there. You and Mr. Ellison are university instructors, historians. The only thing different is you're your time travel technology does not exist."

Josue looked up. "You're sure?"

"I'm not a monster, and I do have a child, so I understand."

Wyatt helped Josue to his feet and then turned to Amanda.

"I have established an institute housing an experimental laboratory where my father and I continue exploring the possibilities of his Engine. A time device there is equipped to take you home."

"Both?"

"You have another suggestion, Mr. Ellison?" Amanda twirled the umbrella, her eyebrows raised.

"Wyatt, don't." He touched Ellison's shoulder. You've been my best friend for years."

"I got into this game for the adventure. Teaching undergrads what year some politician became Prime Minister would be unending death." He glanced toward Amanda. "Could your institute use someone with time travel experience, and advanced knowledge of virtual realities?

"Are you offering your services?"

"If you'll have me."

"Think about it. This won't be home."

"My home was the Wayback."

"Mr. Hunter, as I promised, you will go home to your wife and family. You will, as I do, have two separate memories of reality, but in your case, I imagine you will eventually accept the new version."

Josue listened but he was still looking at Wyatt. Then he sprang forward, held onto the tall man, and cried. "God, I'm going to miss you so much." Finally he pulled away and looked up with tearful eyes. "Take care of yourself, okay?"

Wyatt smiled a little. "You wouldn't want my life to get boring, would you?"

"You can say your farewells at the laboratory. I'm sure father would love to meet you both." She gazed pointedly at Wyatt. "Sure you won't change your mind, Mr. Ellison?"

"I won't, and call me Wyatt."

Someplace, Sometime, the Far Future

"Sorry I dragged you to another bust, Camille." Josue Hunter and his wife, a woman just slightly shorter, sporting long, flaming red hair, and a thin figure draped in clinging linen, walked out of the main doors of the small playhouse with forty or so other people.

She leaned in and kissed his cheek. "Not your fault. The jokes were too old. Probably something that guy you used to work with would enjoy. Next time, let me pick."

A wistful expression passed over Josue's face as he ripped up the tickets and dropped them in a nearby trashcan while recalling that other life. Gazing up, he saw clouds moving in, obscuring the stars. "Looks like rain."

"It's only half a block to the tube. I'm sure we can make it before the storm." She grasped his hand. "How about taking me to that ice cream place near the station first?"

"Absolutely." Among the thinning crowd, they gently kissed, their hot breath mingling, and then walked down the uneven sidewalk of old town, passing under an antique electric lamp and then into the comforting night.

Europe, 1888

Amanda pulled the trigger on her long barreled, brass and copper-plated Carbonic Blaster, shattering the lock and part of the door to the warehouse's interior office. Wyatt slammed into the solid oak door with his shoulder a second later, throwing it wide open. He quickly moved to the left in the dim, box-shaped chamber, and Amanda rushed after him yelling, "Freeze!" Dressed in her leather aviation jacket, scandalously short knee-length wool skirt, and shear black silk stockings, she looked both menacing and alluring.

Wyatt drew his own weapon and motioned Baron Otto Von Schticklegruber's three Bavarian miscreants toward the right side of the room.

"Turn around, hands against the wall. Feet back and spread 'em," Amanda ordered. Wyatt chuckled, recognizing the phrase he'd taught her from a million 20th century cop shows.

Only a single oil lamp on top of the rickety pine desk at the room's back provided illumination. Silhouetted by that light, the man Wyatt knew only as "the Courier" was tied to a metal chair, hemp ropes around the chest, hands bound behind him. His head was hanging down loosely and Ellison saw fresh blood on his shirt.

Moving behind him, knowing Amanda would hold their adversaries at bay, he holstered his Blaster and took out his knife. "You okay?" Placing a lens suspended to his leather helmet over one eye to enhance the illumination, he cut the ropes.

Coughing, the Courier hesitantly lifted his face. His features were nondescript as you'd expect of a spy, typical male pattern baldness, coloring suggested a native of Morocco or Algeria. "I'll make it. Didn't say anything. The PM send you?"

"We'll talk later." The ropes fell to the floor. "Can you stand?"

"Help me up."

Pocketing the knife, Wyatt draped the man's arm around his neck and lifted, then called out, "Time to leave."

"Get him out. I'll be right behind you."

Wyatt and the limping Queen's operative lurched out the doorway and into the dark, vast warehouse, aiming for a distant exit that opened to the deserted shipyard.

"I suggest you schweinhund stay right here unless you enjoy getting shot." Without waiting for a reply, she ran out, but after a few yards, spun back just long enough to fire an explosive shell at the doorway, throwing up flames and debris. "That ought to hold you."

Outside, she saw her father at the controls of the Autogyro with the Courier in the seat behind. The flying machine was silently floating upward into the darkness, emitting bellows of steam. Daddy would fire up the screaming engines when it didn't matter if the noise alerted the port authorities. The rope ladder was hanging down from the aircraft, dragging along the uneven pavement, and Wyatt was suspended just above her extending his palm. "Come with me if you want to live."

She didn't understand most of his jokes, but she loved his dazzling smile.

"Always." She leapt forward letting him grasp her hand, and then ascended the ladder right behind him.

Once they were safely aboard, Carson Westcott, engaged the W-L motors that drove the tri-propellered craft and climbed west into the ebony sky toward the Channel.

In their seats at the rear, Amanda and Wyatt embraced passionately and kissed. They held each other close as he murmured, "The Adventures of Westcott and Ellison have only just begun."

James Pyles is a published science fiction and fantasy writer and Information Technology author. Since 2019, his short stories have been featured in numerous anthologies and periodicals. He has a passion for these genres and is currently working on more compelling projects. You can find him at https://poweredbyrobots.com/

The Predators

by Eamonn Murphy

"**N**o predators?" Chief Science Officer Peter Morgan stared at the botanist opposite him in disbelief. Deputy Science Officer Jill Penny had enough intelligence and charm to capture any man on board but had so far rebuffed them all and focused on her work.

She was good at it. He trusted her. Even so, it was hard to believe what she was telling him now. They sat in his office on the survey ship Endeavour and she had just returned from the planet below with the initial reports.

He frowned. "That doesn't make sense, Jill."

"I know, Pete. The flora is as varied as Earth. There are insects galore as you might expect. Oh, I should qualify my statement: there is predation at that level. Insects eat other insects and much of the bird population eats insects too."

"And fauna?" he asked. "What about animal life?"

"All herbivores as far as we can tell. There are vast herds of grazing animals analogous to the buffalo, deer, antelope, that sort of thing. They eat the grass and feed it with manure in a beneficial cycle that works fine. There seem to be millions of little critters about the size of a rabbit. They eat a green leafy plant that grows abundantly in amongst the grass and mingle with the herds of larger creatures."

"What about the forests?" He stood up. Peter was one of those men who like to pace when thinking.

Jill leaned back in her swivel chair as if she was about to put her feet on the desk, but didn't. "Plenty of forests. There are creatures that live off the produce of trees, storing them for winter presumably and many insectivores." She grimaced. "We had to wear protective clothing against the insects. Some of them pack a mean sting."

He had moved over to the screen on the wall. The exterior cameras showed a view of Planet TC46. The TC stood for Terran colony and the number indicated that forty-five planets were already occupied by Earthmen, albeit only just. Infant human colonies were springing up all over this area of the Milky Way.

"No animal eats another animal."

"Not that we've seen so far."

Peter Morgan was silent for a time as he looked down at the lovely green planet below, almost a double of Earth, and pondered the circumstances that had brought man here.

He was part of a vast Diaspora. Humanity was spreading out to the stars, thanks to the Scorpii, an advanced race who had seen that man must spread out from his own doomed planet or be made extinct by war and ecological catastrophe. The Scorpii had given humanity the secret of FTL drive and the stars beckoned. Earth had become overcrowded but the galaxy was huge and there was plenty of room for everyone.

This thought inspired his next question. "What keeps the population down? If there are no predators and all the herbivores keep breeding they must exceed the food supply eventually. Pretty quickly if they breed like Earth mammals."

"That's the big question, Chief Science Officer," said Jill.

He smiled. Using his title was kind of a joke between them. The colonization program had been organized on military lines with scientists and crew members assigned ranks and given uniforms. It was thought by psychologists that this would instill a sense of camaraderie, purpose and discipline and it was probably true, he reflected. Humankind generally worked more efficiently when they had order, structure and even a hierarchy in which to fit.

He sat down again. The informal briefing was concluded. "I assume you've downloaded a full report into the ship's computer which I can read later to cure my insomnia."

"You have insomnia?"

He smiled. "No. But if I did, reading reports would cure it. Especially yours."

Jill laughed. "I'll take that as a compliment."

"Oh do! Your paperwork is detailed, complete and as professional as an academic paper. It's not meant to be fun. Joe Niven puts jokes in his and I have to edit them out. I keep telling him these things will be read back on Earth and the Colonization Bureau doesn't have a sense of humor."

She stood up and turned for the door. "Joe's like a big, naughty kid," she said. "And Carl Stefano is even worse."

"You mean Assistant Engineer Joseph Niven and Surveyor Carl Stefano, I presume. Please observe the forms Deputy Science Officer Jill Penny," he said sternly.

She saluted. "Aye, aye, Captain Bligh. I mean Chief Science Officer Morgan."

"Which reminds me, I have to pass this on to the Captain." He tapped the console on his desk and began to read through several reports that he would have to summarize. Captain Blaine was mainly preoccupied with transporting them from planet to planet and had little concern with the actual colonization process but he would still want to be kept up to date with the latest information.

"Am I dismissed?" said Jill from the doorway.

He looked up and smiled. "Dismissed, Jill. No, wait. You want to rendezvous for dinner at 1900 hours in the refectory?"

She smiled. "Gladly."

"See you later then."

As the door closed it occurred to Peter Morgan, not for the first time, that he was madly in love with her.

But then, so were half the men on the ship.

#

While Jill had returned to the Endeavour, Assistant Engineer Joseph Niven and Surveyor Carl Stefano had stayed on the planet. They were in an area of grassy plains in the center of the largest continent, at a spot where the plain began to merge with a huge area of forest, giving the survey team easy access to both types of terrain. The trees grew dense about a mile away but there were a few strays near where they stood. Nothing on TC46 had been named yet so they simply referred to their location as the Great Plain. Herds of large grazing animals roamed across it but there were none near. Their only companions were the small rabbit-like creatures that Joe called Smeerps. He laughed when he said it.

"What's the joke?" said Carl.

"Oh, nothing. You'd need to be familiar with William Atheling, Jr. to get it."

Carl made a small dismissive noise and returned to adjusting his laser cutter. He preferred vids to reading. They had been tasked with clearing the few trees here. When they had done so the large robot diggers would move in and scoop out a meter or so of topsoil to make a level foundation for the first colony dome. When the survey was finished and the first settlers arrived they would have a base camp. Meanwhile, it would serve the same purpose for their team.

The laser cutter looked like a big gun mounted on a stand but had no military purpose. Now that there was a galaxy full of resources available and room for everyone, man wasn't going to study war no more. At least that was the theory. Carl didn't believe it would last and had a bit of a yen for being an action hero, like the ones in the vids he enjoyed.

He had set the device up six meters away from a tree five meters tall, just in case it contrarily chose to fall in his direction. He had the thing angled so that the wide laser beam would slice downwards, cutting the tree off very near its base.

"Stand back, Joe!" he shouted. "Firing one."

He pulled the trigger. A burst of white-hot energy came out of it in a flat beam fifty centimeters wide. He had been aiming slightly to the left of the tree and the grass there was blackened. He moved it to the right in a slicing action across the tree trunk. It was cut cleanly and creaked loudly. The grass to the right of the tree sizzled and blackened a bit just before he cut off the beam.

The tree seemed to pause for a few seconds then toppled to the left. Carl ran forward with a fire extinguisher to spray the grass. The last thing they wanted was to start an inferno. Only water was used as they didn't want to introduce new chemicals into the environment, at least, not yet. Carl had just satisfied himself that any potential fires were well doused when he saw something lying in the blackened grass.

It was one of the Smeerps, as Joe called them. Its fur was burnt black and it was clearly dead. He nudged it with his foot.

"Damn." He hadn't wanted to kill anything. "Hey, Joe. You reckon I should report this?"

His companion came closer, looked down at the dead animal. Neither man had ever killed anything before. Both had been too young for the wars that convulsed Earth before the Scorpii came with their FTL gifts and hunting had been a privilege of the very rich for at least fifty years.

Joe shook his head. "No. It might get you in trouble and there's no real harm done. Let's just forget about it."

Carl was looking down at the dead animal. He studied it intently for a few seconds then turned to the other with an almost guilty expression. "Hey, Joe. You ever eat meat?"

When Earth's population had reached ten billion meat had vanished from the dinner plates of all but the wealthy elite. It took 16 lbs. of grain to produce 1 lb. of meat and that simply wasn't viable with so many mouths to feed. Assistant Engineer Niven laughed at the question. "Sure, every Sunday. A big roast joint with potatoes and everything. You kidding? My pa wasn't no trillionaire."

Carl grinned. "Wanna try some?"

#

The next day, Peter Morgan managed to free up a few hours in the afternoon to finally get down to the planet. As chief of the science department, his job was to assess the reports of others and get an overall picture of the planet. Some general had once said that a thousand reports weren't half as good as going and looking for yourself, a philosophy with which Morgan agreed wholeheartedly. He wanted to see planet TC46 for himself, but not by himself. He wanted to see it with Jill Penny. Finally, he had managed to finagle their schedules to make this possible. Of course, he was in charge of scheduling for the science department. There were some advantages to rank.

The shuttle dropped them near base camp. They waved perfunctorily to Joe and Carl who were continuing the work of clearing the area for the first buildings with the aid of three crewmen and several large machines. Then they walked off in the direction of the forest. There had been heavy rain about an hour before and the landscape smelled fresh and wonderful.

"I see what you meant about the insects," said Peter, swiping at his face as some flying beastie landed on him.

"Abundant." Both wore the recommended outfit of tight-fitting coverall elasticized at wrists and ankles. Only their hands and faces were left exposed.

"Perhaps we should wear beekeepers hats as well."

She swiped an insect away from her nose. "Most of them don't bite, they just get in the way but, yeah, some headgear might be useful. I'll check with stores."

Morgan looked around at the abundant grass, the thick patches of spinach-like vegetation and the forest in front of them. He grinned and took a deep breath. "You can almost smell the greenness."

"It's great, isn't it?"

"What's this?" He felt something against his ankle and looked down. A small, furry creature with large hind legs had just brushed against him. It didn't run away but continued without haste on its journey to the nearest patch of thick green leaves. It was about the size of a rabbit.

"That's a Smeerp. Joe Niven calls them that, for reasons known only to himself and it's caught on. The green leaves are TC46 spinach which is extremely rich in a variety of nutrients and edible for us, too. You could live on it for a while, maybe forever."

Morgan made a face. "I had to be forced to eat my broccoli as a kid. Not big on green leafy vegetables." He looked around and saw several more of the rabbit-like creatures. "There's certainly an abundance of Smeerps."

"No predators, remember." They were getting closer to the forest and the number of birds around had multiplied. Some of them sang loudly, some were busy swooping back and forth snatching at insects.

She took his hand. It seemed perfectly natural and neither noticed it particularly. "This is a wonderful planet, Pete. A paradise."

He nodded. They had reached the edge of the forest and he paused. "Has this been explored yet?"

Jill shook her head. "Not properly. We've flown over it but so far only set foot on the grasslands. But I'm sure it's safe. No predators, remember?"

"No predators that we know of yet," he corrected and turned to the right. "We'll skirt around it for now. Head off this way and circle back to the camp. No point in taking unnecessary risks."

"Wimp," she said but followed his lead.

They walked along in silence for a while. Peter became conscious that they were now holding hands and smiled. He heard a noise ahead of them and after a while realized it was water.

"The river," she said in answer to his unspoken question. "It's quite broad so we can't cross. If we follow this bank along a while it will take us back near home."

A few paces later he could see it. The river had cut a channel into the plain and the banks were steep, about a meter high. The water was clean and clear and he thought he could see fish. The planet was certainly abundant with life.

Jill laughed suddenly. "It looks like we're not the only ones who have to turn back." She pointed to their left and he saw a pair of Smeerps approaching the steep bank. They stopped and looked down into the rushing water.

"Can Smeerps swim?" he asked.

"We'll see."

The furry creatures had stopped and sat down. They looked up to the sky.

Four birds dropped down.

Jill inhaled sharply.

"Hunters?" he said.

Two birds dropped on top of one Smeerp. They dug their claws into its thick fur and picked it up. Their companions were doing the same with the other Smeerp. Both pairs rose into the air, just a few feet high.

They flew across the river and dropped the Smeerps on the other side.

"Did you see that?" Jill was pointing and shouting, absolutely elated.

He nodded. "I did. I did." He didn't really know what to make of it. Cooperation? Telepathy? What exactly had they just witnessed?

"The birds helped the Smeerps cross the river!"

"So it seems," he agreed.

"That was wonderful!" He realized even more than he had already what kind of person she was. Jill Penny wanted every creature to be as kind and generous and helpful and loving as she was herself, all living in perfect harmony and not eating each other. TC46 was her version of heaven and a starship had brought her there.

He liked her all the more. But the implications of what they had just seen were enormous. Earth was a planet of contesting species. Planet TC46 didn't appear competitive at all but they had seen no external evidence of communication between the rabbits and the birds. Were they telepathic? This definitely needed further investigation.

Peter looked at his watch. "We'd better get back. Time and Captain Blaine wait for no man."

She was almost babbling on the walk back along the river bank. "This is just the most fantastic ecology. Can you believe it? No killing."

"Except for insects," he reminded her.

"I doubt if insects feel pain. But all the higher life forms live in harmony!" she clapped her hands with joy. "They must have some way of keeping the population stable, though. Perhaps they breed just enough to replace themselves."

"By instinct?" Peter was dubious.

"Instincts can be pretty sophisticated. Have you seen bees dance?"

"Yes." He stopped and turned to face her. "I haven't seen you dance yet, Jill."

She grinned. "I'm sure we'll get around to it." Then she leaned forward and kissed him. He put his arms around her and for a moment there was nothing else in the universe. "Soon," she said, breaking away.

They walked the rest of the way back in amicable silence. As they drew near the survey crew preparing base camp he tugged gently to separate his hand from hers. She gripped him firmly.

"Let them gossip," she said. "Who gives a damn?"

Joe Niven trotted up to them. He looked at their joined hands and raised his eyebrows slightly. Peter was released.

"Officer Morgan," said Joe. "We're just about to cut the last tree. A big one. You want to watch?"

"Sure."

"I've got to get back to the lab," said Jill. "Got some microbes on a slide that just won't wait. See you later, Peter."

He stared after her for a moment then turned to Joe. "Let's see this tree."

Carl was sighting the large laser projector on the last tree. He had it angled downwards as usual and was well back. They usually fell in the direction planned but it was best not to take chances. Peter noticed that a few of the rabbit-like creatures were around, evidently undisturbed by their presence.

There were two of the Smeerps just behind the tree. Carl seemed to be waiting for something. The Smeerps moved.

Peter was about to ask what was the hold up when the surveyor pressed the trigger. The beam, angled downwards, sliced from left to right across the tree trunk cutting it neatly near the base.

It also incinerated the two Smeerps.

Peter grabbed Carl by the shoulder and turned him around. "You did that deliberately!"

The surveyor shrugged off his hand. "What if I did? A bit of Smeerp meat makes a pleasant change from ships rations." He grinned. "You want to try some?"

"You're not a vegetarian are you, sir?" asked Joe. "I know Deputy Science Officer Penny is one, but not you."

"That's not the issue," said Peter. He took a deep breath. He couldn't let it appear that his fondness for Jill was affecting his judgement at work. "Do you know what we just witnessed, me and Jill?"

The crew shook their heads. He told them about the birds lifting the Smeerps over the river.

"It sounds like something from one of those old Walt Disney films," said Joe.

"Very sweet," said Carl sourly. "I still don't see what's wrong with eating Smeerps."

"That's because you're a surveyor, not an ecologist," said Peter. "Look, Carl, you eating a couple of Smeerps isn't going to change much but if an expanding colony comes here and does the same thing what effect will it have on the local ecology? We simply don't know. In fact, we can't be sure that your eating a few won't have any effect. Until we've studied the matter a bit more I'd like you to hold off."

Carl nodded but there was a look in his eye that said he didn't agree.

#

Peter found himself having the same discussion two hours later with Captain Blaine. This time he had Jill to back him up.

Carl had taken the issue to the Captain. Peter couldn't really complain about that. Technically he outranked the Assistant Surveyor but Carl wasn't in his department and was within his rights to argue his case.

Unfortunately, the Captain agreed with Carl.

"Really, I can't see the harm." Blaine was a big man who shaved his chin blue every morning and had his hair trimmed to a military crewcut. He was from the American south-west, land of cattle and the 16-ounce steak in the days when Earth's population hadn't exceeded its food supply. "Hell, with all this grassland I reckon the colonists might introduce some Texas Longhorns." He grinned. "I'd retire and settle here if they did."

Jill spoke with barely restrained fury. "So having wrecked the ecology of Earth you think we should carry on and do it to the rest of the galaxy."

"I agree with her, Captain." Peter flinched inwardly as Blaine raised an eyebrow. Word of their hand-holding had raced around the ship at the usual speed. Some wag had once said that even before the Scorpii's gift to man, gossip had travelled faster than light. Now it was hard to take her side without everyone thinking he was biased in her favor.

He ignored the look and continued. "It's not a matter of us being vegetarian or not. It's a matter of interfering with an ecology that we don't yet understand. You've seen the reports on the cooperation between the birds and the Smeerps."

"Yes. That was very interesting. What do you think? Telepathy?"

He shook his head. "I don't know. There's no real evidence for such a thing outside of fantasy and science-fiction. Thoughts travel around your brain on paths of neurons but how would they get outside to another brain?"

"We don't understand it," said Jill. "And until we do, Captain, I think we should keep our disruption of this planet to a minimum."

"Our job is to make sure it's safe for colonization so it can be colonized," replied Blaine gruffly. "Earth is still packed and half the people are hungry. The starships can barely leave fast enough to move the surplus away. We need every suitable planet and this one looks very suitable so far. I won't let your squeamishness interfere with our…"

"Our Manifest Destiny?" she said, a jibe at his western background. "Pity there's no red men here to slaughter but we can settle for Smeerps."

Blaine glared at her. "You scientists can be all detached and benevolent but real people need real planets to settle. And people have been hunting meat since forever. That's how nature works. It's dog eat dog and an eye for an eye. If that interferes with your fluffy notions of a Disney paradise where birds and rabbits all cuddle together…tough! Now get out."

They left.

Outside in the corridor, Jill muttered furiously. "An eye for an eye, indeed. As if we haven't got beyond that."

Peter tried to calm her. "We did our best."

She was quietly furious, fists clenched. "I know we're here to scout the planet for colonization. I know people are going to come here and settle. I just want to make sure we do it the right way. That we fit into the existing ecosystem instead of wrecking it."

"We're bound to change it," he said. "We're bound to have an impact."

"But hopefully not the same as on Earth. Our impact there was to wipe out almost every other species except for the unfortunate ones we farmed in giant concrete sheds for their milk and meat and eggs."

He nodded. Peter had read his history and knew that ethical concerns once raised about factory farming had long since been crushed under the weight of the need for food. Eventually, even the cost of raising cattle, pigs and hens in concrete sheds had become unviable. Even after most of Brazil had been deforested to grow soya beans there simply wasn't enough grain to feed them. The impact of such places on the local environment had also been disastrous and most were relieved when they closed down.

"Damn it, Peter. Are we going to make the same mistakes again all over the galaxy?"

"I hope not. But meanwhile, the captains in charge and he said Smeerps are fair game. We'll just have to keep researching and see what new information we can gather that might prove him wrong."

Jill frowned and looked unhappy.

#

The Smeerp hunt next day didn't make her any happier. Carl and Joe had organized it and several of the other men had decided to come along. They were not a military ship but were equipped with small arms and some of the crew had rifles.

Peter found Jill by the airlock that led to the shuttle, arguing with Carl. Five other men stood behind him, bearing rifles. Some carried large pouches as well to carry whatever they caught.

"Game hunting is a tradition on new planets. I've done it on my last two missions. TC12 and TC23 in case you want to look them up. Planets suitable for us usually have animal life suitable for us to eat."

Jill was stood in front of the airlock blocking him from leaving. "Other planets have had prey and predator species. This planet is different. It has no predators."

"It does now," said Carl. "Us." He grinned and hefted his rifle.

Pete came alongside Jill and took her arm. "Come on, Deputy Science Officer Penny. You can't stop them."

She twisted free of his grip. "I can't allow this."

"You haven't got a choice, babe," said Carl. "The captain has Okayed this shooting party and there's not a damn thing you can do about it. Now stand aside."

The men behind him grumbled menacingly.

Peter stepped between them. "No need to get rough with the lady, Carl. You men carry on but we'll come down with you to observe." He gently pulled her out of the way. Carl opened the airlock and the small gang trooped through to the shuttle, Peter and Jill bringing up the rear.

"What good is watching them?" she asked irritably.

He shrugged. "I don't know. We can perhaps make sure they only shoot what they want to eat. If they go blasting away at Smeerps and leaving them dead just for the hell of it we can step in. The captain authorized a hunt, not a slaughter."

She took a deep breath, let it out. "You're right. We can do that at least."

Nobody spoke to them on the trip down to the planet's surface. Carl piloted the shuttle and he was focused on his job. One of the men gave them sly sideways glances that Peter fancied might have a trace of guilt in them. The others wore defiant expressions. The shuttle landed and they disembarked in an orderly fashion at the base campsite. The trees had now been felled and a digger robot the size of a large truck was excavating a circular foundation trench twenty meters in diameter to take the first domed habitation unit. Constructed of lightweight plasteel, such domes provided a weatherproof home for the researchers until they left and a first base for the colonists when they arrived.

The hunting party moved well away from the shuttle. The rifles fired bullets and they didn't want to risk any damage to their craft. Carl led them in the direction of the forest, perhaps thinking that there might be bigger game available among the trees.

As usual, there were plenty of Smeerps wandering blithely about. They weren't afraid of humankind. They had no reason to be.

Until now.

Carl, naturally, bagged the first one. The others looked around, looked at Jill and hesitated. She was well-liked and respected on board the *Endeavour*. No one really wanted to upset her. Carl didn't care. He hefted the rifle to his shoulder and took aim.

Peter had never heard a projectile weapon fired before and hadn't realized they were so loud. He flinched at the noise and stared in horror at the target. A Smeerp squawked as the bullet penetrated its side then collapsed, evidently dead.

Joe was next. But he wasn't such a good shot and only hit the Smeerp in the flank. It hobbled away, bleeding.

A third man finished it off with another shot. Its head split open in an eruption of blood and brains as the bullet hit its skull.

"Woo-hoo!" Carl punched the air. "Now we're real men. Hunters!"

Jill had gone very pale: "I can't watch this." She turned to start back to the shuttle.

Pete was inclined to follow but really did want to make sure the men didn't go too crazy. Two Smeerps were dead already. A few more would be enough if their only purpose was to get food.

Suddenly he heard a noise overhead; a loud cawing. He looked up and saw a large black bird of some kind, bigger than any bird they had seen so far. It had come from the direction of the forest.

Within seconds it was joined by several others. More came. The hunters were getting into their game now and all five were looking about eagerly for prey. He heard the crack of a rifle again, swiftly followed by another.

Jill had stopped and was looking up as well. She hurried back to him.

"What are they?"

He shook his head. There were twenty or thirty of the black birds overhead now, all cawing loudly. In warning?

Suddenly the birds swooped down in unison. About four of them attacked each man that held a gun. The hunters were taken completely by surprise. Carl dropped his weapon and swiped wildly at the dark birds clinging to his arm and pecking at his shoulder. Two others were pecking at his legs. Then one flapped up and went for his face. He shouted in alarm, tucked his head into his arms and ran for the shuttle.

Joe and the other three hunters were suffering a similar fate. One had tripped and four black birds were sat on his back pecking at him. One pecked his scalp and he yelled as blood flowed.

Peter and Jill hurried over to help him up. The birds had not yet attacked them, only the men bearing weapons.

They helped Joe to his feet. The birds flew away.

"Let's get him to the shuttle!" shouted Peter. The rest of the hunters were already there or very near. As they retreated the birds circled not far overhead but left them alone.

There was a lot of shouting on the shuttle.

"Damn birds!"

"Why did they attack us? We weren't shooting them!"

"Maybe they're the Society for the Prevention of Cruelty to Smeerps," said Jill. She spoke quietly to Peter.

He nodded and turned to Carl. "Are you okay to pilot us back to the ship?"

The engineer grunted assent. There was a long scratch on the left side of his face and several tears in the arms and legs of his uniform.

Joe turned to Jill and Pete. "Aren't you going to say "I told you so"?"

Peter shrugged. "We didn't tell you so. We had no idea that would happen. I'm just glad no one was seriously hurt."

Joe wiped at a cut on his arm. "Vicious creatures," he muttered.

Jill shook her head. "I don't think they are natural carnivores. The sharp beaks are probably just for breaking twigs and things to build nests. Maybe they eat carrion, though."

"Vicious," said Joe again.

"They didn't kill you."

He glared at her then frowned.

"She's got a point," said Peter. "The birds backed off as soon as it was clear we were leaving."

"Not killers," said Jill, looking pointedly around at the men who had shot Smeerps.

"Not yet anyway," said Peter.

"Not ever," growled Carl. "We'll be ready for them next time."

#

Peter and Carl reported to the Captain as soon as they got back to the ship. They sat opposite him at his big desk but quite far apart. Carl was still angry.

"The birds are dangerous, Captain. We'll have to take measures to protect ourselves against them."

"You had rifles," said Peter. "What else would help? It's very difficult to defend yourself against a flock of attacking birds. Ask Daphne du Maurier. Or Alfred Hitchcock."

The Captain and Carl recognized the second reference. "The Birds. Yeah, it was like that," said Carl. "The birds on this planet are crazy, Captain."

Peter got angry. "The birds are not crazy. They attacked because you were shooting the rabbits or Smeerps or whatever you want to call them."

"Why should the birds defend the Smeerps?" said Captain Blaine.

Peter thumped the desk in exasperation. "We don't know!" he said, emphasizing each word with a bang of his fist. "That's the beginning of science. We don't know. We don't know so we try to find out. Jill had already reported that there were no predators here which is odd. We didn't know how that worked. We still don't. That's why I objected to the hunting party. Not because I'm squeamish about killing little fluffy bunnies but because we don't know how this planet works yet."

The Captain's lips quirked in what might have been a smile. "Don't thump my desk, Peter. Okay, so we don't know. Any theories?"

Peter leaned forward eagerly, enthusiastic. "I've been discussing it with Jill and we think there may be some kind of overmind at work. We see the individual creatures - birds, Smeerps, grazing animals - and assume that they are individuals, like us; like all the creatures on Earth. But what if it's not just cooperation? What if they are part of some collective intelligence so the birds and the Smeerps are just like our arms and legs, operating together in harmony?"

"The Gaia theory? The ultimate Gaia theory," said the Captain. He stroked his chin thoughtfully. "It's an interesting concept."

Peter said, "It's just a theory and a pretty wild one at that. Perhaps they control the population by just not breeding when a certain number is reached. Who can say? We need to know more."

Carl was still looking annoyed but the Captain was more receptive. He nodded agreement. "We know more now. I mean, the bird attack is additional data."

"And I told you about the birds helping those Smeerps cross the river," said Peter. "Two facts about the animals here: one, they don't kill each other. Two, they cooperate."

"Three: they defend each other," said the Captain.

"Good point." Peter turned to Carl. "So what's your solution. Kill them all?"

Even the gun-loving surveyor was looking less militant. He shook his head. "No. no. You can't kill everything on the planet. That would be crazy. And if they defend each other when one species is attacked…" he paused.

"You can't kill anything on the planet," concluded Peter.

The Captain rose to his feet. "That's the way it's going to be then."

#

It was a less exuberant party that boarded the shuttle the following day. Carl was once again the pilot and Joe Niven was in the party as were Peter and Jill. The other three men were engineers and in the cargo hold, they had the materials for constructing the first dome. The excavation robot had been left on TC46 and had now finished digging its ditch. The shuttle carried curved sections of plasteel that would be laid in the foundation. It had fittings on to receive the curved vertical girders that would form the dome. The plasteel sheets to form the walls would be brought down on the next trip.

"At least we'll be safe from birds once we get the dome up," said Joe.

Jill whispered to Peter. "We have to get it up first."

He squeezed her hand. They would take no part in the construction. Their job was to act as lookouts while further studying the wildlife.

"You look worried," she said.

"I am." He nodded down at the great plain they were approaching, visible through the window to his left. "They let us leave after the hunt. Do you think they'll let us come back?"

"They? You talk as if the animal life was intelligent. I think they were just responding to a threat. Instinct."

"I don't know. We'll see."

The landing was smooth. As they disembarked, Carl in the lead, Peter made a quick visual survey of the area around.

"I wish I had a gun," muttered Carl. The Captain had forbidden any firearms.

Joe Niven and the other engineers opened the cargo hold and began to unload the curved plasteel beams which formed the foundation sections.

Jill nudged Peter and pointed. "There's a herd of large grazing animals over there. The big ones with horns, like buffalo." He squinted into the distance. They were about a kilometer distant.

"You notice something else?" he said. She shook her head. "No Smeerps."

She looked around. "You're right. Normally there are loads of them. They're staying away from the landing site."

"Instinct, you think?"

"I don't know what to think anymore."

The work party began to carry the foundation sections over to the large circular ditch. The excavation-bot was an extraordinary piece of heavy machinery that could dig out a trench so that the bottom was exactly level. Obviously, they had picked fairly level terrain to put the dome in the first place. Peter and Jill stayed near but kept watching the nearby forest and the sky. He kept a weather eye on the grazing animals.

Two birds flew overhead and landed in the trees. Peter thought nothing of it. Then another two appeared; then four; then six.

He grabbed Jill's arm. "I think the birds are gathering in the forest."

She looked up. Several more flew overhead in that direction. "Keeping watch?"

Peter shouted to Carl. "Be careful! Something's going on."

He waved an arm. There was no telling whether it indicated dismissal or acknowledgement.

"Listen!" said Jill.

He stopped very still and held his breath. From the forest, there was a raucous cawing.

He ran up to Carl. "Get the men back to the shuttle."

The engineer turned angrily. "We have a job to do. Let us get on with it."

"Listen, you fool!"

Something about his manner made the other man pay attention. He stopped his work and looked up.

As if it was a signal the black birds burst out of the forest and shot towards them.

There were hundreds of them.

"Run!" shouted Carl. "Back to the shuttle!"

Most of the men turned and ran but Joe Niven was in the ditch wrestling with two bits of plasteel that wouldn't go together. He was bent over and intent on his task.

Jill ran towards him. "Joe! Joe!"

Peter shouted at her. "Jill! I'll get him! Make for the shuttle!"

She didn't hear. She touched Joe's shoulder. He looked up and jumped out of the ditch. They ran for the shuttle. Peter was running towards them, his only thought to protect Jill.

Seconds later the birds were on them.

Peter reached Jill. She bent over double to protect herself as best she could. He swung his arms crazily trying to fend off the attackers. It was as if an all-enveloping, writhing black shroud had descended on them. He caught glimpses of sky but the world seemed composed of flapping wings, sharp claws and sharper beaks. His adrenalin was rushing but he still vaguely felt the rips in his trousers, in his jacket, in his skin. He focused on keeping them away from Jill. He bent over the top of her and tried to charge forward but he could no longer see the shuttle. He didn't know which way to run. He kept fighting, swinging his fists, making contact now and then.

Vaguely in the melee, he felt the ground tremble. The herd was thundering towards them! Every animal in the area was on the attack.

A bird dug both claws into his back and he tried to reach round to get it off. As he did so another one went for his face. He went down, pushing Jill underneath him.

Peter blacked out.

#

He came to in the sickbay of the *Endeavour*. At first, he was vaguely aware of murmuring voices and the faint hum of machinery. He realized he was flat on his back. He was sore all over. Slowly, like coming out of a dream, he recalled the battle with the birds.

"Jill!" He sat up. There was a sharp jab of pain in his head, like a spear going through it. He opened his right eye but his left didn't seem to be working.

"I'm here. I'm okay." She was sat by his bedside. She was still in her ripped uniform and a medic was applying bandages to her sorely ravaged hands. She was looking at him and crying.

"Everyone else?"

She took a deep breath before responding. "Joe didn't make it."

"Damn."

She managed to report the rest, speaking in short bursts. "The other men came and got us. Dragged us back into the shuttle. By then the buffalo animals were charging as well. We were lucky to get the shuttle off the ground before they hit it. The Captain says we're not going back."

"Good. "He put a hand to his face. "What's wrong with my eye?"

Jill bowed her head and wept quietly. "Take it easy, Peter. You're safe now." She heard a sound behind her and turned to see the Captain.

"Is he…?"

Peter dropped his hand as he fell asleep, exposing the dark hole to the right of his nose. The Captain stared.

Jill nodded. "Just like you said sir, an eye for an eye."

Eamonn Murphy was born and bred in Bristol, England, many years ago. He misspent much of his childhood reading Marvel comics, Golden Age science-fiction and the heroic fantasies of Michael Moorcock. He's been a reviewer for sfcrowsnest for several years and has published more than forty short stories in small magazines.

Nowhere To Be Found

by Alex Minns

"Hey Chica," Carlos called over his shoulder. He heard a sigh from the back of the next compartment.

"I know you don't want to go to Winera..."

Footsteps rang out against the metal floor as she approached.

"No, I don't but that's not what I called you for," he cut in. He tapped at a unit hanging from the wall beside his head. "I could put any ship back together blindfolded from a Kretian cruiser to a G-Pin but I have no idea what that is or why it is flashing at me."

She peered at the unit, her face stony as she considered it for a moment.

"It's a long-range comms beacon. I re-appropriated it from Mel-Tech and hard-wired it into the ship to boost the signal."

"Reappropriated from Mel-tech? Remind me to stay clear of any of their workshops. So someone's trying to get hold of us? How do we open a channel?"

"We don't. It's more an SOS signal. If we decode it, we'll have the sender's location." She didn't move. Carlos noted her jaw twitch, it was about the biggest emotional outburst he'd seen from her in the six months they'd flown together, including after pulling off the Galatian Shuffle in under two weeks with just the two of them. The score had been more money than he'd ever had in total over his whole life. She had merely smiled, nodded her approval and got down to finding their next mark. To see her frowning at the comms beacon was somewhat un-nerving.

"Should we go help them? Find out who it is?"

"There's only one person who has the codes to send to this module. And they were told only to use it in the direst circumstances."

"So we're staring at it why?"

"Because," her jaw flexed again, "that person is my good-for-nothing brother."

#

They stared out of the viewscreen in silence. The cloaking was still hiding them from the trading post they were orbiting. It was a small, artificial moon that had been commissioned by the owner of the station that sat off to its left. The station's metal structure gleamed; bright chrome contrasted with the blackness of the space around it. There was no sun nearby but the station had enough lights and reflectors to create an artificial daylight that even cast enough light down onto the trading post to give it a day and night.

The station had a central core that could only be described as a palace. Towers jutted up at different heights, walkways twisting round them and shuttle-chutes giving access between. Gyroscopic counterwheels surrounded the whole inner core and slowly rotated at different angles and speeds to keep the central palace stable in position. It had been a marvel of engineering and architecture, talked about on either side of the Rim. And all this had been constructed, trading post and all, in under five years. Carlos titled his head in awe, watching the rings tumble over each other, his eye tracing the line he would take to fly between them.

Every now and then, a piece of debris came close to one of the rings and it would bounce off the protective atmospheric shield surrounding the entire structure. It was an impossibility to create such a large atmosphere in the depths of space and sustain it. Carlos hated to think what it took to power it. He watched a small cruiser fly towards the shield and hover. A wave of blue energy reached out from the shield and flowed over the ship, swallowing it and allowing it to enter without breaking the barrier. It then flew on a pre-arranged path towards the palace where several bays jutted out like piers over water on old Earth.

"Unbelievable," Carlos breathed.

"I know."

"Not that," Carlos waved at the viewscreen. "I mean the fact you have a brother and I had no idea."

"There's a lot you don't know about me." She stated bluntly before turning away.

"Don't I know it." She was right, he didn't know why it was such a surprise, he still didn't even know her first name. He was unsure about calling her Nyradzi, her grandfather's infamous name. It felt like a name that should only ever be whispered in reverence. Her grandfather had been a hero to people like Carlos, a genuine Robin Hood. Tales and rumours of his exploits had been passed down around fireplaces, exciting children all over the galaxies. No-one knew what had happened to him or why he stopped, and Carlos still didn't feel like he could ask her. For now, he contented himself knowing he was helping her follow in his footsteps and create new tales for kids to re-enact on dusty planets. "So, is your brother like you? Is he in the family business?"

"No. My brother is a criminal," she dropped a bag onto the workbench, making implements clatter to the floor.

"Err, you do know you're a… I mean we don't exactly colour inside the law do we."

"That is different. We have honour, a code. I'm an artist. He gives con-men a bad name." She jabbed her finger in the air at him. Carlos stared at her, his eyebrow raised as her words settled. "Worse name then." She shrugged, shook her head and went back to rummaging in her bag. "Rule one where my brother is concerned: trust nothing he says, does or even thinks."

"So why are we here? "

"Because one of these days, he might just be telling the truth."

#

The fake sunlight was very off-putting. She looked up to the spinning monstrosity in the sky and squinted. Yes, it was a technological marvel, but it was also a very large display of just how much money its owner had. And very little of that money had been gained legally.

"Tell me why I can't come with you again?" Carlos was dragging his heels as they weaved their way through the stacks of crates. Billy would be somewhere nearby, the nearest tavern most likely and she was going to meet him alone.

"I need you to do recon. Find out everything you can about what's going on up there," she pointed at the Station. "And you might as well restock while we're here."

"Restock? You've put…" he lowered his voice and leaned closer, "explosives on this list." His eyes searched side to side just in case anyone had overheard. She couldn't help but smile; they were about the same age but he was still so innocent. She patted him on the back and slid a few notes into his hand with practised ease. Even he was surprised when he looked down and saw what he was holding.

"You are going to teach me that one day, aren't you?"

"You should see what I put in your pocket."

Carlos immediately stopped and started rummaging in his empty pockets.

She laughed and carried on walking. "Won't be long." She left the grumbling pilot behind her as she exited the docking compound, flashing one of her many identity documents at the man on the gate. Before slipping it away, she quickly checked the name on this one. Always paid to know who you were supposed to be. Frezia Halden– it had been a long time since she had been the diplomat.

Trading posts were all very similar; the list of buildings closest to the docking compounds always contained some kind of local law enforcement post, a few shipping companies, a medical centre and at least two drinking establishments of varying repute. Other than that, each place had its own additions and variations. She spotted the obligatory two taverns on opposite sides of the central square. She moved towards a fountain in the middle and surveyed her options. The building on her left seemed to be where all the pilots headed: dark, dingy, eyes watching everyone that went past. Exactly the place you would go if you were trying to hide or trying to plan something unsavoury. On her right, was a more stylish establishment where any travelling dignitaries would definitely lurk while they tried to forget they were on such a dismal little rock and wondered why they didn't stay on their class B cruiser instead. It was where the well-to-do and those reaching above their station would frequent. So it was exactly where Billy would be. The man had no sense and an aversion to what he considered slumming it.

The place was heaving, packed to the walls with a who's who from this side of the Rim. She slipped between people making as few ripples as possible which wasn't always easy considering the size and shape of some species inhabiting the tavern. A kordaite was close to the bar with a fairly large space around him. She stayed well away. Although they had a solid core, most of their being was made up of electrical energy. They always reminded her of the make-up of an atom, just on a much larger scale, and of course if you happened to try and move into their space, enough electrical energy went through you to send you to sleep for a fair few hours.

She kept her head down. There were a few faces she recognised, mostly from the news and high-flying circles but there were others too. Ryegus had caught her attention the moment she turned a corner and was faced with a series of booths. She ducked behind a group standing and talking loudly, trying to merge with the group as if she were with them. It was definitely Ryegus. She had run into him once before when she had a job relieving a Prince of his ill-gotten jewels. He had been working his not inconsiderable influence on the Prince, trying to encourage himself appointed as an adviser. Of course, what that really meant was, the Prince became Ryegus' puppet. She'd seen it plenty of times – cartels and mob families were alive and well and Ryegus' operation was multi-global. She slid away from the group and went back to searching for Billy, spotting a few other familiar faces along the way. The First Minister of Cixia was following one of the waitresses back towards the bar. The man was well known for having expensive and less than legal hobbies. His attention was so focused on the girl, he never felt the hand dip into his pocket and remove the paper peeking out. She quickly slid it into her own pocket for later.

She felt someone's attention on her. Reacting slowly, she swept the room with her gaze and saw a familiar, furtive face peering round a mint-green wall at her. His head jerked, urging her forwards.

He'd at least managed to find the most tucked away table in the place. She slid into the booth, happy her back was against the wall and her eyes could track all of the movement to her side.

"What took you so long…"

She held up a hand abruptly, stopping him in full flow. Her eyes piercing him as he recoiled.

"That name does not pass your lips here."

"You're paranoid." Her brother snorted as he folded his arms and sat back, relaxing against the backboard. His brown hair was swept over to one side and greased into place. He was wearing a burgundy suit, one, that if she was not mistaken, was the accepted attire of anyone working for Monteiro Kaliban, the owner of the Station floating above them.

"Last time you said that, you got us into a gun fight with a group of Versians and nearly gave my name to the Marshalls."

"It was an accident."

"That's what you said." She refused to blink and he refused to meet her gaze. "Why am I here? You don't look in danger. In fact, seems like you're doing rather well for yourself. Got yourself a job? Don't tell me, you press the buttons of the shuttle-chutes sending the guests where they need to be?"

"I needed an in. I need to get close to one of the guests." He chewed on his bottom lip and started playing with the cuff of his left sleeve. That was always a dead giveaway.

"Why? If I'm not convinced in three minutes, I walk out of here."

"Come on Sis," he whined. She didn't budge. "Look, I got in some trouble and now I owe someone so they want me to retrieve something for them from a guest."

"Who do you owe?" She closed her eyes, already knowing what he was about to say.

"Ryegas."

She hissed, covering her cursing.

"You see? If I don't get what he wants, I'm a dead man. I can't pull this off alone. I need two people to get into a ship and get past the security."

"What are you retrieving?" His pause didn't ease her anxiety.

"A shipment of Jazz."

"Are you kidding me?" She made to get up. Drugs was a no-go area, no discussion.

"Please. If I don't get it, he *will* kill me. If I do this, I'm free of my debt, no more Ryegas or Jazz."

"That's not how these guys work and you know it."

"Please Sis," he grabbed at her wrist and stared up at her imploringly. He caught her hesitation, a glimmer of hope flared in his eyes. She sighed as he grinned, both knowing she'd already resigned herself to her fate. "You er, you have your ship?" She nodded. "I mean, *the ship?*"

"How did you know I got it back?"

"Word gets around when The Nowhere is in the air." He hopped to his feet and squeezed in front of her, already making for the exit. "Come on, we haven't got long to sort this. You took too long getting here." A familiar tightness crept across her jaw as her teeth ground together. With a growl, she followed him out.

#

"Oh, it's been too long." Billy ran his hands along the side of the ship's hull. "I remember Grandpa taking us out in this."

"Yeah," she nodded slowly before tapping a little rhythm on the metal surface. "Still holding together."

Billy moved to the bay door and waited expectantly.

She paused next to him reaching for the brace around her right wrist before tapping in the unlock code. Billy grinned and nearly leapt forward on hearing the release. He hauled on the door, making her wince; he never did treat The Nowhere with the respect it deserved. Holding her breath, she moved up the steps to join him inside, waiting for any sound of Billy coming across Carlos. No sound came.

Billy was already sitting in the pilot's seat, fiddling with dials and adjusting things when she stepped inside. Carlos would not be happy.

"We need to get up there. When we get close enough, I can use my clearance to get us a docking position."

"Pretty keen to get going."

"The mark leaves tonight, Ryegas has given me a very narrow window to get this done." He gestured at the co-pilot seat. She shook her head. There was no way he was flying her ship. He rolled his eyes and slid out of the seat, sulking as he threw himself down in the other chair.

"Leaving tonight? What exactly is going on up there? Seems very busy."

Billy turned to look out the viewscreen. "There's some tech conference."

"Ryegas goes to tech conferences now?"

"You know the toys you can pick up there."

She nodded and moved to the back of the cockpit, pulling the slip of paper she'd lifted from the First Minister without Billy seeing.

"Been on the lookout for some new comms." She pulled a small tin from her pocket and made a show of pulling the small ear bud out. "These could do with replacing. Gotten quite a bit of use lately. Maybe I can pick myself some new ones."

"Sure, once we've done what I need to do, you can go wild." Billy turned away again and didn't see her eyes scan the words on the paper quickly. Tech conference huh?

"You reckon you can get my cover on the list for the tech conference?" Glancing over her shoulder to check Billy wasn't paying too much attention, she grabbed a pen and scribbled a quick couple of sentences on the back of the paper before tucking it between two units mounted to the side wall.

"Should be easy. I'll sort it when we dock. What's the name?"

"Frezia Halden."

"The diplomat?" His face wrinkled in disgust.

"It was a rush to get here and no-one warned me I needed a tech back story." She fixed him with a glare as she moved back to the pilot's seat and strapped in. "Anyway, all politicians want to get their hands on the best tech for their people. Good for profits."

"Okay." He held up his hands in submission. "I'll get you on the list. Assuming you can fly this up to the Station through the rings?"

"Don't ask stupid questions." She dialled in the start-up sequence and listened to the music of the engines going through their powering sequence. Each cylinder of the claxion generator gave a different note until it sang to her that it was ready to fly. Her eyelids fluttered half closed as she put her hands on the controls. Carlos looked after the flying, but she did love to fly this bird. And just because Carlos was better didn't mean she wasn't really bloody good. Joy filled her face as her hands went on autopilot and brought the ship up to hovering height before inverting and shooting off into the upper atmosphere. Billy was thrown back in his seat cursing as she laughed. Clattering echoed from the back of the ship, making her wince a little and she eased off slightly.

In under a minute, The Nowhere was closing in on the atmosphere of the Station. The ship slowed, giving the control room of the Station long enough to register their approach.

"This is Kaliban Station, Theta sentry, please identify yourself." A voice crackled over the comms system, filling the cockpit. She glanced over at her brother and nodded at him to intervene. He leaned forward, hesitating as he tried to remember the controls. Eventually, he hit the right button and opened a return channel.

"Kaliban Station this is Mox, identification 517 alpha. I am accompanying the party of the Honourable Frezia Halden, who is visiting the conference on behalf of the Nisorrah Federation. There appears to have been an issue with the booking so I was sent down to Beta Site to make sure they arrived without any further hitch."

"Mox, we have no record of Halden or anyone from the Nisorrah on our system."

"Exactly. Complete disaster. Kaliban sent me down here himself to sort it out. He needs to open some negotiations with them for the new Station, if anything messes that up, anyone involved is going to be lucky to work anywhere this side of the Rim by the end of the day and this woman is very hard to keep happy."

There was a pause. They stared at the wire mesh on the control panel, willing the voice to speak again. She gripped the controls a little tighter.

"Look, I really shouldn't but I can add her to the entry list and get you a docking site but that will only get you in the main hall."

"That's all I need, past that I can call Kaliban." A disgusting smug smirk crawled across Billy's face.

"Ok, I'm sending you the path through the rings to your nav system. Dock at port 84.3."

"You are an angel Theta." The comms clicked off as the coordinates started pre-populating the navigation system.

She rolled her eyes at the satisfaction on her brother's face but was quickly distracted by the blue haze coalescing before her eyes and moving towards the ship. The air seemed to crackle in the cockpit as it moved across the hull and enveloped it inside the atmospheric shield. She pushed the navigational instructions up to the viewscreen and overlaid them with the true image she saw through the window. It was like threading a needle between the rings. Some of them passed perilously close to the top of the ship but the timings of the nav instructions were perfect. It almost took the fun right out of it. Feeling somewhat cheated, she brought the ship into position at 84.3.

"Big brother is watching." She nodded out the viewscreen towards a camera that swivelled towards the ship as soon as they entered range.

"Security is very tight round here. There's a camera on every port."

"Well at least I know the ship will be safe. But how are we going to get on the other ship to get your cargo without security seeing us?"

"I've found a weakspot. No-one expected anyone to try and manipulate feeds directly from the cameras. I can fuzz the feed for a few seconds, from the actual camera post. Will give us plenty of time to get round to the main bay door."

"You can jack into all the feeds from the actual cameras. Seems like a pretty big weak spot."

"Well they have plenty of armed security wandering round too so they guess no-one would dare. But with my uniform, people will think it's legit." He stood up and moved to the exit. "We gotta move. The ship we need to hit is in the north quadrant. We'll have to take a shuttle-chute."

#

"Are you literally just plugging into the main line?"

"Will you keep watch or something?" Billy hissed. She shrugged and went back round to keep the rear doors and the armed guard doing his rounds in sight. "Clear?" She waited, watching the path of the guard. He veered to his left, away from them. She gave a sharp nod. "Ok, go." Billy crossed behind her to keep an eye out as she moved to the rear door of the cruiser. She pulled a device out of an inside pocket of her jacket and held it to the frame of the door, listening for a beep. Right at the top of the frame she heard it, almost imperceptible. She hit the jam button and then closed her eyes. She listened to the frequencies, waiting for a tone exactly like the beep she had heard. When it matched, she hit the button again, locking it in place before it moved to the next channel. Once all the channels lined up, the lock was released. She took a step back and the door slid open.

"Forty-five seconds, nice" Billy nodded appreciatively as he stepped inside. She followed closely behind and closed the door. "It'll be hidden somewhere, probably in separate packages in case there was a spot search of the ship on the Beta site."

She chewed on her bottom lip as she thought. "Could be anywhere." Billy had already started pulling open every locker in the rear hold. She moved behind him and made for the mess hall. The ship probably held a crew of at least fifteen which allowed for a lot of hiding places. She systematically started searching, checking for hidden compartments or anything attached to the bottom of drawers. She even took to dismantling the cooker just in case. When she was happy the room had been cleared, she went to the next room along: the med bay. Tucking her bag beside one of the cupboards, she started rummaging in the chemical supplies. Hiding the drug in plain sight would have been the clever move. She inspected the containers carefully, making a mental note of all the details. Her thoughts were interrupted as the door to the bay whistled loudly. She heard boots outside the room. They were not Billy's.

She moved and was instantly round the examination chair and in the doorway when a sharp pain stabbed in her righthand side. Her legs gave out as the electricity crippled her body. The floor smashed into her face but she could barely feel it over the fire coursing through her veins as the shocker did its work. From her paralysed position on the deck, she could see Billy being held by a security agent. The agent had their arm across Billy's throat and a shocker pressed into his side. The blue helmet hid the agent's identity but from the size of his figure they must have been Molok or similar. There was no way Billy was getting away.

A second figure came into view inches from her face. He was wearing the uniform of Kaliban's security force as well.

"Mister Kaliban does not tolerate thieves on his Station." The voice rang out clearly, dripping with scorn and confidence. The head turned to Billy and his companion. "Take him outside. We'll let her stew in here while we get him talking."

"No, look, it's a misunderstanding..." Billy's voice was cut off midflow as the agent squeezed harder on his airways.

"Enough." The guard kicked the back of Billy's knees making him stagger forward and easy to steer out of the ship and out of sight.

The second agent lingered. "He will tell us what we want to know. And then you will tell us again. Just for completeness." He paused and checked her pockets, taking the tools from her coat jacket pocket. Her jaw flexed in anger as he removed the brace from her wrist and along with it, access to her ship. She willed her body to move as he walked across the cargo hold but her treacherous limbs refused to budge. This was going to make things harder.

#

Billy stood at the back of the room surveying the people sat before him. He adjusted his collar, his uniform having been swapped for a much more comfortable suit. Kaliban had left him in charge of overseeing the auction now that everything else was in place. He smirked. He couldn't help but enjoy the image of his sister stuck on that ship, limp on the floor. The only question was how long could he leave her there? She'd find a way off eventually but it would be too late.

The auctioneer tapped his podium drawing the collective attention of the room. There had been a good turnout; his contacts had spread the word far and wide and the tech conference proved a perfect cover allowing some of the more outwardly respectable members of the community a chance to take part. The collective wealth before him was unimaginable. Even just a thirty-five percent cut of the sale would make him a fortune. Perhaps then his sister would give him the respect he deserved. Just like he had deserved the family birthright. That ship should have been his. Now he loathed it and the injustice it stood for.

"Ladies and gentlemen. I believe all participants, or their proxies, are present so if we could get down to business. You can see the merchandise on the videofeed and saw an active demonstration of it being docked. The Nowhere is a legendary ship and can outrun even the fastest Marshall Runners. It has sophisticated cloaking technology and an impressive claxion generator. It would serve as a useful addition to any fleet for more covert operations, or as I know many of you are interested in, it could serve as a useful lesson in backwards engineering for replication in more of your vessels. The historical value of this item cannot be ignored either. The symbol of Nyradzi would be worth every penny, even if for some of you, who may have fallen foul of this figure, it is just in order to destroy it."

Billy shuddered in delight at the thought of the ship being torn apart for spares. It would destroy her. It was almost too perfect.

"If you could all submit your sealed bids on your panels, we will close the window in three minutes. All bids are to be blind, highest offer wins, no further bidding will take place."

The next three minutes dragged on interminably. Billy's eyes scanned across the back of the heads of the wealthiest criminals in the universe and their representatives. Kaliban was going to have to give him a better position in the organisation after this. One of the agents beside him coughed. He shot him a piercing glare, making the agent stand up a bit straighter and stare directly ahead. He was still angry with him. Yes, it had to be convincing, but did he really have to squeeze his throat so hard?

"Check the corridor again," Billy instructed. The agent, now without his helmet, nodded once and moved out into the hallway leaving Billy with the second agent. He went back to surveying his customers. Some of them had clearly checked out, knowing they would never be able to put up a big enough offer. There were a couple of figures who had asked an annoying number of questions when the room was opened. A man in a purple jacket had been particularly annoying, refusing to allow the room to settle until they had seen proof that the feed was live. Billy had been forced to radio down and get one of the engineers to stand by the camera and perform the actions as dictated by the purple suited buffoon. He'd had him dancing like a fool before he'd been thoroughly satisfied.

"Ten seconds left." The auctioneer stared at his screen, monitoring the bids as they came in. "And time is up. Thank you for your bids. If you would bear with me while I check the winning bid and availability of their funds."

Billy smirked as the customers eyed each other, assessing how confident each other looked.

"Thank you for your patience." The auctioneer gave a small cough catching Billy's attention. The man's face was trying to remain impassive but there was no denying the look of surprise trying to break through his mask. Excitement surged, sending adrenaline through Billy's body. It was a big number. "I am pleased to announce bidder 32 has been successful with a bid of thirteen point seven million imperial marks." Billy's eyes bulged. That was over ten times the estimate. He quickly started searching the crowd.

"No…" The man in the purple suit stood up and marched to the front of the room, giving a little wave to the unsuccessful bidders. "Who even is he?"

"I don't know Sir," the agent beside him replied.

"I wasn't asking you, you idiot."

"Thank you." The bidder shook the hand of the auctioneer, pumping it hard enough to risk dislocating the man's shoulder. He was wearing a ridiculous hat that partially obscured his olive skin and young face. He had to be somebody's errand boy, and whoever that person was, had deep pockets. It would be wise to get their name. "My panel." The bidder handed over the bidding panel, proving he was number thirty-two. "I have already started the funds transfer." There was an odd lilt to his voice, an odd rhythm, it jarred with Billy. He moved closer to the podium waving at the wrist brace. "Is that the key to the new ship? My employer will be most happy."

They all felt it first. The floor vibrated under their feet. Then came the noise. A deafening boom made them all cover their ears. Clamouring voices rose up in the aftermath, people demanding to know what was going on.

"What is this?" The bidder screamed, leaping backwards and waving madly at the feed of The Nowhere. Billy froze: his heart stopping as he watched a ball of flames dance on the screen. "Stop the transfer. The ship. What have you done? I want the money returned!"

The other agent burst into the room. "Sir, we have reports of an explosion."

"Really!" Billy jabbed his finger in the direction of the feed. "We need to get down there now." Both agents launched themselves out of the room, Billy hot on their heels. They shouted instructions at people blocking the corridors, sending them scattering in all directions. Indignant voices chased them as they barrelled onwards but Billy ignored them.

"The shuttle-chute is quickest Sir."

Billy followed them inside, his hands curling into fists by his sides. He watched out the window of the compartment as they started to gather speed. Shuttle-chutes did not stop until they reached their destination making it the fastest transportation. Billy watched the rings outside still spinning, moving behind the docking ports, as a cold realisation swept over him.

"We're going the wrong way. The Nowhere is in the east quadrant."

"Yes Sir, but the explosion was in the North quadrant."

"North? But the screen…" Horror descended upon him. "No. No she didn't." He slammed his hands against the sides of the compartment. "That bitch."

#

Sometime earlier

Carlos was careful not to let the packages hit the floor with too much force. The explosives were stable but he didn't see any point in taking chances. It took a couple of trips to get everything off the trolley and onboard; he still didn't really know why he needed half the stuff on the list, but Chica didn't really like to go into the reasoning behind her decisions. Not that he minded that much, it had only been six months but he'd already learned a hell of a lot, including to trust her instincts. And working on The Nowhere was fun. He felt like a hero, righting the wrongs of the galaxy. He smirked; he knew she would be rolling her eyes at him by now. Amused by the image of himself as a spacefaring Robin Hood, he went back to putting the packets of explosive securely in the storage area; there were still plenty of other things she'd gotten him to buy.

The market that sat just behind the docking port was immense and chaotic. He'd had to fend off a raft of ruthless vendors trying to weigh him down with all manner of junk. Thankfully, his new captain had also alerted him to the trade of pickpockets and he'd caught a couple of urchins trying to grab a handful of cash.

It had been stupidly busy. There was talk of a tech conference going on up on the Station but some of the faces he'd seen lurking in the corners did not seem like they were interested in the benefits of modern advancements. The whole thing had to be a front.

A noise distracted him from his thoughts: a rhythmic tapping on the side of the ship. He froze for a moment as it happened again. He knew that tune. He cursed, grabbed the last of the items strewn outside the storage bay and dragged them in behind him, pulling the door as close to closed as he could get. He had just managed to get into hiding when he heard the door to the ship open. A greasy looking human walked up the ramp. Carlos took an instant disliking to him and his overconfident swagger. Holding his breath, Carlos shrank back as the intruder cast his eyes around the ship, worried he would come snooping around. Chica had given him the signal to hide for a reason.

He relaxed a little when she appeared in the doorway of the ship as the man sat in *his* seat. He fumed, barely restraining the urge to leap out there. He took a deep breath and waited; Chica was always extolling the virtues of patience. He almost broke when he saw the man start messing with the controls. He had everything set up just as he liked it! It would take an age to reconfigure everything. His fury almost made him miss Chica speaking. Carlos focused and realised she was glancing in his direction at the gap in the doorway as she spoke. She was holding her comms and talking about overuse.

Getting the hint, he dug in his own pocket and took out his

matching tin. The ear bud was in place and on in seconds giving him much clearer audio of what she was saying. That greaseball was her brother. His eyes widened in shock as he squeezed up to get a better look and was just in time to see Chica wedge a piece of paper between two units after checking Billy was not watching.

"Gotcha," Carlos whispered, knowing Chica would pick up his voice. She seemed to relax a little, her shoulders lowering slightly as she moved to the pilot's seat and kicked out the interloper. Carlos settled in and listened to their conversation, making note of key details and not liking what he was hearing. Then Chica decided to let loose on the accelerator, leaving Carlos biting his tongue in terror as packs of explosives rained down on him.

#

Sitting in the auction room, he was sure she would be able to hear his heartbeat through the comms system. Criminals from every corner of the galaxy milled around, brushing past him as they closed in on the screen to watch his ship being paraded around for all to see. Fine, Chica's ship.

He covered his mouth with his hand as he whispered under his breath.

"Chica? Where are you?"

"On the ship."

"Our ship?"

"No. There was a delay. Son of a bitch used a shocker on me."

"We don't have much time." The rather green gentleman on Carlos' left turned. Carlos nodded and smiled nervously, his ridiculous purple hat nearly tipping off his head. "I'm just so excited."

"Really?" Came Chica's voice.

"I wasn't talking to you."

"You get into the auction ok?"

"Yeah, Frezia Halden's assistant gets red carpet treatment. That auction invite you slipped me did the rest." It was still in his pocket. He managed to use the First Minister's invite to help blag his way into the back room. Thankfully no-one took it from him or they'd have seen the note on the back which read: he's setting us up, get into the auction. That was pretty much all he'd had to go on as she hadn't had many opportunities to talk on the comms. Thankfully, she'd asked her brother enough pointed questions that he'd managed to get the salient points.

"I've already stalled as long as I can. I made a guy to dance in front of the ship to prove it was live feed but I can't do much more before I get punched," he glanced at the other bidders around him. "Or worse."

"The feed here is ready. You set?"

"Yes. I'll have a one-point-three second delay."

"Is that enough?"

"Will have to be."

"Okay, hopefully that's enough explosive."

"I put ten pounds in your bag. That's enough to make a dent in surface underneath." The auctioneer tapped on his platform. "We're starting here."

"Okay. I've already plugged in to the feed. Give me the sign when you're in position." The auctioneer did his ramble as everyone returned to their seats and started eyeing each other warily. Carlos turned to survey the crowd and saw the slimeball at the back of the room, two agents flanking him. He'd sold out his own sister, who knows what he had planned for her after selling their family ship. Safe to say only one of those siblings was worthy of the name Nyradzi.

The auctioneer gave the ten second call. Carlos looked down at his panel. No-one could see the second device tucked underneath it. All the bidding figures were being routed through his device so he could see the winning amount. All he had to do was bide his time. The device countdown hit zero and he hit in his bid; the delay tagging it on the end without anyone noticing the lag. He smiled; his ship was worth every penny.

That was the easy bit he thought as he noisily made his way to the front of the room.

"Thank you." Carlos pumped the auctioneer's hand energetically, positioning himself in front of the screen with the feed. "My panel." He handed over his bidding device, without his additional unit over. "I have already started the funds transfer." He edged forward, totally blocking the screen and pointed at Chica's wrist brace he could see on the shelf behind the auctioneer. "Is that the key to the new ship?" As the man turned to retrieve it, he hit a button on the secondary unit in his pocket, switching the feeds on the screen he was blocking.

After Chica had left the ship, Carlos had set about directly plugging into the feed monitoring The Nowhere. Billy had been kind enough to tell him what he needed to do. It hadn't taken long for agents to turn up to watch the ship so he'd had to work fast and get out of sight. Thankfully, he'd had the foresight to grab everything he needed off the ship including the ridiculous outfit Chica had encouraged him to buy. He didn't realise his new disguise would come in handy so quickly. Now

Chica had tapped into the feed of the ship she had just left, all he needed to do was change the channel. "My employer will be most happy."

He felt the vibrations under his feet as Chica heard his key words and detonated the explosives. He just hoped she had time to get back to their ship.

"What is this?" Carlos screamed in fake outrage and horror. He leapt backwards waving at the display of a smouldering ship. He gulped, that really had been enough explosive, there was nothing left to identify the ship. "Stop the transfer. The ship. What have you done? I want the money returned!" Carlos reached over, wrestled the panel out of the auctioneer's hand and hit reverse.

Chaos reigned in the room. Billy had already disappeared. The auctioneer pled for calm but the room was emptying quickly. Explosions had a habit of making criminals twitchy. Carlos took his cue, taking his hat off and slipping into the throng leaving the auction room. The crowd made it easy enough to slip away and before he knew it, he was in the middle of the tech conference.

"Where are you?" He had to shout to be heard over the noise in the auditorium: everyone had heard that tremor.

"Heading to Gate 3A." Carlos spotted a sign for that terminal and pushed his way through.

"I'm close, I'll meet you." He scanned the faces around him but didn't see her anywhere. "Chica?" Fear welled up in his gut. It wouldn't take long for her brother to realise what had happened. Once he got off that shuttle-chute, he would be headed straight back for The Nowhere.

The doors slid open to the chute parked at 3A. He grinned; Chica stood in the doorway. He pushed a Versian who had seen the new escape route and jumped through as she quickly shut the door.

"Of course," he laughed as the compartment roared off towards their next stop.

"And?"

Carlos rolled onto his backside and pulled out his device. His eyes widened in delight. "Oh, we're good." He showed her the display and even she looked surprised. It would be a while before Kaliban looked at his account and realised he'd been cleaned out. The auctioneer really shouldn't have let him retrieve his transfer. The worm he'd placed in the programme took everything.

"That should keep Billy out of our hair for a while. He's going to need to do a lot of work to get Kaliban to let him out of his dungeon." Chica's jaw was set, no hint of emotion. The shuttle-chute slowed down. Carlos got up but she held him back as the door slid open and she checked the route. "Everyone's too worried about the fire. All the agents are gone."

They moved quickly between the other parked ships, Carlos unlocking The Nowhere's doors as soon as it was in sight.

"Ny!" he called. She turned and caught the brace as he tossed it to her.

"Ny?"

"Can't call you Chica all the time. And your brother gave up his claim to Nyradzi. Time for you to put your own spin on it." They barrelled into the ship and took their places, powering up the ship with practised ease.

"Ny," she shrugged with a small smile before nodding.

"Where to Boss?" The ship started to hover attracting the attention of a few stragglers.

"There's a good casino on Pandemonium, we've got some excess funds."

Carlos nodded, programming in the initial route. He looked out at the moving rings, mapping it out in his brain as he put navigation into manual. This would be fun.

Alex Minns is based in England and has worked in forensics, teaching, PR and been paid to wield custard flamethrowers. She writes sci-fi, fantasy and steampunk and can be currently found forcing her mother to listen as she tries to untangle the timelines of her time-travel steampunk novel. You can find her obsessively creating blog stories and micro-fiction on https://lexikon.home.blog/ and on Twitter under @Lexikonical

The Sting
Of Immortality

by Gregory Allen Mendell

D
r. Pearson's heart tugged on my left arm. It seemed to weigh a ton, though I knew most of the heaviness came from the slurry of ice water and bio-antifreeze it sat in. A blizzard had almost shut down DC, but I had to deliver it to the NIH for study. No poor soul needed it for a transplant, not given its damaged condition. So I decided to go outside and enjoy the weird sense of being inside a snow-globe.

I only needed to walk from the hospital to the Metro station to take the Red Line to Bethesda. While the few others on the National Mall were bundled up like it was Siberia, it didn't seem cold. Then a breeze hit me, and I wished I'd worn a hat and gloves.

A hint of blue caught my eye. Near the Washington Monument a swarm of feathers danced like translucent fairies in the wind, swirling in slow motion. Unbelievable. I ran toward them while a warm feeling rushed down my spine. What a story I'd have for Lori tonight. I reached for the nearest one but missed. It hit the ground and dissolved in the snow.

Looking around, I saw a boy waiting with his rolled tongue sticking out. Gently gliding in, a blue vane touched pink flesh. The boy's scream flung me off my feet. The cooler I had been holding slid down the icy walk.

Out came Dr. Pearson's heart. The boy, clutching his own, ran twitching past me.

I struggled to stand up. A mangy dog appeared, sniffing after what it probably thought was a holiday ham. I couldn't swallow, but somehow I found my voice. "Get away from that."

The dog shied away then circled back. I was about to yell again when

117

a streak of metal flashed across my view. Careening out of control, a motorcycle flipped the dog like a rag doll. The bike and its driver cartwheeled to one side. The chains on the back wheel spun in the ice until the engine coughed to a stop.

I went to the driver, who groaned. Helmetless, with blond hair down to the waist of her leather jacket, she looked maybe nineteen. "Are you okay?" I asked.

She nodded and seemed fine.

I wasn't. Breathing hard, I looked around for Dr. Pearson's heart and then yelled over my shoulder at the girl. "So what the hell?"

"It stung me," she explained, her tone flat. "Poked my eye out."

I stumbled on, the snow and my fury blinding me. "Did you see a heart go anywhere?"

"I was just doing donuts in the street while no one was around."

I turned to the girl. "I'm someone. If you haven't noticed, there's a big red cross on my coat—so I'm someone. Maybe someone important."

"Well I'm the one who needs help here, Mr. Red-Cross, ... and my dog. If you hadn't fallen down he wouldn't have gone running off after ...after ... whatever that was ..."

A wave of nausea passed through me. There was the dog. Not whimpering. Not moving. Had I caused this? I walked closer. It was dead.

A feather looped into view and hovered a few inches above the dog. Amongst its aerogel-like plumage I could see barbs with a drop of sticky serum at the tip of each spine. Then it touched down on a bare patch of the dog's skin and vanished in a fine cloud of mist.

There was a yelp.

To my amazement Fido was up. "He must've been playing freeze tag. He's fine," I said.

"No thanks to you, Dr. Death." The girl got on her bike and Fido joined her, all frisky. "By the way, there's your heart." She pointed to a red lump partially covered in snow.

She rode off with the dog. "Your eyes seem fine," I called after her in a huff.

I retrieved the cooler. At least there was still some ice water left inside. After adding snow I took it to Dr. Pearson's heart. With my bare hands I scooped it up and dropped it in. I tried to shake the gunk off, but no amount of shaking would do. Before I could close the lid a feather floated in and landed on the antifreeze-filled heart. It didn't dissolve.

#

At home, Lori was unimpressed.

"You dropped the heart?"

"It was icy."

"Chasing after a feather?"

"I wanted to catch one for you."

"Why were you on the Mall?" Lori's tone curled the linoleum of our apartment floor.

Clearly it was all a big mistake. One of many I'd made during our eight years together. Given her reaction to the feathers, it seemed there was no point in making things worse and telling her the real story about where I'd been. So I lied. "Foggy Bottom Metro was closed. I was walking from GWU hospital to Smithsonian Station. It was the only one open."

"And NIH knows that you brought the heart here. So you're fired?"

"No, I didn't tell them I brought the heart here. I'm not an idiot."

"So they didn't fire you?"

"Er, I told them I left the cooler on the Red Line … by accident. Then they fired me."

"And why? To show me a feather?"

"I knew you wouldn't believe me if I didn't show you one."

Lori shrugged. "Jimmy, everyone knows about the feathers. It's all over social media."

#

Lori was right, of course. She was always right. The blue feathers had been a worldwide event. Space debris, NASA said. And then there were the reports from the nutcases, from people who said they had been stung and cured, stung and saved. Lori showed me one from Senator Jack Haw. "Come look at this jaw flapper. He looks like he has a hedgehog squatting on his head."

Haw had revealed on his reality show he had a brain tumor. Now today's news showed him declaring he'd been on his way for a scan when a feather stung him. His tumor was gone. Furthermore, he knew the feathers were sent to announce the end-times. And further-furthermore he knew in his heart he was now immortal. The end of the video showed his young wife pulling his hair. "It's real," she proclaimed.

119

#

After that, each day I had to sneak to the fridge.

"You're not getting ice for your blue feather of happiness again, are you?" Lori yelled.

I ignored her. Once back in my office, where I had started to sleep, I peeked in the cooler at the feather. Stories of feather stings and miracle cures played on the TV, interspersed with pundits interviewing believers and skeptics.

When Jack Haw appeared on screen with a meat cleaver, Lori bumped into me and almost gave me a heart attack. She patted me on the back.

I thought we were about see the scene from *Stand and Deliver* where the teacher cuts up an apple in front of his calculus class. But Jack's hand went rolling off his desk.

I covered my mouth and tried to squeeze my eyes shut.

Lori reacted with a laugh. "That's so stupid."

Through my squint I saw Jack Haw's hand grow back.

#

We thought it was a trick. So did most people. But several security cameras in DC showed a feather landing on Haw's head. There was no doubt he'd been stung. And Haw's critics, who he'd invited to the demo, had cell-phone videos of his stunt. Why would they go along with it?

So Lori and I got talking.

"It could save you."

"From what?" she asked.

"You know."

"Remind me, I'm getting old."

"Very funny. Your mind is as sharp as the day we met. And your rich mahogany-colored locks … you look great. But you know—"

"What? That some people in my family cannot recognize the difference between a loaf of bread and a book by the time they're forty-five? That I'm thirty-eight? That I haven't been tested? That I should get tested? What difference would it make?"

"It would make a big difference to me."

"You know I've chosen to live without letting this thing hang over my head."

I knew she hadn't lived like that at all. But all I said was, "You're all hope, Lori. Your enthusiasm—it makes you irresistible."

Lori rolled her eyes. "What *made* me irresistible was that I was studying to be a sex therapist when we met and I needed someone to practice on."

"Are you implying when we met I looked like someone who needed a sex therapist?"

"No, it wasn't the way you looked." She got closer to me. "It was the way you acted—desperate." Her eyes twinkled. "Desperate for me to practice on you."

#

Besides always being right, Lori was perfect.

Except, she wasn't. Lori, who insisted she didn't think about the future, had married her high school sweetheart at sixteen, thinking she had better start out young. But she left him after finishing her degree in psychology for her therapist, who, as she put it, turned her on to counseling, but not much else. She also liked to say life was way too short—for everyone she added—to waste time in bad relationships. I wasn't about to point out that according to her, when we met, that's what she had done for the past fourteen years.

So I didn't.

That was eight years ago, soon after her second divorce. She was thirty, I was twenty-two. When it began, our relationship was good. I worked as a tech in various labs and took care of the house. And when she wasn't studying for her master's degree, she took care of me.

Then two years ago she said she needed something new. I was relieved to learn the new thing was a grad program in astronomy education. She had taught herself enough physics to join an observational group but she chose a philosophical topic. Alien life was her real interest, she insisted, though some wondered why in such a big universe we had yet to see a sign it existed. "It's a paradox. One I've always wanted to figure out," she explained. "Like men." Her eyes did their twinkle thing again.

#

"Jimmy, do you remember when you dreamed of finding a cure for something? Maybe this is your chance."

I was about to show Lori the feather, but she put her hand out.

"I don't want to see it."

I rested my arm on the cooler lid.

"You know," she continued, "you should take it to NIH. Let them extract the serum. Maybe they can figure out how to make everyone immortal. At the very least, tell them what really happened. Maybe they'll give you your job back."

"Dr. Pearson's lab is closing down. The complications of his own gene therapy caused his death—it's not like the funding is going to get renewed. So there is no job. Besides, I don't think this feather would survive their scrutiny. Once it triggers, poof, it's gone."

Lori gave me her lecture look. "There has to be a residue. Nothing can just disappear."

"What about love?"

"What?"

This put her off guard, so I pressed on. "How does love disappear?"

She stood silent for a moment. "Is that what this is about? I thought you were going to show me the feather." Her eyes found mine. "You've always said you wanted to go to grad school. Here's your chance. Take it to NIH. You know more than anyone what was going on in Dr. Pearson's lab. Even if it dissolves, analyze what's left. That's got to be worth a PhD."

"That's not why I want to show it to you."

"Why not? Worried you can't figure it out? So sting yourself. It might take a thousand years, but I've always believed in you. You could do anything—"

"You're wrong Lori." The metaphysical impossibility of that statement sucked the air out of the room. I'd always told her I had ambitions. I thought she must have known the truth, though maybe not. "I'm a slacker," I finally said. "You think I want to go to grad school and end up in some basement lab pouring my best years into test tubes like Dr. Pearson?"

"Weren't you already doing that?"

"At least I was home most days by four."

"Okay, maybe you're not scientist material. But what about your writing?"

"It's crap," I said. "There are no new ideas."

"It sounds like you're feeling frustrated." Lori's switch to her therapist voice could have come across as patronizing, but didn't. I remained silent. So she added, "Of course, you're right. There are no new ideas. There's just your own unique truth."

#

That night I realized this was my opening. Lori had started giving me mini-lectures about the universe, about how she thought it was infinite but the number of possible human genomes was finite. There were only so many ways to arrange a few billion nucleotides. But it went further, she explained. There also were only a finite number of quantum states a finite sized object could attain. That meant in an infinite universe, there were infinite Earths identical to this one. And infinite Lori's and Jimmy's too, living the exact same lives, thinking the exact same thoughts.

"So no need to reproduce," she explained. "There's already enough of us to go around."

I knew she was hedging her bets, but instead of calling her on this I asked her my favorite leading question. "Why do you love me?"

"You know I hate that. It makes it sound like you're not sure if I do." She did a full circle of the room. "What is love anyway?"

I suspected Lori had an answer, but I gave her mine. "For me, it's knowing when you're gone everything will feel pointless. I could get a million PhD's or write a million novels, but without you—"

"Hah." Lori laughed. "When I'm not around it's the sex you'll miss. Right?"

"Um ... and the other things ..."

"Name some."

There were many ... I knew there were.

"Hah, here's my proof. If I stopped having sex with you, would you leave me?"

"That's hypothetical right?"

"I'll take that as a yes." Lori's eyes gleamed. "But if I stopped doing all the other things except having sex with you, would you leave then?"

"That sounds like a trick question."

"I'll take that as a no. Okay, to sum up, you'd leave if we stopped having sex, but not if I stopped doing anything else. Therefore, you stay with me only for sex. QED, Jimmy."

Lori was smart. She also had a way of deflecting things to avoid the big stuff. But too much was at stake. Shaking, I knelt next to the cooler. "Lori, the point is, I love you."

"I know ..." She looked down. "I know ... I've been busy ... but after I defend my dissertation, we'll have lots of time. Besides, we aren't debating love here, are we?" She swished the toe of her shoe in a circle. "What we're debating is who should live forever."

I nodded and opened the lid. "I'll be around for a long time. You can be too."

"Then let it sting you, Jimmy. You're gifted. I've always seen that. You can figure out how it works. Then everyone can live forever."

"I've already pointed out I'm not as great as you think I am. Admit it, you chose me because you needed someone after the divorce. Someone younger who could take care of you."

"The initial reason doesn't matter. It's just a game I like to play …"

I thought she might finally say she loved me. But she didn't. I wanted to stop and beg her to sting herself, but decided she needed more convincing. "I also know you thought you might need me to take care of the babies. But—"

"I don't want to talk about that. Jimmy, we need to think about this logically."

"We need to talk about the frozen embryos. I know you only plan to use them if you still have your wits at age fifty. But this way you can use them now, with your future guaranteed."

There were tears in her eyes. "That's just what we need," she said. "Immortals reproducing. How will that work out?" She pulled her hair over her face. "No sting of death? What about the sting of immortality?" She came closer and collapsed to her knees beside me. "I've watched too many people in my family die, Jimmy. I'm not going to watch you."

She reached in the cooler and grabbed the feather by the shaft. Before I could move, she swiped it across my forehead.

#

I should've seen that coming. I should've stopped her. She was so impulsive. Maybe she did it out of love. Maybe she did it for the reason she gave. I didn't want to think about it.

If I'd only known what would happen next.

Because after that sting I did know things, things I shouldn't have known.

For example, I knew the feathers had gone out millions of years ago, that they were designed to fill interstellar space and eventually collide with every planet in our galaxy. I also knew the Feathermakers were coming. They'd be here in ten thousand of our years.

I knew all this because something in feather's serum had rearranged my brain.

Of course I explained this to no one except Lori.

I also told her when the Feathermakers came they would ask three questions. What is mass? What is consciousness? What is love? And we had to prove our answers … or else.

"That's so stupid," Lori responded. "Why would aliens millions of years more advanced than us come to Earth to ask questions? And why now? You know, this screws up my thesis."

"Maybe they want to prepare us—"

"Or maybe the Feathermakers don't know what love is." She gave my chin a gentle stroke. "Maybe that's what they really want to know. The other questions are just a setup to make sure we're not complete morons."

I nodded, sure she was right, like always ... at least about things like this.

#

"If the first child's a girl, what should I name her?" I strolled with Lori across the Mall.

"Lise," Lori replied.

"After your favorite—"

"Yep. But you can name the first boy Jimmy Junior if you want."

"No," I said, "not that. But maybe something less common?" She smiled at me, but I hated this conversation, hated to think about why she'd frozen her eggs. She was now forty-two, but her brain was as bright and impulsive as ever. Would it be in another few years? I changed the subject. "Now that Haw is president, maybe we should move out of DC."

"Haw? I'm not going to worry about him. He may have convinced some folks he's a prophet, that the end-times are nigh, but I know better. I have you."

I told Lori I thought his brain must be like mine, but maybe had received a different message. Still, there was nothing to worry about. The Feathermakers wouldn't be here for a long time. I looked at the bare cherry trees and pictured the blossoms to come. I tried not to worry.

A maple seed spun down. It landed at our feet and we both looked up.

"Haw keeps saying to watch for a sign," Lori said. "Um ... do you see something?"

She was pointing past the trees. The wind picked up and a few more seeds fell. Lori's long hair began to stream.

Then the sky filled with them—millions of tiny helicopters whirling towards the ground. They were beautiful, growing larger, the sun glinting through their translucent edges.

"Feathers?" Lori pushed on my arm and moved behind me.

We turned. Bricks started flying off the Washington Monument.

Then we heard the buzz of a million saws.

"Run," I shouted.

I took Lori's hand and headed across the grass, away from trees, which were getting trimmed down to size. Farther away I saw people fall. Then something sliced me and Lori pulled away. The sound was now deafening. On the ground I rolled over and kicked up in defense. "Stop it!" I yelled. Both my legs were severed, but there was no blood, no pain.

On my side, I saw Lori. She'd kept down.

And the sound … it was gone.

Somehow I managed to sit up. I had to be in shock.

Looking over at Lori again, I thought about crawling to her.

Except my legs were back.

On new bare feet, I looked around. Everything was flat. What had happened? I ran to Lori. Thank goodness she'd stayed on the ground.

"Lori! Lori!" She looked so peaceful.

But she was dead.

#

Five hundred years after Lori died, I still remember the phrase of the day:

Jack Haw, stung by a featha, lived fo'eva.

I knew then there were other messages. Ones I'd been given but blocked out.

The cutters, like the feathers, were spreading through the galaxy. They were made of yellow diamonds and spun thousands of times faster than maple-tree seeds. And every planet they reached was given a bad hair cut.

After this, President Haw declared himself the Everlasting Ruler of the World, or what was left of it. People started to rebuild. It seemed the cutters were sent to impede but not completely destroy technology. Electricity returned first, then computers.

But space travel didn't come back. Haw outlawed it.

He also rounded up as many of the immortals as he could—not as friends, but as slaves that could work forever. If they didn't, they were starved until they petrified.

Like Larry the Stump—Haw placed him in the Rose Garden as a warning.

After that, outside of DC, the rest of us immortals were mostly forgotten. Within a few hundred years no one paid attention to the Everlasting Haw anymore, though every year he made a pronouncement that we were to wait for his next revelation.

Gradually the rumors about him changed from immortal to android and the world split into the usual factions. People merely intensified whatever beliefs they already had.

Except once I ran into a group of freaks. They believed in the immortals and wanted a show, wanted to try out different tortures just to watch a hand or leg grow back. Even after I'd escaped them, I always had to move on when those around me grew older.

Finally I moved to an uninhabited island in the Pacific and I lost hope of ever finding anything interesting about life again. That doesn't mean nothing happened in five hundred years. Every bad or good thing that humans were capable of did happen somewhere.

I was also able to learn there were only a few thousand immortals and most of us were in hiding. And I learned suicide was hard, but not impossible. Usually the immortal went into a petrified state, like Larry. The other example was Pete the Pancake. Pictures of him were on the freak sites. He'd jumped from the Leaning Tower of Pisa and never recovered. Almost no one realized he and Larry were still alive.

I also came to understand if we couldn't give the Feathermakers the proofs they wanted the 'or else' meant they'd abandon us. What I didn't know was how many other immortals, like Haw, had placed their bets on the Cuttermakers taking over after that.

So far, I knew how to prove mass was energy. And someone had shown consciousness was also energy, but I didn't know the proof or even if there was one.

And love? After computers came back, android companions became common. But by then it was also hard to tell what was human and what was not. So I told myself it didn't matter.

To know what love was? It was hopeless. I needed Lori.

#

After many tries I finally tracked down the girl and her dog. They'd traveled with different circuses in Asia, which came back into fashion every other generation. The girl remembered me and cursed me. But she let me take blood samples. She asked why I wanted them. I said I hadn't learned the secret of immortality. Not yet. However, I had learned how to petrify things.

I'd learned that even before Lori had died.

#

Lori was right. I was the only one who could have done it. I was slow to learn, but I'd been given the luxury of time … and the motivation.

I travelled to DC. Getting in wasn't hard. Jack Haw had built a wall around it, but the guards let anyone in stupid enough to ask for admittance.

Getting to the Smithsonian Institution Building was also easy. Everything was in ruins, but the secret crypt underneath it was still there. It was the one thing I'd never told Lori about.

Two miles down, it had power for five centuries. Originally it was built to withstand nuclear war, then terrorism, then to test the rejuvenation of soldiers on the battlefield. Only Dr. Pearson had no intention of creating immortal army men. Knowing his experiments would cause his death he had taken me to the crypt and shown me how to freeze his body for the future.

So after Lori's death, I'd taken her here. Besides freezing her, I had isolated an agent from my own blood to put her almost in the same state as Larry the Stump and Pete the Pancake. But if Lori hadn't already been dead I could never have injected her with the petrifying solution.

Before I pulled her from the refrigeration unit I thought about how the poor doctor hadn't made it here. GWU hospital had cremated the body after the autopsy. That saved me from having to make room for Lori's. Now, I gently took her out and managed to lay her on a portable surgical table, which I cranked down almost to floor level.

Something creaked, probably the cooling pumps, and the lights flickered. The power wouldn't last another week. Before this I would never have risked losing her … forever. Now I had no choice. If all I got were another two minutes with Lori, it would be worth it.

I prepared the injection and touched her cold arm.

"Stop."

"Lori?" But I knew it wasn't her. The voice came from behind. I turned. Jack Haw was holding an axe.

"Come here Jimmy, I want you to do something for me."

"For you? How do you know my name?"

"I've been watching, and a ruler has his spies. The people, they need to believe again."

"In God?"

"In me!" Haw's lips curled like mating worms. "In the Prophesy. So here's what I want you to do. Come up to the White House. I had this passage built." He motioned behind him. "Then cut off my head with this axe. I want to see if my body grows a new head or my head grows a new body. We'll send out the video and I'll be back in business, spreading the word."

"Why would you need me?" I didn't take my eyes off the blade. "Don't you have aides just waiting for an opportunity like this?"

"Don't get smart with me. It's insurance son. Insurance. I might need that serum you've got. Also, I need an immortal that hasn't run away or been petrified … for a test run."

I dodged Haw when he came at me. He turned to Lori and gave me a knowing look.

I knew then whatever love is, it must also be energy. I didn't hesitate to sacrifice my right forearm to get to Jack and hit him square in the chest. He crumpled like a cardboard box filled with wet sand and fell to the floor.

Before he could get up I grabbed the axe with my remaining hand and did what I had to do to give myself time to save Lori. I knew there'd be no blood, no pain. Not that it mattered.

Then I pushed the hypodermic through her stone-like skin.

A rush went through me and all the heaviness I'd carried around for five hundred years disappeared. Lori blinked. I thought she was staring at my arm growing back. But she pointed behind me. I turned to see two Jack Haws rising and we ran for the passage to the White House.

#

"Now you know everything I know."

"That love is energy? That nothing else matters?" Lori smiled. She looked glorious, like she had just woken from a fairytale dream. "I agree."

"So you're saying it? Right—"

"Saying what?" Lori shook her head. "I always believed in you … but I can't really believe I'm here. Without love, I guess I wouldn't be. Maybe that's the beginning of a proof."

We were four hours from DC, in a mountain cabin.

When we had entered the White House it was empty. But we found Larry in the Rose Garden. I injected him and he pointed us to the robo-limos out back—our way out. We kept looking back, but it seemed Haw had the test results he wanted. On the screen in our cabin we saw his new broadcast. It ended with four of him preaching about the

Cuttermakers. Soon there'd be eight, then sixteen … then an army of Haws sent out to make way for our future rulers.

It was horrifying. We didn't sleep. We worried we'd never be safe. We worried someone would ask about the limo parked outside. We talked all night about what we should do.

But the next morning we learned that Larry the Stump had triggered the White House defense systems, sending out the robo-dogs. After that, the Haw bits were too small to grow into new ones. The news showed the petrified pieces being scattered in the Rose Garden.

#

On my island in the Pacific, Lori liked to sing a song from the *Wizard of Oz* about how the evil Haw was gone. Then we'd laugh and fall into each other's arms.

One night we talked about having kids and whether we should we make them like us or let them live life without the sting of immortality.

"I never wanted this for myself. But is it really that bad?" Lori asked.

"It was, without you." Looking up at the night sky, I wondered about other things. I asked if she really believed there were an infinite number of Lise Einsteins in the universe, if she was the one to prove mass was energy in every galaxy.

Lori replied, "Maybe there could be a continuous set of small perturbations … and eventually big ones too. So do I think everyone in the Pearly Trail Galaxy exists ad infinitum?" She looked into my eyes.

"No. I think some of us are unique."

"So you do love me? Is that why?"

"I'll tell you when the Feathermakers arrive," she replied. "I'll have my proof by then."

I'd almost forgotten. Ninety-five hundred years to go. I didn't know if I could wait that long. But if we stayed together, wouldn't that be enough? So I said, "If that works for you."

Lori's eyes twinkled.

Yes, waiting could work. Waiting could work.

Gregory Allen Mendell is a gravitational-wave astrophysicist, science & nature lover, and a moonlit scifi reader & writer. When writing, he likes to explore key mysteries about the future and the meaning of it all. He published his first novel, *Finding the Elsewhere*, in 2019.

Secrets To Keep

by David Cleden

D ooley knew they were coming.
—Not from any outward signs, but maybe there was something below the normal threshold of hearing, some subsonic rumble that was felt rather than heard.

So. One more performance, one last huzzah. One more go-around wondering if this time, *this time* after so many lies and deceptions, he would stumble and let them discover the truth.

Dooley drew in a slow breath of cool mountain air, holding still so as not to disturb the kingfisher he'd been observing. It sat poised on a low branch overhanging the riverbank. Now the bird dived; a glorious flash of blue and orange. Moments later, it rose from the shallows, something silver and trembling in its beak.

Yes. There was a sound. No mistaking the low whine of an aero-engine moving up the valley, like the spinner of a fishing rod unwinding.

They were coming for him again.

Alarmed, the kingfisher took wing, flying low and fast. Dooley wished he could do the same.

They would be flying direct from the Facility's airstrip down in Sentiana, an hour-long flight to Dooley's mountain hide-away. Oh yes, he'd been given the promised privacy and independence: a thousand acres of remote, wooded valley to ward off prying eyes and a Facility-owned cabin to do with as he pleased—but they kept him close, too. They came every quarter, like the changing of the seasons. For how long now? Eight years? Ten?

The whine of engines grew louder as he hurried up the path, wanting to be back at the cabin before they came knocking. He could hear something different in the engine tone as it passed up the valley. Not a 'copter this time. Maybe one of the new VTOL flyers he'd heard about, the latest product of the Facility's spin-off tech division. A VTOL's body was a sleek, bean-shaped glass pod grown from a single crystal-composite; incredibly resilient. Held aloft by sonically-damped, triple-adaptive mesh rotors, the craft was powered by a tiny activated-lithium fuel cell you could heft in the palm of your hand. It was personal flying transport straight out of The Jetsons. However you looked at it, the VTOL show-cased remarkable advances in materials science and engineering prowess, just one of many such developments to emerge from the Facility in the last few years.

That irony wasn't lost on him. But with all those billions sunk into the Facility, naturally someone expected a return on their investment. Those billions had paid for the Facility to develop a world-beating range of diagnostic and fabrication equipment—everything from state-of-the-art neutron-beam scanners and ultra high-temperature furnaces, to atomic-scale extruders and molecular fabricator looms. Mossman—the last operative to visit Dooley—had boasted that the Facility had the tools to tear apart *anything* and then put it all back together again—only better. But Dooley had laughed at this, making Mossman scowl.

Their last meeting had followed a well-worn pattern. Mossman civil, yet not afraid to push hard if he felt the line of questioning justified it. *Did anything seem unusual before it happened? Anything at all? Think hard. Was there some kind of message?* And finally, exasperated: *Why choose you for First Contact?*

Why indeed?

He'd mostly told them the truth, embroidered with a few lies where it seemed sensible. What mattered was what he didn't tell them. Those secrets were his to keep until his final breath. He had a duty.

So just relax. You've handled this before. You can do it again.

But what if he couldn't? Sometimes all he wanted was to tell someone. Wanted it so badly he could weep. He had dreams about screaming it from the top of his lungs into the silence of the mountains. He might have done so too if not for the conviction that they watched him every waking moment, listened to every murmur and curse under his breath, waiting for a moment of carelessness.

His silence, in some bizarre fashion, was his gift to humanity; the ultimate act of selflessness.

Dooley broke clear of the stand of trees, reaching the eastern corner of his cabin which was dug into the sloping ground. The 'copters always set down in the strip of meadow by the river, giving him a minute or two to compose himself while his visitors climbed the path to the cabin.

He rounded the corner and found a stranger standing on his veranda.

She wore dark combat-style fatigues, and something that looked like a weapons belt around her waist. She also looked mightily pissed. A few yards away, a sleek VTOL pod rested at an impossible angle with no obvious means of support, like an object in a Dali-esque painting. Some kind of self-leveling mechanism apparently kept the pod horizontal despite the sloping ground.

Dooley wasn't sure which unnerved him most, the woman or the dark brooding presence of the flyer that sat right by his front step.

"Where's Mossman?"

The woman regarded him for a moment with the kind of look a specimen hunter gives a rare species too long in the finding.

"Mossman's retired. You have me instead."

"Retired?"

She gave him a thin little smile. "Are you surprised? Mossman didn't come back with answers last time, did he? So—" She shrugged. "Retired."

"Do you have a name?"

"Ageira."

He waited but she volunteered nothing more. "Well, Ageira—"

Her presence unnerved him. He wanted her gone. At least Mossman had shown him... civility. He forced himself to take a step towards the woman.

She shifted, tensing. A coiled spring, ready to be triggered. *Dangerous.*

"Come inside, then. I'll brew us some tea."

#

He pretended not to see as Ageira set up the recording devices. If ever his story changed—minor inconsistencies or exaggerations creeping in over the years—then they would know. Every word Dooley uttered, every hesitation, every micro-expression that passed across his face, was scrutinized. Somewhere, a backroom team analyzed the recordings, extracting every last ounce of meaning and intent from his words, alert for clues. Or deceptions. That was why he stuck as close to the truth as he dared.

On the night in question he'd taken Benji for a walk, wondering the paths through the tract of woodland out beyond the town boundary. A popular spot for dog-walkers, although he'd seen no one else that particular evening. It was getting late and the weather had turned cold, keeping most folk indoors. Since Suzie had walked out on him, he'd begun venturing further afield, often losing track of time. Now with the light fading rapidly, the old retriever had shown no signs of tiring but he was down for a night shift on the sheet-metal line at Besselman's Steelworks and needed to get back home.

Something had made him look up. A wash of speckled light swirled in the gap between two Douglas firs. Benji had barked a warning.

"It made a fizzing sound," he'd told Mossman. "Like the crackling hum of powerlines when it rains. Not loud but... I don't know. *Powerful*. Like a machine with a lot of pent up energy."

And they had talked about what kinds of machine he meant (even though he didn't know himself), and the exact tone of that hum. (But it was just a hum). Later, Mossman had played him sequences of humming, crackling, sparkling noises and asked him to make choices. *This* one? Or more like *this* one? What about this?

Only none of them had been quite right and, though he didn't say it, he wondered if his memory could even be trusted any more.

Then Mossman had said, "Describe the portal. How big was it? Did it expand from a point of light or was there already an opening? How did the Artefact come through?" And off they'd go again. Doing the dance of truth and evasion, as Dooley had come to think of it.

Make her the damn tea and let's get this over.

Dooley lifted the pan of water he'd heated on the stove and poured. "Shall we make this easy?"

He was suddenly aware of Ageira standing right behind him. She had moved with the stealth of a cat, no creak from the old pine floorboards.

"Sounds good," he said, not turning round.

Her breath tickled the back of his neck. She took his arm, gently at first. Then he felt the hardness of her fingers digging into his muscles. She didn't let up. Tomorrow there would be bruises—always assuming there was a tomorrow.

"I think you've been holding out on us, Dooley."

She relaxed her grip for a second then tightened it again. Dooley winced.

"Time to tell all."

"Ask your damn questions. I'll answer them all."

"I know you will. And that's how you fobbed Mossman off for so long. But I want the answers to questions we haven't thought to ask yet."

When he didn't answer, she let go his arm and began to prowl around the cabin's interior, picking through ornaments on the mantelpiece, lifting and discarding photographs.

"Did you hear? A new round of investment's been approved. That's thirty *billion* this year. Another twenty after that. You can do a lot with that kind of money. Build the best damn facilities in the world—"

Dooley chuckled, unable to resist the bait. "Ten years on and you're still promising to have the Artefact figured out any day now."

She whirled round, a nasty little smile on her face. "And what happens to you when it is? What value do you have left to us? Kiss goodbye to all this. If there's any justice, you'll be spending the rest of your life behind bars on a charge of obstructing a Federal Agency."

"What am I supposed to be hiding? I gave you the Artefact. I've told everything there is to tell. —Please be careful with that! It belonged to my mother."

Ageira paused as if only now noticing the little painted china doll in her hand. She let it fall and it shattered against the stone hearth.

"Oops."

He could feel the pulse pounding in his neck, his anger mounting. *She's only trying to provoke you. See if your guard will drop.*

"You're the real puzzle Dooley. You could have had it all: fame and fortune. The news channels and investigative journalists would kill to get ten minutes with you. You've no idea how hard we work keeping your identity and location a secret. Why? Why not cash in, Dooley? You'll always be the first human contacted by an alien civilization. That must mean something."

"You already know what I think. The Artefact isn't mine. It was meant for all of us." He shrugged. "I just happened to be in the right place at the right time."

"How noble of you. How selfless."

"It is," Dooley said, thinking *if you only knew.*

When he was seven, he'd stolen a comic book from the neighborhood 7-11. Of course, his pa had soon discovered the theft, marching him back to the store where, mortified with embarrassment, he had been forced to apologize and return the item.

Later, when they returned home, his pa had said, "Son, show me how you did yer stealin'."

"Papa, I'm sorry. I won't ever—"

"You just show me! Do it right now, you hear?"

And his pa made him act it out, reaching up with his right hand to a make-believe shelf like he had done when the store-manager's gaze had been elsewhere.

Pa grabbed his hand. "This one, was it?" He dragged him to the kitchen range, and pressed the offending hand flat to the blackened metal of the oven door. It didn't seem so bad at first because the heat wasn't scolding. But Pa held his hand to the hot metal, giving no sign he ever intended letting go and suddenly what had seemed uncomfortably warm before was now a searing heat. Tears came thick and fast as he begged Pa to stop. But Pa held his hand steady.

"Yer nothing but a selfish son of a whore," he said, baring clenched teeth like he'd become some feral animal. "Thinkin' of no one but yerself. Maybe this will learn yer."

When he couldn't hold back a scream, Pa let him go. He pulled his hand away, sure that the angry red welts would leave scars.

But Dooley was wrong about that, as in so many things. What scars he was left with were all on the inside.

"I've read the transcripts," Ageira said. "I've listened to the expert analysis. And you know what? It's all bullshit. Some piece of this puzzle is missing—and you know it."

When he didn't answer, Ageira began to pace the length of the cabin's living space. "Why, Dooley? They sent humanity this Artefact, this weird *thing*, but we can't figure out what it does. A gift? But what do they expect from us in return? What's the trade? And why pick the middle of the goddamn backwoods to do it?"

"Maybe because the portal was difficult for them to control. It drifted across the ground, as though they were struggling to fix it in one place. Maybe the location was never planned, it was just where it happened to be? Maybe they tried many times and there was never anyone to see."

"But why, Dooley? Were they sending a threat? A warning?"

"How should I know?" He held her gaze, defiant and resolute.

But he *did* know. He knew because of the images that had filled his mind the moment the portal had opened, as clear as voices in his head. They had done this before, this reaching out across immense distances in some unfathomable way, sending a message—and a token—of their existence. *We are here. You are not alone.* And they had done it not once but many times, the voices said, across many different worlds. Like a father reaching out to guide his children, helping them grow and flourish. Well, some fathers, Dooley supposed.

Ageira pulled something from a pocket. It fit snugly in the palm of her hand: a black, vaguely cube-shaped thing that reminded him a little of a fire-blackened Rubik's Cube. Suddenly he couldn't tear his gaze away.

"My god! Is that—?"

Ageira watched him intently. The various surveillance devices would be recording his every move, the fluctuations in skin temperature, heart and respiration rate, and god knows what else.

"You brought it *here?*"

The Artefact never left the Facility, as far as he knew. It was the most studied object in human history, the reason for the very existence of the Facility and its vast network of scientists and engineers and affiliated research groups around the world. The *thing* was unique. Priceless.

"Here. Catch."

Ageira lobbed the object to him.

Dooley felt every muscle in his body tense, every bad memory from his schooldays suddenly flooding his brain. *Catch it Dooley, you doofus! Easy catch, man. Don't drop the easy catch, Dooley! And then the sting of the baseball against his hands—so much harder than he had expected—and even though it hurts so bad, he's forcing his fingers to close around it, but the ball is like an animal wriggling from his grasp, burrowing its way through his stiff, hurting fingers and—*

He caught it cleanly.

Straight away, he knew he had been tricked. Its shape and color were right, but not the texture. Or the weight. Because how could they reproduce those impossible contradictory things?

"Interesting reaction," Ageira said. "You really believed. Just for a moment."

He turned the object in his hands. It had the same odd arrangement of faces he remembered, the same coal-black coloring. Mossman had said it looked like a dodecahedron sat on by an elephant. One face was smooth, the others notched and indented in ways that reminded him a little of the folds in a human brain.

There wasn't a person alive who hadn't looked at the Artefact and thought, *What the hell does it do?*

He closed his eyes. He remembered how you could squeeze it, feel the texture and surface give beneath your hands. But open your eyes and the surfaces were still diamond-hard—harder, in fact, since not even the Facility's 3-petawatt laser could put so much as a scratch on it, never mind vaporising enough molecules for spectroscopic analysis. And they had *tried*. Boy, had they tried.

And then there was its variable weight! One moment it had the heft of a granite paperweight; the next it scarcely seemed to weigh more than a wad of tissue paper. No reason for the change. No pattern to it. And certainly no workable explanation. It put the physicists into a frenzy, this ability to tweak its interaction with Earth's gravitational field. What was it trying to do?

Haptic jiggery-pokery, Mossman had called it.

Dooley preferred magic, plain and simple.

Whatever it was, the Artefact was one hell of a conundrum.

It kept the Facility busy. Yet the more state-of-the-art machines they developed to probe its properties, the greater its mysteries. The bedrock of long-held scientific principles trembled. Cherished theorems were brought down by the incontrovertible existence of the *thing*. But new theories rose in their place. Research in a dozen related fields burgeoned and prospered—even if they still couldn't answer the most fundamental question of all: *What was it for?*

"A copy," Dooley said. "And not even a good one. Is that the best you can do?"

Ageira touched something on her belt. Dooley heard noises outside: clunks, then a chorus of humming that diminished rapidly.

"Those are drones deploying," she told him, unable to keep the smirk off her face. "Pre-programmed search patterns. It's clever tech—multi-spectral hi-res optics, ground-penetrating radar, chemical sniffers. Nothing within a twenty kilometer radius escapes analysis. If I have to widen the search area, I will."

Dooley spread his arms. "What have I got to hide?"

Ageira didn't answer straight away. "There's a new theory doing the rounds. Suppose there was another part to the Artefact? A piece of the puzzle the tech boys are missing? And what if good old Dooley—that right place, right time guy—decided he'd keep quiet about it? Plenty of governments around the world would let you name whatever price you liked just to get a piece of it."

"Don't be ridiculous."

"See this smooth face, right here? Looks a little bit like a join, doesn't it? An interface. So I have to ask myself, is there some missing part we don't know about?" She drifted closer until she was standing over him. "Is there?"

"Sure. Because despite all your surveillance, years ago I snuck out and buried it in the woods." He held her gaze defiantly. "Come *on*."

"You don't get it, Dooley. We *will* follow through. We'll pull this cabin apart log by log if we have to. We'll move heavy equipment in, trample your little plot of land to mud, burn the forest. We'll dig and excavate and sift. Whatever it takes."

"And then?" he asked quietly. "When you don't find anything?"

She moved to the window, watching distant drones flying their automated search patterns.

"What did you really see? Through the portal, I mean."

"Nothing. As dull as that sounds, there was nothing except a dazzling white light. It was too bright to see anything beyond."

"How convenient. No extra-terrestrial to hand you the Artefact? No delivery chit to sign?"

Dooley sighed. He knew she had read his testimony. Knew that she knew that he knew...

"Like I said, the portal didn't stay in one place. It drifted, and I saw this thing left behind on the ground—it hadn't been there a moment ago. I thought how weird it looked, lying there in the mud. Pretty soon after, the portal closed. Just shrank to a dot and was gone."

"What did you do?"

"Picked the thing up. I'd never handled anything like it before. It felt—"

"Could the portal have sliced some part off as it closed?"

"I guess. But I didn't see anything."

"Could you see *anything* through the portal? Maybe another version of the Artefact? A copy?"

"No."

"And no attempt to communicate? Other than sending the Artefact through?"

"No."

She held his gaze, trying to sweat something more out of him. Dooley fought the urge to swallow, to wipe sweat from his brow.

She touched his arm. "Don't be scared, Dooley. It's okay to tell the truth. Even after all this time."

"I've nothing more to tell."

Her hand moved to the back of his neck, cupping it. If the gesture was meant to comfort him, it wasn't working. Then her hand shifted and she was gripping his wind-pipe. A gagging noise came from his throat involuntarily.

"You're holding out on me. I don't like that. There's something you're not saying, something you never told Mossman."

Her fingers dug deeper and there was a rising whistle in his ears. His vision began to shrink to a small circle of light in a much larger tunnel of darkness. *Steam train coming.* The woman was insane, out of control——but he'd known that from the first moment.

Why not just tell her? Let the secret go.

And lose everything that he'd worked so hard for.

Even if he told them, their minds were too stuffed full of the obvious questions. *What does it do? What gives it those strange properties? Why gift this thing to us?*

And why you, Dooley, out of seven billion humans to choose from?

He didn't have the answers. Ageira, Mossman and all the others would never understand that.

But there was something.

He knew what it was *for*.

#

Ageira stood suddenly. Dooley massaged his throat, forcing himself to remain calm. In the doorway, she turned. "Till next time, Dooley," she said, and winked.

Moments later the pod lifted into the sky, bringing a whirlwind of dust through the open door. He realized he still held the copy, gripping it hard enough to whiten his knuckles. He let it tumble to the floor.

He washed the tea things, straightening the place until he could almost convince himself there had been no visitor. Then he shrugged on his jacket.

Outside, he took a moment to savor the landscape; distant peaks and dappled sunlight on the wooded valley slopes, the whistling call of a woodchuck somewhere close by. It might all be gone soon if Ageira followed through on her threat.

He raised his gaze, spotting a tiny black dot high in the sky, holding motionless against the backdrop of drifting clouds. He didn't doubt they were watching him—they had always been watching him—hoping for some clue in their never-ending quest.

But they were looking in the wrong place.

Near the riverbank, he found a bloody smear of feathered gristle in the grass where some hapless bird had met the whirling blades of a survey drone. A splash of blue and orange feathers amongst the gore made his jaw tighten.

He could end this right now. Go back to the bland life he had been plucked from—working a dead-end job, struggling with debt and a crushing lack of ambition; finding solace in the bottom of a beer glass in some rowdy bar. That future could still be his. Why should he be the one to shoulder this burden?

He knew why.

Because he had to prove his Pa wrong. He wouldn't be that selfish son of a whore.

It could have been anyone, but it had been *him*.

He stooped and scraped out a shallow grave for the bird in the soil. Something else had come through the portal. An *idea*. The concept had lodged in his mind like the vivid recollection of a childhood memory. They—whoever *they* were—had meant it to happen this way. And that made the responsibility his.

Study.

Learn.

Understand.

And they had shown him what that meant. Curiosity was written deep in the universal code of life. You only had to look at how humanity had reacted to the Artefact: no effort spared trying to understand its function, drawing the smartest minds from across the world. The Facility had blossomed from nothing to a world-leading research center, developing ever more sophisticated techniques for study and analysis, spinning off theories and new lines of scientific advance the way a catherine wheel throws off sparks.

The Artefact had switched humanity onto a developmental fast-track. Not as an easy gift; this progress had to be earned. We had to do it ourselves, humanity boot-strapping itself, driven forwards by its insatiable curiosity. The Artefact itself did nothing, of course—*that* was the missing piece of the puzzle—other than act as a catalyst, for as long as its true purpose remained hidden.

Why had they done this? Dooley wished he had an answer to that. Some cosmic gesture of benevolence? An intervention to save us from ourselves? Or just the out-reaching of a kindred spirit, alien though it might be, far across the universe, driven by the need to communicate and… eternally curious.

One day the portal would open again. Or maybe it was down to us to open our own portal and show that we had learned and were ready.

Dooley smoothed over the little grave. Then he stood, reached back and hurled the copy of the Artefact far out over the water. It dropped into the river with scarcely a ripple.

He wondered who that ambassador would be. Would they be surprised to discover they were not truly the first to make that journey? Undoubtedly.

Funny how no one had ever asked where Benji had gone.

David Cleden is a previous winner of the James White, Aeon, and Writers of the Future awards and has had fiction published in "Interzone" and the "Fall into Fantasy 2020" anthology, amongst others. He's still trying to decide whether he prefers typing first drafts or writing in long-hand. (This story was long-hand).

Carbon Dating

by Louis B. Rosenberg

I t was a quiet restaurant filled mostly with young couples on dates. At a small table in a shadowy corner was Gordon Pines, all alone, his eyes glued to the empty seat across from him. Balding and wearing oddly thick glasses, he looked older than his 65 years would suggest. He also looked tired. That's because he was tired, exhausted by life itself.

"Water?" rang a voice.

Gordon slowly turned. From his grim expression, you might think he was annoyed about being stuck in that cramped little corner by the kitchen, but he had requested the location. Hell, he would have asked for a table in the kitchen if he could.

"Would – you – like – some – water?" the waiter repeated, loud and slow, now assuming he was speaking to someone hard of hearing.

"No – I – do – not – want – water," Gordon fired back, deliberately louder and slower than the waiter. Then in a normal voice, "But, I could use a drink."

"We have a wonderful wine list," the waiter smiled. He then gestured oddly above the table, as if unrolling an invisible scroll. "As you can see, our selections range from-"

"Forget it," Gordon interrupted and abruptly looked down at his menu.

Perplexed, the waiter retreated with a nod.

Silent seconds passed, then a tipsy woman giggled at a table nearby. The sound made Gordon cringe, as it reminded him how much he hated being alone, especially for meals. Of course he also hated being with other people, so –

"Dad, I'm sorry," a young man rushed over. "I had a meeting that just wouldn't end."

This was Lonny Pines, dressed sharp.

"It's 8:30," Gordon noted with tone.

143

"I know, I know." Lonny took off his jacket and sat. "And believe me, I realize how much you hate doing restaurants alone, but-"

"It's fine," Gordon huffed. "You get used to it."

"Dad…"

Gordon's gaze fell back to his menu. Lonny didn't press the issue, instead welcoming the silence. That's when another giggle rang, this time from a middle-aged couple lifting wine glasses for a toast. Gordon glanced over as the man drew an invisible circle in the air with his finger, making a large smiley face between him and his date. The pair admired the invisible drawing and then clinked their glasses upon it, laughing.

Gordon stared for moment then scoffed, "I'm obsolete."

"That's ridiculous," Lonny tossed. "They say 65 is the new 50."

"Yeah, and I'm the new Brad Pitt."

"Jeez Dad, you need to snap out of this funk. It's been–"

Lonny suddenly fell silent, distracted by something off to his left. An apologetic smile, then he reached upward, tapping an invisible button in the air. "Hi Honey," he said to an unseen person before him. "Yeah, I'm out with dad. No, he's… *great.*"

Gordon grunted.

Lonny listened to words that only he could hear, then replied – "I agree, they should be punished." He then looked off to his right. "Do you kids think it's okay to leave a mess like that in the bathroom? Do you?"

A tense silence, then Lonny hit another invisible button, ending the link.

"Sorry, it's been a crazy day."

Gordon ignored him, brooding over his menu.

Lonny studied his father, recalling how happy he once was, how optimistic, the life of every party. That's when Lonny blurted – "You need to start dating."

Gordon tensed, but didn't look up.

"It's not like it was when you were young. They have terrific new apps."

"I've seen the apps," Gordon spat.

"No, *Carbon apps.* You need Carbons."

"I've got Specs," Gordon defended, gesturing to his thick coke-bottle glasses.

"Jesus… that's half your problem. Those glasses make you look ridiculous."

"You gave me these."

"Five years ago – I'm surprised they still work."

"They work fine." Gordon pressed a button on his glasses and the lenses brightened. Now, as he gazed upon his son, he saw a panel of simple data floating in the air – basic facts about the restaurant, local weather and traffic, even how many times he and Lonny had eaten together over the last six months.

That's when the waiter returned. "Do you gentlemen need more time, or-"

"Any specials?" Gordon asked, eager to change the subject.

"Of course!" And with a grand gesture, the waiter slid his arm over the table, his palm upward, as if supporting a tray of food. Of course his hand was empty, at least to Gordon whose hardware didn't support immersive overlays. "As you can see, we have organic braised-"

"Forget it." Gordon shot.

Lonny smiled at the server, *"I think we need another minute."*

As the waiter departed, Lonny got firm. "Dad, this isn't just about dating. You're missing out on half the world. It's like you don't... fully... exist."

Gordon's eyes went wide.

"I'm sorry," Lonny softened. "It just pains me to see your life passing you by."

"I'm good," Gordon insisted.

"No, you're not."

Father and son shared a moment, eyes locked, the younger Pine holding firm.

"Fine," Gordon exhaled. "I'll get a pair. Happy?"

"Of Carbons... good ones?"

Gordon nodded, surprised how relieved his son looked. Was this really so important? Either way, he pushed back lightly with a smirk – *"But they better not bug my eyes."*

"You?" Lonny laughed. "How could anything bug you?"

#

A small woman in a white lab coat stood beside large optometry machine, its surface covered in dials and levers. Flipping between settings, she asked – "Better, or worse?"

"Better," replied Gordon from behind the contraption.

"Brighter, or darker?" She adjusted a lever. "Brighter or–"

"Brighter."

"Perfect," and the technician pulled the machine forward, revealing Gordon squinting as he reached for his old glasses. She grabbed them first. "You don't need those."

"But I have to wait for—"

"No waiting," and she led Gordon out of the exam room.

It was one of many such rooms on the far side of a busy Apple store. The place was bustling with customers, everyone fingering the air as they explored apps that Gordon couldn't see. He followed the technician past a circle of young kids playing on the floor.

"Steady…" a mom said to a small boy as he reached towards an invisible object at the center of the group, his hand outstretched, eyes wide.

"Go… Go… Go," other kids chanted as the boy got onto his tippy-toes.

A tense moment, then he opened his hand and smiled big.

Hoots and hollers erupted all around.

Gordon just stared, confused.

"This way," the technician called, leading Gordon to a glass wall, a brightly lit room beyond. It reminded him of the glass wall he peered through when Lonny was born, filled with newborns being swaddled. But there were no babies here – just tanks of steaming liquid, dozens of them, each with a robotic laser aimed into the fluid. Gordon watched as the flickering beams etched out precision sets of Carbons, each pair robotically lifted from its steaming tank, then washed and dried and deposited into a small black jewelry box. It was mesmerizing – box after box shuttled down a silver conveyor to an exit window.

"Here you go" the technical said, handing a box to Gordon. "I recommend you try them out before you leave. Our dressing rooms are over there."

Gordon glanced down at the box, nervous.

Noticing his angst, the technical added – "Or, if you need a little help, a class starts any minute." And she gestured to a table where a few older men and women were waiting.

That's when Gordon spotted a young boy opening his own little box. "Do they have night-vision boosters," the kid asked a salesman, "and instant-replay?"

"These are Carbon 22's," the salesman smiled. "They have everything."

The kid popped the Carbons into his eyes like it was nothing.

"Everything I need is in the box?" Gordon asked the technician.

"Plug and play!"

#

It was a small white room no larger than a walk-in closet. Gordon was seated at a smooth white counter, the little black box before him, a large mirror ahead. A nervous breath and he opened the box, revealing two contact lenses, black as charcoal, and tiny wireless earbuds. That was it – nothing else, certainly nothing that looked like instructions. Gordon huffed, unsure what to do next. In response, a bright green light began flashing on the earbuds.

Gordon pondered, then grabbed the buds and popped them in, pushing them deep.

"Greetings Mr. Pines," rang a cheerful female voice. "Can you hear me alright?"

Gordon nodded, motion sensors in the buds detecting his response.

"Wonderful!" the voice gushed. "It's *sooooooo* exciting to meet you."

Gordon grunted, skeptical.

"From your profile, I see this is your first pair of Carbons. Is that right?"

Gordon nodded again

"Stupendous!" And with that, a little green light began flashing inside the box, this time beside the contact lenses. "Go head, touch one with your fingertip."

Gordon slowly reached. The instant he made contact, the lens shimmered, still black as charcoal, but now oddly reflective. It clung to his finger by electrostatic attraction.

"Perfect," the voice encouraged, "now put it in."

A deep breath and Gordon slowly lifted his finger, guiding himself in the mirror. But each time he got near his instincts stopped him from touching his own eye.

"The first time is hard," the voice eased. "Try looking past your finger, not at it."

Gordon tried again, hand shaking, eyes tearing, until... the lens leap off his finger and jumped onto his eye, driven by electrostatic force. Then, as if by magic, the lens began to shimmer, becoming reflective for a moment before going perfectly transparent.

"Good job!" the voice exclaimed. "You're halfway there."

Gordon smiled, reaching for the other lens.

It took a few tries, and a few angry snarls, but he did it.

"You rock!" sang the voice in his ears. "Now, double-blink."

"Double-what?"

"Blink twice, fast... it's how you turn them on."

Gordon blinked as instructed, and flash – a glowing grid appeared over his visual field. It began as a sheet of simple green lines but quickly molded itself to the contours of the room, coating the smooth white walls and the glossy white counter. Another flash, and the grid melted away, replaced by virtual overlays. The featureless walls were now covered by elegant velvet wallpaper, the drab counter replaced by rich mahogany, the linoleum floor now Italian marble.

"Whoa…" Gordon whispered.

"Amazing, isn't it? These are Carbon 22s. Everything is spatially registered with near perfect precision, not to mention the optimized color-blending."

Gordon wasn't listening. He was too busy admiring the antique wooden moldings around the impressive oak door. "It looks so real," he muttered.

"I set your defaults to *Classical Décor* with *Victorian Accents*," the voice explained, "but you're welcome to change the settings. There are over 2,000 variations to choose from."

That's when something small fluttered into Gordon's view. For a moment he thought it was a dragonfly, but then saw — it was a tiny flying woman, like a modern Tinkerbell.

"I'm Una," she burst, giddy as ever. "I'm here to help."

Gordon gaped, "You're… *a fairy?*"

"Technically I'm an elf," Una laughed, "an *Electronic Life Facilitator*. Because your settings are Victorian, my aesthetic adopts the *fairy genre*. Would like to reconfigure me?"

"What… why?" Gordon reeled.

"Because I'm yours," the fairy replied. "I'm your Life Facilitator."

Una fluttered closer, now hovering inches from Gordon's nose. "Life is hard these days," she explained, "not just for you, for everyone — so many places to go and things to do, endless details to track and decisions to make. I can help you, with… *well…* everything."

Gordon just stared, speechless.

That's when Una flew towards his right shoulder.

"This is where I usually stay," she said, hovering by his ear. "From here I can help without getting in the way. Only you can see me, nobody else. I'm *your* elf."

Gordon eyed his reflection in the mirror, dumbfounded by the adorable fairy floating over his shoulder. Finally he asked, "So… can I go home now?"

"Of course!" beamed Una. "But we should get your halo installed first."

"My what?"

"Your halo. It's how you present yourself to the world."

Una gestured, and flash – a glowing cloud appeared over Gordon's head in the mirror, his name printed boldly upon it, along with his age and interests, his favorite music and movies, and even a mention of his profession – retired middle school teacher.

"People can see all that?" Gordon gasped.

"It's just the default. You can add whatever you want – images, videos, theme songs…"

"No, no, no." Gordon interrupted. "I don't want all that. I don't want *any of that.*"

"Why not?" Una seemed surprised.

"Why not?"

Una waited, her algorithms highly skilled in the use of awkward silence.

"Because…" Gordon struggled, "…just, *because!*"

Una smiled kindly, as she detected a rise in Gordon's stress from the blood pressure readings in his earbuds. "How about we go minimalist?" she offered. "Just your first and last name. We can add more once you get familiar with the features and benefits."

"Fine," Gordon shot.

Una gestured and the glowing halo condensed to just his name in a plain font.

"So, can I go home now?" Gordon asked with tone.

"Of course!"

#

Exiting the changing room, Gordon barely took two steps when his eyes went wide. The store was now an explosion of images and animations, appearing and dissolving, expanding and contracting, fluttering and flickering. In every direction, people were fingering objects in the air, tapping and stretching and pulling, while elaborate halos floated over their heads.

"Amazing, isn't it?" Una whispered in his ear.

Gordon was silent, overcome by a sudden need for fresh air. As he rushed across the busy store, glowing advertisements leapt out at him, bursting into view with big smiling faces that touted the benefits of some new product or service. Each time it happened, Gordon recoiled and stepped around the garish ad.

"You can walk through them," Una laughed, "they're harmless."

But Gordon wasn't listening, his attention drawn to the circle of kids on the floor. They were now cheering a small girl as she reached upward, hand outstretched. It was just like before, but now Gordon could see the medieval castle of simulated blocks at the center of the group.

"Careful!" a boy exclaimed.

Gordon watched as the girl delicately placed a block atop the tallest spire.

The simulated tower swayed, drawing gasps, but didn't fall.

Cheers erupted all around.

Even Gordon smiled.

#

The city was ablaze with color and motion, pulsing and throbbing, every inch vying for Gordon's attention as he walked down the street. It wasn't just the storefronts, which erupted onto the sidewalk with leggy supermodels strutting the latest fashions, or the restaurants that tempted passersby with steaming plates of simulated food, it was all the apartments above too. Every window was splashed with colorful nonsense, from local gossip and personal ads, to shrines to favorite musical groups and movie stars.

"It's a lot to take in," Una whispered, as if she could read Gordon's mind. Of course, she couldn't. She simply had access to Data Central, the vast database that correlated human sentiments to the speed of their gaits and the stiffness of their shoulders, even the dilation of their pupils. Using this data, Una determined with 98% certainty that Gordon was feeling utterly overwhelmed. "Change is hard," she said softly, trying to put him at ease.

"Change is for the young," he grumbled.

Just then, a sim-airplane crossed the sky. It was pulling a long glowing banner that read, *"JENNY, WILL YOU MARRY ME?"* All around, people were smiling and pointing.

Suddenly, a sim-rocket roared into the air. It exploded into sim-fireworks, the embers spelling out, *"YES DAVE, OF COURSE!"* Applause erupted from everyone on the street.

Everyone but Gordon.

Una noticed. "You'll find someone too," she said kindly.

Gordon grunted.

"You will," she insisted, "and I can help you."

Gordon looked at the tiny fairy hovering over his shoulder.

"I can," she repeated.

#

Early morning light filtered through the curtains, casting soft rays onto Gordon's bed. His eyes popped open and he released a lavish yawn. But before he could sit up and stretch, Una floated into view, hovering just above him. "Morning Gordy," she bubbled, "beautiful day!"

He rubbed his eyes, groggy.

"They're forecasting clear skies," she added, "mild temperatures in the 70s."

Gordon sat up and glanced around. His apartment was now enhanced by elaborate overlays, giving his normally dull bedroom the stately feel of an old English manor.

"Would you like the ten-day forecast?" Una asked.

"I'm good," Gordon mumbled.

"How about the headlines?" Una continued, making a glass sheet appear in the air, the latest news from around the world glowing upon it.

"I'm good," Gordon repeated, firmer.

"Also, Lonny left you a message while you were-"

"Give me a minute," Gordon huffed. "I'm still waking up."

He then stood and headed for the bathroom. Una followed, silent, hovering over his shoulder. It wasn't until Gordon was standing at the toilet, pants around his knees, that he noticed her floating there. "What the hell?" he snapped. "Some privacy!"

"Sorry," and she eased backwards out of the bathroom. Then, as the sound of peeing rang, she added – "Just so you know, my input comes from your Carbons and the spatial database, not from the projected location of my animated-"

Slam – Gordon shut the door.

Una made a mental note, *no bathrooms*. She was designed to be adaptive, adjusting the needs of her host, even to quirks that defied logic. Gordon was far less adaptive, wondering as he pulled up his pants, if this was a big mistake.

He exited the bathroom and headed across his apartment.

Una followed over his shoulder. Gordon couldn't quite see her there, but he could sense her presence, as he might sense an unseen person in the room with him. And although he wanted to remain annoyed, he couldn't help but realize – it felt good not to be alone.

Una detected the mood change from the blood pressure readings in his earbuds. And because she had access to Gordon's full history, including the fact that he lost his wife to a tragic illness five years prior, she knew that loneliness and isolation were the biggest burdens in his life. In fact, her algorithms had already begun formulating a plan to help him.

"So, Gordy…" she eased as they entered the kitchen, "what exciting things do you have on the agenda for today?"

Gordon had nothing planned and suspected Una knew that. Still, he was happy to make small talk – "I can't decide between skydiving and drag racing. What do you think?"

"I think you're avoiding the question," Una returned with a grin. Then, as Gordon reached for a bag of French Roast, she flew in front him. "Why not go out for coffee?"

"Go out?" Gordon stiffened. "I can make perfectly good coffee here."

"I'm sure you can, but you're not going to meet anyone here."

Gordon scoffed and stepped to a cabinet, reaching for the sugar.

Una flew out in front of him. "There are nine coffeehouses in easy walking distance," she pressed, "and three are frequented by single women in your age-group."

"My age-group?" Gordon fired back. "What does that mean?"

"It means, you're avoiding the issue."

Gordon grunted.

Una held firm – "You want to meet someone or not?"

#

Gordon sat at a small table in a busy San Francisco coffeehouse, a steaming mug in hand. As promised, the clientele was mostly his generation, mostly singles, and mostly women. This was no accident, as the majority of patrons had been coached here by their Carbons, with younger generations and couples directed to other establishments.

Setting down his coffee, Gordon scanned the room. Almost everyone here had bright halos hovering over them, their names aglow along with their favorite books and movies, and of course, photos of their kids and grandkids. Every so often, Gordon noticed someone rise and walk to another table, introducing themselves then sitting for a conversation.

"Excuse me," a bald man said to a chubby woman, "do you grow roses?"

"For thirty years," the woman smiled. Of course, the man already knew this from her halo, which was swirling with images of her award-winning flowers.

"I'm just getting started," the man said. "But already, I've got black spots." He opened his hand, revealing the floating image of a rosebush, its sickly leaves dark and splotchy.

"Oh, that's fungus," the woman explained and invited him to sit.

As Gordon watched them fall into conversation, his confidence grew, thinking this might not be as difficult as he feared. After all, he wasn't bad looking and knew he could be charming when he tried. That's when he noticed a silver-haired woman across the room. There was something about her – a kindness in her face that drew him in.

Una too was aware of Gordon's interest, for his Carbons tracked not only the direction of his gaze but the intensity of his focus and rhythm of his pulse. So when the woman stood and walked toward Gordon, Una was monitoring his rising anticipation. But then, as the woman walked past and sat at another table, Una also noted his abrupt disappointment.

"We should update your halo," Una whispered. "It's a barrier."

Gordon glanced to his shoulder, skeptical.

"Do you want to meet someone or not?"

Gordon wanted to argue, but everyone here had elaborate halos.

"Fine," he conceded, "but keep it simple."

"Of course!" And with that, Una flew out in front of Gordon, a sim-mirror in her hand. She held it up so Gordon could see his own halo. As before, it was merely his name in simple letters. With a few quick gestures, Una added colorful elements – images of Gordon with his kids and grandkids, old classroom photos from when he taught middle school, even a few favorite album covers of Miles Davis and John Coltrane, as he was a lifelong jazz fan.

Gordon felt ridiculous.

"Sure you don't want to add my medical history," he tossed, "and credit score?"

"No need," Una returned, ignoring the sarcasm. "But I do recommend we install *Matchmaker Plus*. It gives me access to advanced Romance Features."

"Romance Features?"

"The success rate is very high."

That's when Gordon noticed another woman walking towards him. He assumed she would walk past, but she stopped and smiled. "Anyone sitting here?"

"Um, no…" Gordon stammered, gesturing at the empty seat. "It's all yours."

"You're a doll," and the woman dragged the chair back to her own table.

Gordon released a heavy breath. "Fine, install it."

"Fantabulous!" Una exclaimed. *"System, install Matchmaker Plus."*

A flash of light, then a tiny pink heart appeared in Gordon's peripheral vision. Another flash, and Una's wings began to glow the same pink color. She fluttered them for a moment, as if trying them out. This sent a puff of pink glitter into the air. "It's so exciting!"

"Now what?" Gordon asked.

"Now this," and Una sped away from the table, a trail of pink behind her.

Gordon gawked as Una blazed around the coffeehouse – a tiny comet darting from table to table, woman to woman, hovering over each for just a moment.

And then… she was back, stopping inches from Gordon's nose. "There are two women here who have potential," she said out of breath, "but neither has a Compatibility Index in the highest data-bracket. I recommend extending the search. How about a half-mile radius?"

"Um… sure," Gordon reeled.

"Stupendous!"

And with that, Una blasted across the room and out the front door, a steaming trail of pink left behind. Gordon expected everyone to be stunned by the spectacle, but there was no reaction, for only he could see Una. That's when Gordon wondered how many other little fairies were buzzing around this place, whispering in ears, nudging and coaxing and prodding. Was this really a good thing for us all, or–

Whoosh – before he could finish the thought, a tiny pink comet shot back into the coffeehouse, blazing to a halt right in front of him. "I found someone!" Una burst.

"You did?"

"She's just down the street," Una beamed, "and her Compatibility Index is 97.8!"

"Is that good?"

"It's remarkable!"

#

Gordon followed Una down a busy sidewalk, struggling to keep up with her pace. Along the way, countless advertisements leaped out at him, pitching everything from vitamin pills to health clubs. That's when a familiar voice rang. Gordon turned and saw his barber stepping out of his shop. At least it looked like his barber – really, it was a virtual overlay. "Gordy, I haven't seen you in weeks," the sim-barber gushed. "I'll give you a trim for half-price if you jump in the chair right now." Gordon kept walking. He reached every intersection with perfect timing. This was no accident – it was because Una, like all elves, monitored traffic signals, modulating the walking speed of her host for optimal efficiency. It was a public service, ensuring everyone got where they were going without crowds waiting at the crosswalks.

"How much further?" Gordon asked, now feeling the pace in his legs.

"Almost there," Una replied. "Her name is Caroline, by the way. She's 64 years old, widowed for three. She lives in North Beach but is currently in Washington Square Park walking her dog. He's a twelve-year-old schnauzer named Frankie."

"A schnauzer?" Gordon interjected. "I had three schnauzers. I love schnauzers!"

"I told you, she's a remarkable match."

As they rounded a corner, Una kept up the pace, determined to get to the park before Caroline left. Fortunately, Caroline had her own elf running Matchmaker Plus, which meant Una could coordinate the encounter over wireless channels. This was important, as Frankie had just completed his *morning business* and Caroline was about to head home. Her elf intervened, noting that the old dog was panting and might need some water.

Caroline responded as expected, taking a quick break on a bench.

That's when Gordon entered the park. The place was packed with people – jogging and cycling, pushing strollers and walking dogs. He might have had trouble finding Caroline if not for the pink dotted line Una projected on the pavement. "I feel like Pac-Man," Gordon snarked as he followed the glowing dots. "Should I be looking for ghosts and cherries?"

Una didn't respond.

Meanwhile, Caroline was focused on Frankie, trying to get him to drink.

"Don't look up," her elf whispered, "but it appears you have a suitor coming this way."

"*Wonderful,*" Caroline sighed, "just what I need."

"His name is Gordon Pines," her elf continued. "He's 65 years old, widowed for five. And you'll be interested to know, he was a middle school teacher just like you."

"*Big deal,*" Caroline grumbled to her elf, who wasn't a fairy like Una, but a wise old genie named Kai. He had a long gray beard and floated on a tiny flying carpet.

"His Compatibility Index is quite strong," Kai insisted. "The best so far."

"I told you, I'm done with Matchmaker Plus."

The little genie rolled his eyes.

That's when Gordon approached. He hadn't felt this awkward since he was a pimply teenager seeking a date for the spring dance. Sensing his unease, Una whispered – "Just smile and take a breath, then comment on her dog."

So Gordon did. "Nice whiskers," he said boldly, forcing Caroline to look up at him. "And such a big fella – too big to be a Standard, but not quite a Giant."

"You know schnauzers?" Caroline replied, skeptical.

"Outlived three of them," Gordon returned. "Best breed there is." This was followed by an awkward silence, but after prodding from Una, Gordon added – "So, what's his name?"

"Frankie." Caroline softened. "He's a Standard, but a very big boy."

Another silence, then Una whispered, "Tell her your name."

"Oh, I'm Gordon, by the way."

"I'm Caroline," she returned politely, but didn't invite him to sit, even though Kai was suggesting it quite forcefully in her ear. She just wasn't sure it was a good idea.

That's when Gordon reached out and let Frankie smell his hand, for he knew that was the proper way to introduce yourself to a dog. He then scratched behind Frankie's ears, as skillful as any serious dog-lover. The schnauzer stretched and wriggled, indulging in the attention.

"He likes you," Caroline noted, her gaze softening.

"He's such a big fella," Gordon smiled, genuine.

"Please, sit…" Caroline finally offered. "It'll make Frankie's day."

So Gordon sat, instantly getting a large dog in his lap.

Silent seconds passed as both Caroline and Gordon pretended to focus on Frankie, but really, they were stealing glances at each other's halo. Gordon noticed Caroline's love for old movies. Caroline noticed Gordon's passion for jazz. And then, at the nearly the same instant, they both said with feigned surprised – "You taught middle school too?"

"Jinx," Caroline joked. "*Some coincidence*, huh?"

Gordon laughed. *"Totally random."*

They shared a moment, both wondering if this might not be a disaster after all. But then Caroline squinted as if annoyed. Gordon thought he must have done something wrong, but then realized – her irritation wasn't aimed at him, but at her own shoulder.

"No," she whispered, "that's a terrible idea."

Gordon was instantly charmed, as he'd never seen someone argue with their elf before.

"Sorry," Caroline turned back. "Kai says I should ask what school you taught at."

"Well, if Kai insists," Gordon snarked. "Laguna Middle, for thirty-five years."

"Thirty-five years at one school!" Caroline was genuinely impressed. "Did they at least give you a gold pen when you retired?"

"Silver," Gordon teased, "budget cuts."

They shared another moment. And another silence. That's when Gordon glanced at his own shoulder. He tried to be subtle, but Caroline could see he was resisting a suggestion.

"Let's hear it," she pressed.

Gordon turned back, surprised he was that obvious. "Ok, well... Una says I should ask about your grandkids. Seems cliché to me, but she's confident it will go over well."

"Cliché indeed," Caroline tossed. "I think you might need an upgrade."

"Just an upgrade?" Gordon matched her tone. "I definitely need a total overhaul."

Smiles – real smiles – possibly the first real smiles either had shared in weeks.

And yet, both were at a loss for words.

For Gordon, it wasn't that he lacked things to say. It was that people these days were usually put-off by his comments, discounting him as *grumpy* or *out of touch*. In truth, he just didn't understand the obsession everyone had with constant change. *Lose your wife of 35 years*, he wanted to tell people, *then see how much you like change*. Of course, that wasn't what Una was suggesting. She was prodding him to mention his love of photography or his fondness for travel. Meanwhile, Kai was coaching Caroline to bring up her passion for playing piano. It was a reasonable suggestion but it just *didn't feel right* to her.

That's when they both realized, they were eyeing their own shoulders for way too long. At almost the same moment, they turned back to each other and laughed.

"Should we just talk about our grandkids?" Gordon joked.

Caroline smiled, then fell serious. "To be honest, I hate these things," she admitted, gesturing to her eyes. "I mean, they're remarkable devices, useful for sure, but sometimes I wonder, if... well..." She paused, searching for words.

"I thought it was just me," Gordon offered, saving her the trouble.

That's when a chatty group of young parents walked by pushing strollers, their halos aglow with rainbows and unicorns – an arms race of digital cuteness. One of the moms stopped and knelt down, scolding her daughter for tossing a candy wrapper onto the pavement. It was a reasonable interaction, and yet Gordon couldn't help but wonder if it was really the mom who was disciplining the girl, or an invisible elf whispering in the mom's ear.

"This can't be the way things were supposed go," Gordon pondered as the bubbly group walked away. "It can't be, and yet nobody questions it – nobody seems to mind at all."

"Oh, they mind," Caroline returned, "but what choice does anyone have?"

Gordon nodded, solemn and serious, but inside he was smiling ear to ear. That's because somebody finally said what he'd been thinking for years – that none of this was a choice, even if nobody was willing to admit it out loud. And yet, the world seemed a little different now as he sat there on that hard wooden bench, gazing upon all the busy people rushing past, everyone glowing and glistening, moderated and facilitated, augmented from head to toe.

"Maybe this is all just growing pains," he finally said.

"Growing pains?"

"A mix of good and bad, but eventually we'll figure it all out."

That's when a teenage boy walked by, his halo filled with bikini-clad women and gory posters from horror films, plus an animation of himself barfing in a toilet, again and again.

Caroline smirked, *"Growing pains?"*

"We can hope," Gordon tossed. Then serious, "The truth is, I have no idea where this is all headed, but I do know one thing for sure," and he gestured to his eyes. "Without these, you and I wouldn't be sitting here right now, and I for one am sincerely glad we are."

"Me too," Caroline smiled.

And with that, she handed Frankie's leash to Gordon and stood from the bench, gesturing for him to join her. So Gordon did, feeling nervous but surprisingly hopeful.

Together they strolled the park, laughing and smiling and getting to know each other. Of course they had their awkward moments, but mostly they were amazed by how easy it was to keep the conversation going, mile upon mile, hour upon hour, long after they had powered off their Carbons. And it wasn't just while walking Frankie, but over coffee, and over dinner, and over the days and weeks and years to come. It turns out, they really were a remarkable match.

Louis B. Rosenberg is the author of four sci-fi graphic novels (*Eons, Upgrade, Monkey Room,* and *Arrival Mind*) and the award-winning web series (Lab Rats) from Frostbite Pictures. He is also a longtime technologist, best known for having designed the first functional Augmented Reality system when working for U.S. Air Force Laboratories in the 1990's.

Butterfly In Glass

by Matthew Chabin

The woman upstairs was cussing out her silent, no-good heap of a man again— "You jerk, you junkie, you goddamn fool!" Only it wasn't the same, not quite. Carol was fairly certain because it was 1939 and profanity wasn't such a casual thing back then; one noticed it more. Now she noticed its absence. She sighed and tipped her head against Dan's chest as they swayed to the music, a mutual sweat soaking their clothes where they touched. "Why does he bother?"

"Hm?"

"Felix. It's waxy again."

"Mm."

She nodded. *I wasn't just that poor woman.* The raspy scat riff coming through the radio was flattened and bell-tone clear like no radio sounded back then, and the smells from the alley stayed out on the fire escape and did not nose the drapes like big yellow hounds, and the wasp sting on her calf was little more than an angry itch, not half what she'd earned dancing the Big Apple on that dauber's cocoon on the porch at Funky Butt Hall. Nothing omitted—not entirely—but everything tidied-up, a Vaseline-on-the-lens general burnishing that Dan (though he tended not to notice it so much) had dubbed 'Felix's nostalgia-wax.'

"Let's go in the bedroom," said Dan. "He can wax it all he wants."

Carol laughed and clutched him through his cotton trousers. "Think we can make him fry his…?"

Her eyes drifted to the corner, the little table with the flaking blue paint, the way the sunlight jelled around it like ethereal ore and made the votive candles glow like they really contained the numinous visions advertised…. That wasn't waxy, that was just *strange*. "Hey, Felix, flip your digits. It's '39, not '63." A shadow at the corner of her eye crawled spiderly up the wall, and despite the heat her skin broke out in gooseflesh.

"Hey," she whispered.

161

Dan was way down in the groove bibitybopping along, but he stopped when he felt her tense up. They stood still in the center of the room, listening to happy shouts in the street, the parade unraveling at the Nero Street loop just down the block. She slipped out of his arms and went into the bedroom, to the portable Zenith on the windowsill, and touched the dial. There was a third voice behind the dueling jazzmen. She tapped the dial and teased it out of static as another shadow ran along the baseboard, gone before her eye could track it.

"...*defense budgets, or aid to the freedom fighters in Nicaragua, or teaching America's young people the meaning of...*"

She looked at him. "That's Ronald Reagan."

He leaned against the doorframe, muscular and sleek in his silk tank-top and suspenders. "Ol' time's out of joint. Dutch always was a little behind the times."

She gave him a look.

He shrugged. "A glitch, babe, so what?" He thumped his fist twice on the wall. "Felix?" He sniffed his drink. "Hooch is still hooch." He tossed it off. "Felix!"

"Shh! You don't feel that?" It wasn't just the radio. There was a hum, a tuning-fork vibration in the air, and it felt like the room was tilting.

"Damn," he said under his breath. Another shadow ran across the floor and Carol fought the urge to jump up on the bed. Outside, the shouts and laughter had become a clamor of mingled, indistinguishable noises. Dan set his drink carefully on a high shelf next to a lace-bound volume of the Kama Sutra and ran his hand over his strong-parted, tight black curls. "Best get up there and have a look."

#

The O'Meara's lived in Florence six months out of the year and summered in Alaska, but their legal address was stations 30 and 32, Peeway 4, C-Deck, near a utility elevator. They'd chosen the Full-Cognizance+VR Capability package (the brochure showed a fit, silver-haired couple riding a jet ski into a sunset, the man grinning intensely ahead while the woman threw a wink at the camera—*Know Thyself*, the caption read). They knew, therefore, unlike the vast majority of their fellow riders, that Simstate wasn't real (at least in the strong materialist sense). Still, it was always a jolt coming out of it.

The body, or rather the sensation of having one, dissolved with a tickly, granular rush, and what remained she couldn't feel, so that for a chilling instant Carol always felt that she'd dissolved quite out of existence. The visual, when it came online, was fed by a camera strip that ran the diameter of her tank, so she saw, in panorama, a length of corridor lit by neon ground-lights, with Dan reassuringly to one side, and their reclusive neighbor, Mr. Webber, to the other.

Normally.

This time, the first thing she saw was the cherry flash of an emergency light pulsing evily in the shards of glass and globules of liberated solution that floated around her like jellyfish. For a panicked moment she thought the ruined tank was her own, or Dan's, before she realized with a sickly relief that it was Webber's. The out-facing, convex side was shattered, disgorging its liquid contents in drifting, opalescent blobs. Little flags of black filaments that might have been hair clung to the jagged edges, moved by some kind current (there wasn't supposed to be any gas on this deck while in transit, only what was fed into the tanks). Mr. Webber's brain was nowhere in sight.

"Dan!-*Dan!*" Her voice, relayed back to her by wire, had an unfamiliar lag and echo. There was no answer. "Felix?-*Felix?* Something's happened!-*happened!*"

"I'm here." Dan's voice sounded strangely distant. "Something wrong, though. Can't see."

"You can't *see?*" The audio, at least, was stabilizing.

"Totally in the dark, no visual. Felix?"

A rhetorical cough announced Felix breaking into the channel. "Terribly sorry, Mr. and Mrs. O'Meara" said the ship's virtual-concierge in his genteel German accent. "There's a situation developing on the ground and we've lost satellite contact. In addition, we've suffered power interruptions due to an electromagnetic—" His voice faded.

"Felix," said Carol. "Where is Mr. Webber?"

"Felix, I've got no visual feed here, at all. The only thing I can hear is my wife, and you. Copy?"

Nothing.

"What's this about Webber, babe."

"He's gone. Dan, something broke the tube."

He started to say something but his voice cut out and a burst of static crackled through the wire.

"Dan?"

A black shape, vaguely humanoid, blotted the flashing light. It drifted, still as a slack marionette, then suddenly broke into movement, swimming languidly in place. It had something in its hand, a long length of pipe, which it transferred to its foot as it caught the bolted ribbing of the corridor and hung, weightless, the light striking one side of its hairy body and showing half its face. Carol had braced herself to face some kind of alien terror, but this uncanny visitation from dear old Earth was somehow worse. It was an ape. It was a goddamn chimpanzee.

"Felix! Dan?!"

No answer, but the round head with the skull-shaped face shifted in her direction as if it had heard her instead, eyes flashing redly in the signal pulse. A big male, by the look of it, but skinny, its ribs showing. *It's hungry*, she thought. *Dear god, it's starving!* It's eyes, it's avid grin…. *Oh God, Webber!*

"Carol, are you—"

"Dan, do you see it?"

"What's that babe?"

The god of death, she thought wildly. *We fled him, and he followed us, found us, even here.* Hadn't she always known in her heart that immortality was wrong, a betrayal of life? Hadn't she always known this day would come? Naturally it would assume some impossible form, a mockery of their fantasy-flight, their glorified paramnesia. Death was a great joker. Death was Groucho Marx in a monkey suit.

"Carol, I can't see my hand in front of my face. Of course, I don't have a hand, but—"

"Dan if you joke right now, I swear to—!"

"Okay, okay. What are we dealing with?"

The impossible, that was what. Damage, wrongness, chaos run all through the ship like sudden cancer, spawning deranged visions.

"It's…it's…." A haywire Simstate residual, a mistake, a clot of wandering nightmare-stuff—had to be. But it was moving along the wall rather too purposefully for her liking and transferring the pipe back to its hand. "Oh no, oh no!" Her thought-scream was a burst of static on the wire as the chimp launched itself off the wall, mouth gaped, red eyes blazing with naked predation. It struck with the pipe. The blow hit below her vantage, momentarily blurring her view, but the glass held. It fetched up against the tube and she got a good orthodontic look down its throat as it clashed its teeth against the glass. Then it repelled and sailed off at an angle into the darkness and she lost sight of it.

"Dan!"

"What, what's happening?"

The ape, apparently well accustomed to zero-gravity, had regained the opposite wall and was launching itself a second time, this time at Dan's tank, both hands gripping the pipe. The attack was more forceful than precise, and landed with shuddering, silent impact and glanced off leaving a white mark in the glass. Only then did she realize the reason Dan couldn't see; his camera lens was opaque with cracks and pressure bruising. How long had they been under attack?

The ape, rebuffed again, flung its weapon and flailed in frustration, showing pink gums and long, yellow fangs. Just as suddenly it stopped its tantrum and hung in the air, resting, its small eyes glittering as they took in the room. It's hands, she saw, were ragged and scraped, and a laceration on its foot leaked floating dollops of blood into the air. *Not a god,* she thought, *just a brute. A dumb, hungry animal, clinging to life, like us.* Wouldn't matter, though, if it had its way. Within Death's old, raggedy sock-puppet was still the hand of Death.

It drifted into the wall and nimbly pushed its way down to the floor as its weapon drifted away into the shadows. It didn't look angry anymore. Now it looked more curious, though Carol had a notion that its curiosity might be more dangerous than its rage. It paddle-crawled over to the base of Dan's tank and started sniffing and poking around the casement. Not much mischief it could do down there, she thought. Now, if Felix would just pull his head out of his stupid mainframe maybe he could suck the oxygen from the compartment, suffocate the bastard, or at least kill the light so it couldn't see (though the thought of being surrounded by a darkness that contained an enemy like that was hardly reassuring).

The chimp pushed off the floor and sailed gracefully through the air. It moved down the corridor, where more tanks reposed in the red-pulsing dark. Fear had held her in such a grip that relief felt like a second loss of body, a dissolution of the clammy substance holding her together. "Dan? Felix?"

The fear returned as she saw it coming back, gliding swiftly along the floor like a great, hairy octopus with the pipe once more in hand. She thought it would launch another direct assault, but instead it sailed under her gaze and caught the base of Dan's tank. *What's it doing?!* It was too damn smart. *No-no-no!* It had pushed the pipe through the ventilation grate and was using it like a crowbar to dislodge the panel. She tried to think—what was down there? Just a filtration system. All the vital feeds and relays came from the top down. Still, it could jam something, or break something, or….

Eight magnetic rollers crawled up the inside of Dan's tank like speedy snails, dragging between them a white, silicone net. It took her a moment to understand—it was a cleaning cycle. If the sensors found impurities in the solution, the net would hold the brain while the tube was flushed and replenished. The ape, its hairy rump still visible as it rooted in the compartment, had triggered it somehow.

"Carol?"

"Dan! Yes, I'm here!"

The net reached the brain and billowed up around it, so that it floated in a white, finely knit sack.

"Babe, what's going on?"

There's…. It ate… It's trying to… "I don't know. Dan…"

The fluid in Dan's tank was dropping, spiraling down as a gentle suction, pulled from below. The manual had assured them the procedure was safe—the nets retained enough solution to keep the brain cozy and moist until the refill kicked in. Still it was distressing to see him floating in dry air like that, naked in his little hammock. The fluid was almost completely drained now, and she imagined the phlegmy, sucky sound it would make if she could hear it. She couldn't see the ape anymore, it was all the way in there. Maybe it would electrocute itself. That seemed as likely as anything.

"Felix isn't responding, Dan, and there's a…a situation. I don't know how to—"

She stopped. The inner base of his tube was moving. She watched, helpless, speechless, as the round black head forced itself through the rubber seal. Shoulders followed, hair matted with the mucous fluid, then a hairy arm scrabbling at the side of the tank.

"Felix! Help! Do something now!"

It opened its mouth and howled silently up at the tantalizing fruit that floated almost within reach.

"Carol? Babe?"

"Oh Dan…."

The chimp was stuck at the waist, trying to claw its way up the slick walls of the cylinder, the flashing red light dancing in its ravenous eyes. Stuck, but not stuck fast. Lubricated by the solution it was gaining inches through the breach.

"Dan," said Carol, trying to keep the panic out of her voice, "I've got a crazy game we could play. Tell me quick, Love…what would you say if…if I were about to die?"

"Carol, are you…."

"Because I know what I'd tell you! I'd tell you, let's it all over again! I'd say I love you to the stars and back, but everything's gonna be okay, because…because, Dan…?"

It broke free.

"Carol?"

She clamped down and forced herself not to scream as it

happened—she didn't want that to be the last thing he heard—as the starving animal took the last physical remnant of her husband, the precious receptacle of his mind and soul, and *bit*. It tore right through the net and released a great, gelatinous bubble of red that broke across its pale muzzle and became a spill of crimson pearls. Carol screamed at last, if only in her mind, and fled away, deep into the machine.

#

"My *deepest* condolences, Mrs. O'Meara. Would you care for a game of chess?"

She stared at him. He couldn't help it; the tidy little man in the checkered suit always had to offer a game of chess following his first words to a customer. It was his programming. He was a product of the same production company that had sanitized Grimm's tales for WASP America and turned the French Revolution into a romance about Princess Marie of Savoy. What could she expect. Still….

"You know what, Felix?" *you simple, inhuman prize idiot…* "that sounds…swell." *Might be the one thing to keep me from losing my mind right now.* Felix, nodded graciously (he had the face of his namesake, Felix Mendelssohn, and the courtier style to match). He swept his arm across the table and an elegant red and white crystal chess set appeared between them. *He can do magic,* she thought. *He can raise the dead, just can't bring them back to life.*

"How many survivors?" she asked as she brought out a pawn.

"Sixty-two," he said, matching her.

"Full-cogs?" She brought out a second pawn beside the first— King's Gambit, still a fashionable choice in her day, practically suicide against Felix. She wasn't looking for long game.

"Seven," he said, taking the gambit.

Seven, down from ten. One other besides Dan and Webber.

"Who else?"

In the ensuing skirmish they each took a pawn.

"I'm afraid I can't say. Privacy rules, you know."

They dueled back and forth, bishops and knights, each looking to flank the other.

"You mean someone pulled their own plug? Bit the death pill? Hit the kill-switch?" Their contracts had an out clause; they could always commit suicide if immortality became a drag.

She took his queen.

"You're free to deduce, Madam." He put her in check. She castled out of it.

"What can you tell me?"

He sighed, looking down at his hands. "It's very bad, I'm afraid. I've restored most shipboard systems, but we've lost contact with Earth, and the professional crew have all abandoned ship. Our remedial options are contractually limited, pending a vote by all Fully Cognizant signatories and shareholders."

"Well that should happen sooner rather than later, no?" A line of attack had lit up for her as he spoke, and now she moved in, cutting through his line on one side while the trap lay set on the other. All she needed was for him to move that rook. Despite the tide of grief and rage she was holding at bay, she warmed to the idea of finally beating Felix. Then maybe she could check out, take the chop-suey express. How long could she go on dancing with Dan's ghost?

"To that end, Madam, Mr. Artem has requested all cognizant hands on deck. Checkmate."

She stared dully at the board.

"If I may, Ms. O'Meara, I'd say you were focused on your attack to the neglect of your own defenses. Otherwise, very well played."

She waved her hand and Felix vanished. *I can do magic too.* She swept the pieces off the board and the cozy English drawing room dissolved around her into darkness. Alone, she put her head down on the board and gave in to her grief.

#

Roger Artem, founder and CEO of the company and owner of the ship, was of her and Dan's generation, and it showed in his taste. He sat in a high-backed, brass-studded leather chair below a mantel bearing a bust of Theseus or somebody, his bronze, velveteen smoking jacket flecked with ash from his pipe, stroking his pencil-thin mustache with a manicured thumb. He was a hundred and thirty years old, but appeared to them a hale forty, the same age as he was when his studio came to prominence in the early part of the last century. His dark, penetrating eyes moved over the assembled company. "Felix," he said, "would you bring me that ashtray?"

Felix was at the piano, playing Duparc's *L'invitation au Voyage* (or rather moving his fingers to a recording of Brigitte Engerer playing it). He broke off, took a crystal ashtray from a roll-top desk, carried it across the room and set it on the end-table beside Artem, then stood back against the wall.

Carol had come early and staked out the opposite corner, a midnight-purple chaise lounge beneath a leaded glass lamp with a design of vines and hollyhocks. She's aged herself to a statuesque sixty-ish, the better to discourage sympathy and other useless overtures. She wore a black gown of embellished mesh, her hair up in a silver chignon. Her fingers, the nails painted bright red, twirled one of Dan's Chesterfields. She wanted to smoke the damn thing, but she was afraid she'd lose if she did, so she tapped the armrest and fantasized about menacing Felix with Dan's old Army-issue .45. *We have ways 'a makin' you talk, see.*

Artem said something inaudible over his shoulder and Felix nodded. He cleared his throat to the room. The chatter fell off. "Good evening…"

Now there was something odd. Everyone who purchased real estate on the Artem Universal Covenant (popularly derided at the time of its conception as the Artem Brain Barge or Uncle Roger's Galactic Noodle Farm) owned stock in the company, but for obvious reasons only the Full-Cogs sat on the voting board. Normally there were ten of them—ten little brains who knew they were brains. Felix had said seven had survived, but there were *eight* people in this room (nine if you counted Felix, but nobody counted Felix, not even Felix). So that meant….

"Carol." She looked up and caught Artem's eyes. "I'm sure I speak for everyone when I say how sorry I am for your loss. Dan was such a fine gentleman. I grieve with you, madam."

There were murmurs of accord around the room, and Gracie Lehman mumbled something to her left. "Thank you," said Carol. "I'll be happy to receive condolences in due time, but I'm sure *I* speak for everyone when I say we need some answers. If you'll pardon me, Roger, we need to know what the hell's going on."

Artem nodded solemnly. "Yes, well—"

"It's some sort of attack, isn't it," said McWhorter, the shipping magnate. McWhorter was a neurasthenic old queen at heart, but he posed as the last Great White Hunter, with his beard and those ridiculous snakeskin boots. "My money's on extraterrestrial." He slapped his thigh. "Roswell!" He was also halfway out of his mind.

"I just want to know if Simstate is stable," said Gracie Lehman. Mr. Lehman had not survived the decerebration procedure (only six in ten did back then) and Carol had always thought of her as The Widow (she'd have to think of her something else now). "I was having a lovely day, drinking tea by the canal in Venice, and suddenly the tea was gone and so was the water in the canal. The fish were *swimming in air.*"

"Not a fan of surrealism?" said McWhorter. Gracie stared daggers at him. He raised his eyebrows and moued at his fingernails.

"Are you stable now, Gracie?" asked an impatient Liu, the Chinese media mogul, his lips out of synch with his words (they never had perfected the translation software). "We are here. No fish. Let the man speak."

Carol rubbed the bridge of her nose, mired in the thought that she didn't especially like any of these people.

Artem cleared his throat again. "Felix, the visual please." The panel above the fireplace, which a moment ago had been a Baroque landscape in oil, now showed a dark orb hanging in space with a sheen of borrowed light on its ten-o-clock edge.

"What is it?" asked Liu.

"Earth," said Artem.

"God almighty," whispered Boulay, the televangelist. He'd convinced his congregation to fund his decerebration on the promise that he'd defer his eternal reward, bear living witness to the End Times, and commend the souls of his followers personally to the Risen Jesus. If God existed, thought Carol, the ape would have gotten Boulay instead of her Dan.

"Why is it dark?" said Gracie. "Why is it so far away?"

"We've lost all contact," said Artem, "so that leaves us, you'll pardon my saying, somewhat in the dark as well. But based on the last transmissions we received, you're looking at the aftermath of innumerable atomic events and the onset of nuclear winter."

Silence filled the room. Even Boulay, assured of Heaven as the was, looked pale. Artem knocked his pipe into the ashtray and Felix nodded gravely.

"The ship took a hit around the same time, likely space debris from destroyed satellites. The damage was bad enough that the professional crew evacuated. At that point everything switched over to the automated system. Felix at the helm."

"You were all in Simstate at the time," said Felix. "The neural relay systems had to be fully tested before I could risk bringing you out. In the meantime, protocol mandated an immediate withdrawal from low-earth orbit to our current position. We are now 2,000 miles from the planet's surface."

Artem had refilled his pipe and Felix popped up to light it for him. He spoke in puffs of smoke. "We're also at geosynchronous orbit now, so we can't see the other side. They may be lighting Christmas trees in Korea right now, but I'd say the odds are against it. We have to consider the very real possibility that we are, or shortly will be, the last survivors of humankind."

"I'm sorry," said Carol, raising her hand. "We left Simstate when things started to get weird in there."

"Yes," said Felix, the anomalies you experienced were—"

"Anomalies? Felix…. A fucking monkey…*ate*…my husband."

"Dan is with God now, Caroline," said Boulay. She glared at him so hard he blanched and turned his head indignantly.

"I take full responsibility," said Artem.

Now she turned incredulous eyes on him.

"As you know, it took considerable resources to make this dream of ours a reality. You all paid your shares, I know, but we needed the kind of money governments command." He set his pipe down, took a breath. "The Russians had a program to use chimpanzees in space. They wanted to use neural relays, the same technology that supports Simstate, to hijack the animal's brain and use it like a kind of living puppet that could operate in high risk, deep space ventures. The dream of an expendable body, cognate, you might say, to our dream of transcendence. It was all top secret, which is why we couldn't tell you about it."

"We had Russian chimpanzees on the ship?" said Liu.

"Technically it was a different ship, the Admiral Gorshkov, just attached to our facilities. Sovereign state property, like an embassy."

"Legally a different entity altogether," added Felix.

"Naturally," said Carol.

"Their animals starved after the crew's bugout. All but one. It got into the vents, and…caused a tragic situation. I'm so sorry Carol."

She looked down at the cigarette in her hand, thinking Dan would have found this hilarious. "Go on," she said. "There's more, and we don't have all day."

"What are we gonna do?" said Mrs. Hawkins' a middle-aged socialite who had bought her ticket after fleecing a Kuwaiti oil sheik and was now Boulay's 'disciple.' "We'll starve up here too, won't we?"

"Brains take very little oxygen, relative to our stores," said Artem. "But we do have to consider the future." He glanced up at Felix.

"As you know," said the concierge, "the Artem Universal is an active research station, and our advances in neuroinfomatics have continued apace since our launch. We now have the ability to scan, copy and upload a full map of human brain into digital format, compatible with Simstate and independent of any organic correlative."

"Whole brain emulation," muttered Liu. "It's possible. My own company was working on it. You're saying you've perfected the process?"

"We've—"

"We're satisfied that we can do it," Artem broke in. "Think of it as the next step in human evolution. You'd still be able to live in Simstate, exactly as before, but your material brain would become redundant. It would not only prevent tragedies like the one we just suffered, it would allow us to run the ship at minimal power."

"To what purpose?" said Carol.

"The Earth is dead," said Artem with a crosswise sweep of his hand. "We're still working out some models, but we have to assume it will remain uninhabitable for some time. The good news is that we have everything we need to affect that rehabilitation when conditions allow. We have a wealth of human DNA, yours and the non-cogs'. We have cloning technology and enough built in automation to pull it off. In due time, you all will be the fathers and mothers of a new human race."

"Felix," said Gracie, "you can do all that?"

Felix wrinkled his brow. "Well, this is a small matter of legality."

McWhorter huffed. "Roger, you've just told us we're 2,000 miles above a dying planet, old boy. What jurisdictional authority are we in hock to?"

"The one codified in Felix's programming," said Artem.

Felix gave an abashed nod. "The automated systems are behind firewalls that I lack the authorization to breach."

"The lawyers are dead!" crowed McWhorter. "Long live the Law!"

"We have a workaround," said Artem. "A loophole, if you will."

"We've developed an additional capability," said Felix. "We can integrate a single whole-brain entity, not just with the Simstate drive, but with the ship's motherboard itself. This entity would have total control of all shipboard functions and be able to cut through the red tape, so to speak."

"You mean," said Carol, "one of us would become the ship's brain. Beyond the law."

"In layman's terms, that is essentially correct."

"But who?" spouted Tahvo. Tahvo was a louche little creep who'd struck it rich in crypto-currencies. He didn't socialize. Rumor had it he enjoyed historical recreations, like torturing suspected witches in a medieval dungeon and smoking opium in turn-of-the-century British Saigon. He seemed vaguely resentful of the others, and the consensus was that he'd gone Full-Cog purely out of paranoia that someone would pull the plug on him. "You're saying this person would have total control over our fates," he said, fidgeting on his divan and flipping the hair out of his eyes. "Who can we trust with that?"

"I suppose that's what we're about to vote on," said Carol. "Felix can patch the upload, but he needs all of us authorize it."

Felix bowed. "Astute as always, madam."

"So dammit, who's the lucky one?" said McWhorter. "I don't suppose you have someone in mind, eh Roger?"

Artem frowned and pecked at his pipe. "It might just as well be you, Marty, if you carry the vote." McWhorter guffawed. "Or Mr. Liu, or Ms. O'Meara. Everyone gets a say in this, and everyone is equal."

"You wouldn't refuse the office though," said Tully Pfifer, a taciturn old aristocrat who'd known Artem at Yale and had a vague rapport with him.

Artem shrugged and looked thoughtful. "It's a terrible responsibility. I wish I *could* refuse it. But consider my qualifications." Knowing glances crossed the room, but no one else spoke. "The Artem Universal was my dream, in which you are sharing. I never intended it to be the last refuge of humankind, but that's exactly what it's become. Without my vision, you'd all be down there." He tipped his head at the darkened orb on the screen and waited a moment for this to sink in.

"Now we stand at the threshold. All of you are successful people, people of vision, people who built great things. But I am the architect of actual, working utopias. Did my visions not preserve the very best of man's heritage while stripping away all that was corrupt, all that was ugly and harsh? But now…." He looked down in a fair show of token humility. "By god, if you empower me to do it, I will make the world that humanity deserves. I'll *do it*."

He emptied his pipe with one resolute tap, and stood. "You'll want some time to think it over. Let's reconvene in, say, five hours, and we'll put it to a vote. I will abstain from that vote, the better to court your unforced mandate. Agreed?" There were murmurs of assent. Others rose to leave.

"Felix," said Carol, "you said—"

Artem and several others turned to look at her.

"Yes?"

"Nothing," said Carol, after a beat. "I'm sorry, I'm not thinking clearly."

\#

The ape had been too clever for its own good. The refill stage of the cleaning cycle had kicked in almost as soon as it was through the breach, and the pressure had resealed the tank, locking it in. Now it floated weightlessly in the restored solution, its face downcast in grave, tragic mien, its eyes closed, mouth open, one hand raised overhead in a vaguely prophetic gesture. Carol watched it with dull indifference in the roaring silence of space.

"Where the hell are you, Dan?" She'd closed the outgoing com-wire, so not even Felix could hear her. It was just her in here, and.... "Dan?"

A bubble slipped from the beast's nostril and wandered forth like a newborn universe.

"Silence, huh sweet prince? You used to talk a good game. Jesus, talk-talk-talk. You said once that you could walk into any room and make your play because you knew the gal behind you was the smartest person in the room. Well, if you're waiting for me to figure a way out of this one…"

Without eyes, lungs and a diaphragm, the impulse to weep was just a frightening paralysis, a contraction with no core.

"We had a good run, didn't we. Like Paolo and Francesca, braving the goddamn whirlwind! Dan. I think I'll lie down with you now. Roger's got his vote sewed up, I think, they'll vote him in because they don't trust each other. He'll control everything. I'll need his permission to hit the kill switch. Frankly I don't fancy it, his kitschy Genesis reboot, or—"

The eyes opened.

The spike of static on the wire told her she was screaming, or trying to, and she watched, unbelieving, as the head turned ever so slightly and the dead eyes dilated as they fixed on her. The mouth opened and a red cloud of blood issued from its throat. *"Eight…"* it said, its voice like an ellipse, a hollow in the silence. *"…out of seven."* The red cloud bloomed out, enveloping its head in a scarlet nimbus. Suddenly Carol knew that she had to hang on, that if she could keep from losing her mind in the next few seconds she might grasp something terribly important.

\#

Artem set the tone for the second meeting by a change of venue—a grand conference room with a red-draped, circular table under a coruscating chandelier. Four elegantly tortured bonsai trees were set in soft-lit, recessed alcoves, and three high, statin-draped windows looked out on starry space. The man himself wore an elegant black tuxedo, his hair slicked back along his skull, black and shiny as his shoes. He nodded to Carol as she sat across from him. "How are you keeping, my dear?"

She gave him a prim, tired smile. She'd dressed for the occasion as well—a red sequined evening gown, black, gossamer shawl, and a diamond necklace to rival the chandelier. "I never fancied being a woman without a man," she said, stripping off a lone long satin glove and laying it on the table. "Then again, most men aren't fit to stand in my Dan's shadow, I'll have to revisit the idea."

"I couldn't agree more. Forgive me, but the providence of your fortune…oil, wasn't it?"

"Mostly luck." The others were filing in, taking places around the table. Felix was greeting them, discreetly offering them each a game of chess. "But yes, he inherited his crazy old dad's land. Turned out there was oil under the cows. He expanded into Texas and Arizona. Give that man a hand to play…"

"I can only imagine."

"You know, it's funny," she said, peeling off the other glove and laying it beside its mate. "All that time in Simstate, all our lives to relive—you know how much we cared to wallow in the fat years?"

He raised his eyebrows half a centimeter.

"Hardly at all." She gave the smallest of shrugs. "No, we liked the hardscrabble days, back when you could still get your nose bloodied. When winning meant something because you could actually lose. When was the last time you really lost something, Roger?"

His smile was more in his eyes than his lips. He didn't say anything, just looked at her across the table while the others settled in. She didn't have to count to know there were eight.

"Well," he said, looking around the room, "I hope you've all had some time to reflect."

"Bastard," muttered McWhorter.

"What's on your mind, Dick?" Artem's voice was mild, but with a hard hook in it.

"Oh come off it, you know you've got us bushwhacked! We're here to vote you in as, what…God? I mean, lemme get this straight…." He sounded drunk, and he wasn't the only one who appeared inebriated. Tahvo was on the nod, and several others looked soused. It was Simstate, so they could purge the effects of whatever they'd been into with a silent appeal to Felix. They were doped because they were stuffing their fear. *Cowards*, she thought, looking around the room.

"Once you get the ship, the contracts will be void," said McWhorter.

"No, Clive, you're quite mistaken."

"But you can wipe your ass with them if it tickles you. You'll have that power."

Artem sighed. "If the responsibility of helming the ship falls to me, you have my solemn word that your contracts will be—"

"Honored, yes," said Carol, "but this is the last time we'll be able to insist on anything."

All eyes shifted to her. Artem looked thoughtful. Felix nodded. "Strictly, speaking, I suppose you're right," said Artem. "Look, the life support systems are running well at the moment, but we'll all be much safer once we've transitioned to digital consciousness. If anything is as pressing as that, then by all means, let's—"

Carol raised her hand.

"Yes?"

"We've got rotting carcasses of apes onboard," said Carol. "I don't approve. Can the automated systems expel them?"

"All organic containment units can be automatically emptied into the bilge and ejected," said Felix. "The protocol was installed as a precaution against infectious disease. Unfortunately, five of the six cadavers in question are aboard the Admiral Gorshkov, where I have no authority to—."

"That's great Felix. What about the one next to my tank, the one that—" Her voice broke and she covered her eyes.

"Naturally," said Artem. "We're starting clean. Transcending the corruptions of the flesh."

"Hallelujah!" said Boulay. He was watching Artem with a look of pious esteem. She wondered if he'd been promised something special on the side.

"I'd like an informal, binding vote now. I'm sorry Roger, I just don't trust that you won't forget as soon as you're God, or captain, or whatever. Who's in favor of expelling all dead-stuff from the Universal, effective immediately?" Hands went up as she looked around, Artem's last.

"The motion passes," said Felix. "Commencing purge of all lifeless, organic matter."

"Are there any other immediate concerns?" said Artem.

No one spoke. Carol picked up a glove and dabbed at her eyes.

"Very well, to the main business, then. Under your napkins you will find a pencil and a piece of paper. Please place a check in the right upper corner to authorize your own whole-brain emulation. Then write the name of the person you wish to see take control of the ship." Carol wrote quickly, folded the slip and held it up. Felix moved around the table collecting the votes as they were raised.

"Do we have a winner, Felix?"

Felix shuffled through the slips. "The winner is you, sir. By a vote of six to one."

Artem raised an eyebrow. "I don't suppose you can be more specific?"

"I'm afraid protocol forbids it."

"Naturally. How long until we're integrated?"

Felix addressed the room. "Each of you will be transferred to digital consciousness within the minute, without interruption to your Simstate experience. It will take about eight minutes for your elected representative to fully integrate with the ship and assume operational control."

"White man's burden, eh?" sneered McWhorter.

"Yes," said Artem, more to himself than to McWhorter. He produced his pipe and packed it with deliberate care. Felix stepped forward to light it for him. As he puffed, he became aware of Carol studying him. "Something on your mind, dear?"

"I'd prefer if you didn't call me that."

He frowned, leaned back, and blew a series of smoke-rings.

"You're a careful man, aren't you Roger?"

He spread his hands invitingly.

"Wary of new technology, even your own. You wouldn't have trusted whole-brain-emulation, not without insurance."

One side of his mouth ticked up and his eyebrow rose. "Wouldn't I?"

"You authorized Felix to upload you to digital consciousness, but you kept your brain viable, like a backup drive, in case the digital copy proved faulty."

Now both eyebrows rose.

"But that essentially made two of you, one organic, one digital. I supposed you realized that while the two Roger Artems were initially two versions of the same person, they would evolve different motives, even conflicting ones, as their interests diverged. That must have been an experience, colluding with yourself to decide which one of you had to go. But the answer was obvious, wasn't it? The organic original had to make way for—how did you put it?—'the next step in human evolution.' Roger Artem's brain consented to die, so that Roger Artem the eternal entity could win our votes and become God."

Artem's laugh was so violent and sudden that the whole table flinched, all but Carol. "I always knew you were a superior woman. I dare say the first children of the new Earth might just be yours and mine. What say we do it the old fashioned way, eh?"

"Not likely, Roger."

"Oh-ho, contraire. I think it's getting more likely by the minute. Felix, the time?"

"Five and a half minutes to full integration, sir."

"Mortals don't say no to gods, Carol. But tell me, how in *my* name did you figure all that out?"

"Deduction," she said, staring levelly back at his leering face.

"Balls!"

"None at all. It was Felix, his lovely protocols. You may have noticed he can site numbers, but he can't put names to them. Like just now, when you asked about the vote."

Artem laughed again. "A perfect kike, isn't he? Accommodating, discreet, singular...." Felix looked bemused at this. "But go on. How did Felix tip you?"

"When I came out of Simstate, after the accident, I asked him how many Full-Cogs survived. Seven, was his number. But I counted eight at your first little conclave." Artem was shaking his head in disbelief. "Which meant that one of us no longer registered as a physical passenger. It was you, wasn't it? Already in your digital ascendency. A spirit walking among us."

"But why," sputtered Liu, the first of the others to gain his voice. "Why wouldn't he tell us the upload worked, that it was safe?"

"Probably because he didn't want to turn over any cards," said Carol. He wanted you thinking about your own little existential journeys instead of wondering what he was up to. Just what are you planning, Roger? You've had your vote, now what's in store?"

Artem's cracked smile had become a glimmering, wolfish grin, and he seemed to be swelling in his suit, drinking the air in deep, lusty breaths. "Oh, I'm going do it *right*, by Jove. First I'm going to root out the traitor here that voted against me and cast him...or *her*...down into a very special place. A pit of my own creation. A reiterative nightmare, a *real* Hell, one you just better believe in, boys and girls!"

"Sounds harrowing," said Carol.

"Oh, that's just the start. When the dust of the old Earth has settled, I'm going to seed it again. No more fractious wandering and philosophizing. It's going to be a *pure* race, an *obedient* race. One that will build my eternal kingdom on the scaffolding of the stars. Ar-Tem, shall be their alpha and omega, the sacred syllables that ring through the cosmos. Believe it!"

"And the mess down there. I'm starting to wonder if you didn't have something to do with that as well."

"Ha! Earth? Earth was a tinderbox. I struck a few sparks through my old proxies and subsidiaries, sure. But ask my people in a thousand years, they'll say Artem did it all. Because that's what gods do. They destroy"—he clenched one fist while opening the other—"and they create."

Gracie Lehman was biting her knuckle and weeping silent tears. Boulay was tipped back in his seat with one hand raised, eyes closed, moving his lips in prayer. Liu was staring at the table, and McWhorter gaped in disbelief. Tahvo, who'd been staring blankly at Artem, suddenly jumped up from his chair, eyes glazed with dope and fervor, and bounced a spastic Roman salute off his breast.

Carol dipped two fingers into the front of her dress and took out one of Dan's Chesterfields. "Felix?" she said. Felix walked around the table, struck and match, and lit it for her. The taste of rich, cedary smoke, the rush in her blood, the tickle in her throat—suddenly Dan was with her, now, and always, whispering in her ear that she was still the smartest person in room. She blew out a long cloud of smoke as Felix stepped back and stood behind her.

"Now let me tell you where you screwed the pooch, Roger."

His smile widened aggressively, but not before a flicker of uncertainty showed in his eyes.

"The technology for whole brain emulation was a recent achievement. The ship's protocols predate it. There is therefore no legal standing for a disembodied, digital consciousness to be counted as one of the crew. Or as one of the board."

"The board," he said mockingly. "Do try to keep up, dear, Rome is not a Republic anymore. I have the ship. *Screw* the board."

"Read the fine print, Roger. Only a physically present, Full-cog board member can access shipboard systems."

"Ah, but I am present. Station One, C-Deck. Look at the name on the tank, it says Roger Artem. Felix, does it matter if my mind occupies different hardware, as long as the remnants of my body and my mind are both present?"

"No sir, it matters not."

He sat back and smirked at Carol. "Otherwise, I wouldn't have been able to log into Simstate. This conversation wouldn't be—" He dropped his pipe.

"You abstained from voting," she said. "If you had voted, Felix's tally would be exactly the same, and that might have tipped you, but your arrogance did you in."

Artem was trying to pick up his pipe but having difficulty. "Felix?"

"The tank at Station One does say Roger Artem, and will for some time, but it's an empty tank. When your organic doppelganger hit the kill switch it became non-living organic matter, a lump of dead meat. And if you'll recall my little motion, we just voted to flush you with the chimp."

"Felix?" He tried to grab the table and rise but his hand passed through the surface. "Felix, what is this, what's happening?"

"You've been logged out of Simstate for the last five minutes, twenty seconds. At the five-minute mark the automatic timeout begins. It's gradual, so as not to cause undo shock to the brain, but in your case that's not really a concern. Your brain is now approximately 1,185 kilometers from the ship, and quite frozen, I'm sure."

"Felix, don't you toy with me. I'm right here, dammit, confirm!"

"You have about thirty seconds before your digital hologram dissipates completely, at which point you will remain in an inert 'sleep' mode unless the motherboard's archon elects revive."

"Hard to imagine why she would," said Carol.

Artem stood back from the table, looking wildly around the room. "But...I won the vote. Felix, confirm."

"You won the popular vote," said Felix. "But as you are not officially on board, control of the ship goes to the runner up."

"I'm sorry, Roger," said Carol. "I'm afraid the traitor voted for herself." She took a long drag of the Chesterfield and blew the smoke across the table. Artem was gone.

A strangled, rooster crow came from Tahvo as he threw himself down and genuflected in Carol's direction. Everyone else was just stared at her.

"Upload complete," said Felix, glancing at his watch. "Mrs. O'Meara has the helm. Mr. Artem, such as he is, is in the hard drive."

"Shall I delete him?" said Carol. No one spoke. She stubbed the cigarette out in the ashtray and sat back in her chair. Like Artem had been when he uploaded his brain, Carol was now literally of two minds. It would take her some time to imagine the sort of world she would create, and whether it would have any use for a devil.

Matthew Chabin is a writer from Portland, Oregon. He worked as a journalist in the US Navy and studied literature and philosophy at Southern Oregon University. He is the winner of the 2015 Miglior Press

Essay contest, and his work has appeared in literary journals as well as anthologies from several publishers. He currently lives with his wife, daughter, and two cats in Nagano Prefecture of Japan.

Doppelganger

by Tony Conaway

"When you were thirteen, you let Billy Nederhopper feel you up," she said.

"You really liked him, but you stopped him from going any further," I said.

"So he got mad and told all his friends that you were a slut."

"And your relationships have gone downhill ever since."

We both laughed.

It felt good to laugh. I'd been feeling down for…weeks? Months? A long time, anyway.

"Well, your relationships with the male of the species, anyway."

"It's Billy Nederhopper's fault that you became a lesbian."

You both laughed again, until the portal glitched once more. This was like trying to converse over a bad Skype connection.

Except that it wasn't a Skype conversation over a computer.

It was a conversation through a portal the size of a soccer goal. A portal to an alternate Earth.

And I was having this conversation with myself. Well, with an alternate version of myself.

My father nicknamed me Baby, and the name stuck. I was thinking of this alternate version of me a "Ybab." That's "Baby" backwards.

Well, she was an alternate version of the way I used to be. I already explained to her that, about two years ago, I'd been kidnapped by a demon. The demon kept its victims here in the heart of Manhattan, but transformed so that no one would recognize and rescue them. It had changed me so I looked like the kind of immigrant refugee that a lot of people tend to ignore: a young black Somali woman.

I looked at the image of Ybab, now frozen like…well, like a bad Skype connection. Ybab was a 27-year-old redhead. Mixed Scandinavian and Irish ancestry. Pretty enough to be an actress.

The image unfroze. "And we're back," Ybab said, looking at her

183

watch. "Three o'clock. A year ago, I'd be performing on Broadway right now. A Wednesday matinee. You ever make it to Broadway?" She made a few tap dance steps when she said "Broadway."

A wave of bitterness swept over me. "No. I never made the big time before I was…changed. Aside from a few bargain-basement road shows, I was still performing in church basements and school multi-purpose rooms."

I forced a smile on my face and flung my arms out like a game show hostess. "But who needs Broadway when you have all this?! Rat-infested tunnels and all the cockroaches you can eat!"

Ybab smiled grimly in return. "I know what you mean. I never wanted to be Jake Rosenthal's assistant, but here I am. He didn't survive the pandemic, by the way. Besides, you said you have a pandemic, too. Aren't your Broadway theaters closed?"

"Sure. We've had…somewhere between four and five thousand fatalities so far. There are lots of restrictions on where you can go, and what you can do. We have a vaccine, but it's taking forever to get to everyone."

"Wait," Ybab said. "That's four thousand fatalities in New York, right? Or is it just Manhattan?"

"God, no. We're approaching five thousand in the entire United States."

The alternate me looked away for a moment. When she turned back to the portal, her voice was shaking.

"Five thousand dead in the entire USA. We…we have that every day, right here in Manhattan!"

"That's not…."

"We have electric trucks roaming the streets every day. 'Bring-Out-Your-Dead' vehicles, just like in the Middle Ages. And New York City is handling it better than much of the country. Some places, like Detroit or St. Louis, they're war zones. The military tried to restore order, but they finally gave up. There aren't enough healthy soldiers to do the job."

Ybab collapsed into a chair. Despite being in a filthy underground tunnel, there was an ornate, gilded, high-backed chair for her to sit in. It almost looked like a throne. "Everything's falling apart here. There are people who seem to be immune to this coronavirus, like me. It won't get us. But I'm not immune to a bullet. If New York gets like those other cities, it'll be a free-fire zone. The government censors the news broadcasts, but they can't stop the entire Internet."

"What are you going to do?" I asked.

"My Earth is done, at least for the near future," Ybab said. "I want to come to yours."

#

Jake Rosenthal is the go-to guy for handing weird things underground. He's been doing that for over 30 years, and he's still #1. Me, I'm being trained to replace him. That makes me #2. The #3 person is a young guy named Rollo, who does what he's told and keeps his mouth shut about the strangeness down here. But he's not the sharpest crayon in the box, so he really can't take over the #1 spot. We're all members of Laborer's Local 146, better known as the Sandhog's Union. Our union digs the tunnels under the city.

There is no #4. Oh, Jake sometimes gets help from some of the younger Union guys, but he doesn't tell them anything. They mostly just carry stuff from one place to another.

At the moment, most of our regular Union guys were unavailable. One had COVID-19, and the others had family members who were immunocompromised. They don't want to risk giving the virus to their relatives.

So Jake got Rollo to bring in his cousin, Milo. Or Mmm-mmilo, as women usually refer to him.

It's not just that Milo is drop-dead gorgeous. He's also about 6' 6" of solid muscle.

(Hey, just because I'm a lesbian doesn't mean I can't appreciate one of the top ten gorgeous men I've ever seen.)

I'd heard about Milo from some of the other women in the Sandhog office, where I work when I'm not helping Jake.

That morning was the first time I laid eyes on Milo. I made a fool of myself trying to talk to him for about two minutes, until his cousin mercifully said, "Uh, Milo is deaf. He doesn't read lips, so he doesn't understand you."

Milo's expression never changed. He maintained the same bland, non-committal smile as he turned from me towards the donuts that Jake brought in.

"OK," said Jake, stirring milk into his coffee. He spoke slower than normal, so Rollo could interpret for Milo, using what I assume was American Sign Language. "Here's the plan for today: Baby has pointed out that we don't even have an inventory of our trophies." (Trophies are what Jake calls the bizarre technology we've acquired. They include: exoskeleton battle suits from the future, magical artifacts from the past, and who-knows-whats from who-knows-where.) "So she's gonna do an

185

inventory of the items in the lockers under Central Park. I'll check in on her periodically to identify any trophies that aren't labeled, which is most of them." He stopped to drink down his coffee in a single gulp.

"You two," indicating Rollo and Milo, "have a nasty job to do. We'll be scouring the area for kobolds. Dead kobolds."

Jake was the one who named these underground dwellers kobolds, after the elves that haunted German mines. No one knew what our critters called themselves, because no human could speak their language. They communicated in a birdlike twitter. Kobolds lived deep underground, digging new tunnels. Why they were there, what they wanted, what they lived on – all of that was a mystery. Basically, the kobolds didn't bother us and we didn't bother them.

We pretty much ignored the kobolds until recently. Then came COVID-19. It turned out that the kobolds were extremely susceptible to the disease. As a result, there were dead kobolds everywhere in the tunnels. Kobolds that were starting to decompose and stink.

"Far as we know, the kobolds don't have any funeral traditions for us to worry about. Or maybe they're just ignoring kobold corpses like…well, like the plague. But we gotta get rid of those corpses before the stink reaches the outside, and people start coming down here to find the source of the smell. So, we'll wear hazmat suits, and we'll put the corpses in a cart for disposal. We've got two industrial furnaces at our disposal."

Rollo spoke up, "You just guide us to the corpses, boss. Milo and I will do the heavy lifting. These little critters ain't that heavy, but you're just outta the hospital."

I was glad Rollo said that, though it irritated Jake. He doesn't like to admit weakness – not even his recent heart surgery.

"Fine," Jake said, a sour look on his face. "Let's get started."

#

The morning went smoothly. There were three lockers of trophies under Central Park near the subway stop, and I got through the first one in a few hours. Almost all the trophies were labeled, which made it easy. The ones that weren't, I put aside for Jake to identify.

Jake came by twice. Some of the unlabeled trophies were from before his time, so even he couldn't identify them.

One item intrigued me. It was a square metal box with a metal…thing on top. The thing looked like a cross between a Tibetan prayer wheel inside one of those rotating cylinders with slots that predated the movies. A zoetrope, I think they were called. You looked through one of the slots while you rotated the cylinder. The device had pictures on the inside cylinder. The arrangement created an illusion of motion.

Curiously, there were metal shutters for each slot. About a third of the slots were closed off by one of the shutters. I tried to open a few of the shutters, but they seemed to be permanently shut.

I had a folding table to work on, and an uncomfortable chair. When I placed the box-and-wheel machine atop my table, it was just at the right height for me to look through the slots.

Jake came back then, bringing my usual lunch order: a falafel, a piece of fruit, and a sweet tea. Today the fruit was a nectarine. Jake fished my lunch out of a big bag – no doubt containing lunch for himself, Milo, and Rocco.

After he handed me my lunch, Jake spun the cylinder atop the trophy, clockwise. "Haven't seen this in donkey's years," he said. "You want it to work, you gotta charge it up by spinning the top part."

"Then what does it do?" I muttered, my mouth full of falafel.

He pointed to a button on the right side of the box. "Then you press here, look through one of the slots on the wheel, and you can look through into another world."

"Once you've established a target, it will stay visible as long as the charge holds. Or, you can keep the button depressed while you keep spinning the wheel. Then a mirror rises on the inside and it projects an image just beyond the trophy. You can make it big, very big, if you want. When it's that big, you can even hear what's going on from the other side. It's much easier than squinting through one of these slots."

"What are they images of?" I asked.

"As far as I can tell, other Earths." He counted the slots, starting at a place where three slots in a row were closed off by shutters. "I really should've labeled these," he said. "Here it is." He gave the wheel one last clockwise spin, pressed the right button briefly, and looked through the slot. "All of these show alternate Earths. Some of them are very strange, very dangerous. This one shows an Earth in the middle of an Ice Age. Look."

He moved so I could look through the slot. Yes, it showed a frozen vista.

I few months ago, I would've reacted in amazement. After two years of working with Jake, amazing things no longer elicited that sort of reaction.

"So," I said, "if I want it big, I keep spinning the wheel and keep the button pressed down."

"Yup."

I was sitting at a ten-foot folding banquet table. "How big?"

"You can make the image as big as a movie screen, if you want. I never counted exactly how many spins that took." Jake spun the wheel for a few minutes, while pressing on the right-hand button. In front of the table, an image appeared, as if projected in mid-air. It grew into an oval that was longer than the table.

Jake pointed at the image. "At this size, you can just see buildings buried under the snow."

Sure enough, there were some stone buildings almost completely enveloped in snow. In the distance was a mass of ice which I took for a glacier. Despite the ice age, this Earth was – or used to be – populated.

"What happened to the people?" I asked.

I was staring at the image, but I could hear the susurrus of his corduroy jacket as Jake made one of his characteristic shrugs. (Yeah, I said it. "Susurrus." As in "faint noise." I've got a Word-a-Day Calendar.) "Who knows? Maybe they froze to death. Maybe they moved closer to the equator. I've viewed this Earth several times, and all I can tell you is they ain't here."

"They're not here. Maybe they all moved to Florida. Can this trophy gizmo search elsewhere?"

"Not as far as I know. It only shows more or less the same location – just on a different Earth. We're underground in a tunnel, so a lot of other Earths are completely dark. Apparently, they don't have a tunnel here."

"This ice age Earth isn't in a tunnel," I said.

"There's a glacier in the distance." The image was still in front of the table, and Jake pointed to the huge mass of ice. "We're only - what? - thirty or forty feet underground. Glaciers can dig much deeper than that. Didn't glaciers dig the Grand Canyon?"

"I have no idea."

As if it disapproved of our lack of Earth Science knowledge, the wheel slowed and the image of ice Earth faded away. After a few final desultory rotations, it came squeaking to a stop.

"So that's what it does. Play around with it, if you like. Just don't press the red button on the left side."

"Why? What does that button do?"

Jake gathered up his bag of sandwiches. "Instead of an image, it creates a portal. You don't want to let some other-worldly berserker warriors into our world." He tucked the bag under his arm. "I gotta get

Milo his sandwiches before he decides to find out if dead kobolds are edible."

As Jake left, I pondered the machine. This was just like Jake: casually leaving me in control of a potentially-deadly machine. Every day was a test, working with him.

I took another bite of falafel and examined the machine again. I spun the central cylinder while I finished my lunch, charging it up. No harm in looking at a few different Earths, I figured.

Rather than try to peek through the slots, I viewed them in the big projection. Moving the circular screen on top, I was able to see the alternate Earths. A lot of them were dark. Some of them were the ones with the closed shutters. I guessed the other dark ones led to Earths without a tunnel like the one I was in, or where the tunnel had collapsed.

And then I found Ybab and her world.

#

Jake had specifically warned me of the danger of opening the portal. But this wasn't about letting a horde of warriors enter our world. This was about saving…well, me.

A version of me, anyway. A version of me from before my transformation.

A version of the way I was supposed to be.

A successful version, even. She'd made it to Broadway. I never would, the way I looked now. There just weren't that many roles for black actresses. And I'd be starting from scratch – no one would believe that the resume of a perky redhead belonged to me. A coal-black girl playing Nellie Forbush in a road show version of "South Pacific?" Impossible! The character's own arc was about overcoming her racism.

Didn't the world deserve a successful version of me? Didn't I deserve to enjoy her success, at least vicariously? Our world had a vaccine against the coronavirus. It would be months before our world was back to normal, but it would happen. The theaters would open again.

All I had to do was open the portal and let her in.

But I knew Jake would be back to check on me. And I knew he'd forbid this. I needed time to think.

I got out of my chair and stretched. It was a molded plastic chair, and a long way from comfortable. I decided to stall for time.

"That throne of yours looks a lot more comfortable than my chair. Where'd you get a chair like that down in the tunnels?"

Ybab smiled. "Believe it or not, it's from Central Park West. Not far from here. Immunes like me are in big demand. The surviving doormen in a few fancy buildings give me loot from the apartments of dead millionaires in exchange for helping drag corpses out. This chair isn't half as heavy as the bloated corpse of the stockbroker I dragged out last week. Paper money isn't worth much right now, but barter always works." She pointed at the nectarine peels on the table. "Was that an orange? We haven't had fresh fruit in the city for weeks."

I looked at the sad pile of peelings. "Nectarine. It's spring here, but they still ship out-of-season fruit to us from South America."

Ybab ran her fingers through her red mane. "Nectarine. Even if you don't want to let me in, sending me a crate of fresh fruit would make me as wealthy as those Central Park West residents."

I didn't look at her. How could I leave her – me – in a hellhole like that?

I reached for the red button on the left side, the one that would open the portal.

"Yes!" said Ybab.

"No," said a voice from behind me.

Jake's hand grasped my wrist. "You can't. Not even to be merciful."

I slumped back in my chair.

Ybab started to beg. "Please! Don't leave me here! You don't know _"

Jake closed the shutter to that world, cutting her pleas off. Sealing that world off forever.

Jake and I were both silent for several minutes. I spoke first.

"So, am I fired now?"

"Fired? No. I stopped you, so no harm done. Obviously, we can't open a portal to a plague world. There's no guarantee that it's the same coronavirus we now have a cure for on our world. It could be just a fatal here as it is there."

"I know," I said. My voice was very small.

"But now you know that temptation to violate the rules isn't just about getting rich. Temptation…can be about pity. For me, the hardest is guilt." He smiled. "But what do you expect? I'm a Jew. We're born feeling guilty."

I started to gather up the nectarine peels. "OK. I'll get back to work, then."

"No," Jake said. "Take the rest of the afternoon off. I'll finish up cataloging this locker. Start fresh tomorrow. Or not-so-fresh, if you need to get drunk."

"I...I think I'll put on my jogging clothes and run until I collapse."

"Whatever works for you." He started writing out a label for the machine that had caused all this trauma. "Now git."

I got gone.

#

When Jake was sure that Baby had left, he took out a flask of whisky and drank. He downed the entire flask in a few gulps. Then he took a small, odd tool out of his pocket. He used it on the shutter he'd just closed a few minute ago – the supposedly un-openable shutter. Using the tool, he opened the shutter in less than a minute.

Immediately, the image of the other world reappeared.

"Hello, Jakie," said the woman on the throne. But it wasn't the other Baby anymore. It was a pleasant-looking, middle aged woman.

It was Jake's late wife.

"I knew you'd stop her from opening the portal," she said. "How long were you standing there in the dark?"

"I'd already given the boys their lunch. I sat just out of view, eating mine, the entire time." He grimaced. "The thought of seeing your tricks gave me indigestion."

"Are you sure, Jakie? You just had heart surgery. For the rest of your life, every time you have pain in your chest, you'll wonder if it's heartburn or a heart attack."

"Enough about me, temptress" Jake said. "Are you going to tell me anything about Baby or not?"

The woman shrugged. "You know most of it. She was about to succumb, to open the portal. What you don't know is this: she's been depressed for months. For a moment – just a moment – she considered changing places with me. Well, what she thought was her doppelganger."

Jake started. "Why? Why would she even consider going to a dying world?"

"She's clinically depressed. Why do depressed girls cut themselves? To feel something, anything. There were many thoughts going through her mind. Letting what she thought was the "real" Baby replace her on this world. And ending the pain she's in by changing her entire living situation. Living some kind of 'Mad Max' fantasy – there's nothing like putting your life in danger every minute to change your attitude."

"Thank you. That's enough for now." Jake reached for the shutter.

"Jakie!" the temptress said in the voice of his dead wife. "Come

191

back to me soon."

And then the shutter was closed, sealed from anyone who didn't have the tool.

The old man sat for a minute, then said, "work to do." And he finished cataloging the artifacts in the locker.

There was no one there to hear him pray in Hebrew while he worked. A Kaddish for his wife.

Tony Conaway has written and ghostwritten everything from blogs to books. He has cowritten non-fiction books published by McGraw-Hill, Macmillan and Prentice Hall. He writes fiction in just about every genre except erotica and romance. But make him an offer — he'll do those, too. He can be found on Twitter as @TonyConaway and on Facebook as Author Tony Conaway. He interviews other authors at wayneaconaway.blogspot.com.

Thank you…

Thank you for taking the time to read our collection. We enjoyed all the stories contained within and hope you found at least a few to enjoy yourself. If you did, we'd be honored if you would leave a review on Amazon, Goodreads, and anywhere else reviews are posted.

You can also subscribe to our email list via our website, Https://www.cloakedpress.com

Follow us on Facebook http://www.facebook.com/Cloakedpress

Tweet to us @CloakedPress

We are also on Instagram http://www.instagram.com/Cloakedpress

If you'd like to check out our other publications, you can find them on our website above. Click the "Check Our Catalog" button on the homepage for more great collections and novels from the Cloaked Press Family.

Printed in Great Britain
by Amazon

42856785R00116